THE
PLAYGROUND

BOOKS BY S.D. ROBERTSON

Time to Say Goodbye

If Ever I Fall

Stand By Me

My Sister's Lies

How to Save a Life

The Daughter's Choice

THE
PLAYGROUND

S.D. ROBERTSON

bookouture

Published by Bookouture in 2023

An imprint of Storyfire Ltd.
Carmelite House
50 Victoria Embankment
London EC4Y 0DZ

www.bookouture.com

ISBN: 978-1-83790-644-4
eBook ISBN: 978-1-83790-642-0

For Mum and Dad

PROLOGUE

A hefty shove from behind sends me sprawling forward against my will. Through the gate. Onto my hands and knees on the soft, springy surface of the playground.

I'm gasping for breath.

The world's spinning all around me.

I'm gasping for breath.

I can't move.

I can't think as they laugh and jeer at me, ready to do their worst.

I'm overpowered. Helpless. Terrified of what comes next.

'Please, no,' I whimper, still floored and lacking the strength or courage to get back up. 'Please don't do this.'

But as these desperate words leave my trembling lips, to further jeers, I accept they'll make no difference. There is no sympathy here. Only hate.

I can't let this happen. I can't.

I must find a way to stop them before it's too late.

ONE

NOW

Beth

I trip on the steps down to the pavement as we leave the dental surgery, narrowly avoiding falling on my face by grabbing hold of the cool metal handrail. It's not an elegant save, but it's far better than the alternative scenario, in which I could have crashed into my eight-year-old daughter, a step ahead of me, and sent us both tumbling. Somehow, I manage not to swear.

'Are you all right, Mummy?' Daisy asks, her freshly inspected teeth clenched.

I force my lips into a tight smile. 'Yes, love. Don't worry.'

The receptionist sticks her head out of the door, wincing as she too checks I'm okay.

'Fine, thanks,' I say.

Well, today's off to a great start. I take Daisy's hand and lead her back in the direction of school.

I'd rather not be taking her out of classes so soon after the summer holidays. She's only been back a few days. But what was I supposed to do when she kept complaining that one of her teeth didn't feel right and then, on close inspection, I spotted a hole? This was the only available appointment.

The dentist examined her and confirmed the cavity. 'How often does Daisy brush?' she asked, peering down her nose at me.

'Twice a day,' I said. 'Right, Daisy?'

'Yeah,' Daisy muttered. 'Mainly.'

My heart sank.

'Brushing needs to be twice a day, every day. You don't supervise, Mum?'

'I, er, will in future. Definitely.'

'Does Daisy have an electric toothbrush?'

'No, I thought she was too young. Would it be better if she did?'

'I would recommend one, yes. At least it's a baby tooth, so she'll lose it before too long. I can do a temporary filling in the meantime that's not too intrusive and should keep things in check.'

As Daisy and I continue towards school, I ask her how the tooth feels now.

'Fine, I think.' Gingerly she runs her tongue across it. 'Yeah, a bit weird, but better.'

'You did well in there,' I say. 'Very brave.'

'I *was* a bit scared. I thought it might hurt, but it didn't.'

'Good. Let's use this as a lesson and make sure there are no more holes that need filling in future. We'll get you an electric brush, like the dentist recommended. And I'll be watching from now on, so no more skipping. Twice a day, every day, yeah?'

Daisy nods.

'Promise?'

'Promise.'

'Good. And a few less sweets would be an excellent idea too, I think.'

She pulls a sad face.

My phone vibrates in the inside pocket of my jacket. 'Hold on a sec, love.' I stop to pull it out.

We're right next to the entrance of the playground, which as usual I don't want to look at or think about. I try to steer clear whenever possible, but passing by is unavoidable when visiting the dentist. I turn my back to it and try to pretend it's not there.

'Hello?' I say into the receiver, having already spotted that the call isn't from a number in my contacts. I barely notice Daisy's hand slip free from mine as the male voice on the other end of the line says something I can't make out, thanks to a noisy passing truck.

'Sorry, what was that? Who is this?'

'I believe you've been involved in a car accident that wasn't your fault,' the man says. 'I'm from—'

'Let me stop you there,' I tell him. 'You and I both know that's a load of old cobblers. You have no idea who I am. You're fishing. I won't bother asking where you got my number from. Please don't call me again. Hello?'

He's already hung up on me. Idiot. That's what I should have done. I usually do, but I'm so sick of these calls. I'd have been much ruder if Daisy wasn't within earshot, but... Wait. I spin around and, with a rising sense of panic in my chest, see she's no longer next to me. What the hell?

'Daisy!' I yell. 'Where are you?'

'Over here, Mummy.'

Thank goodness. I still can't see her, though, and she sounds far away. 'Where?' I call.

'On the swings.'

These three words give me heart palpitations. I hadn't even considered she'd have gone into the playground.

She knows she's not allowed.

She knows I can't go into that place. Ever.

Shit, I can see her now, swinging backwards and forwards, waving at me like it's the most normal thing in the world. She's alone in there apart from two shifty older boys in tracksuits on a bench – likely truants – vaping and mucking about as they play fetch with a big dog.

'Daisy.' I try to shout, but her name leaves my mouth as a sluggish croak. I want to tell her to come out of there immediately, but I can't get the words out.

It's hard enough to stay standing. To breathe.

There's not enough air. I'm panting. Can't seem to get what I need.

My head's swimming, and I feel myself keeling over, until something – someone – stops me. Grabs hold of my shoulders. Someone standing in front of me. Looking, speaking. Brown eyes and a beard. Lowering me to the ground. Leaning me against a lamp post. How? It can't be, can it?

Dad?

'Breathe. But not so fast. Slow and steady, like this. Copy me. You're all right. I've got you.'

I do as he says, blanking my mind to focus on the breathing, and gradually my fear and anxiety start to recede. I'm coming back to myself as he asks me my name.

'Beth.'

He smiles. 'Hello, Beth. Nice to meet you. I'm Billy. I—'

'You're real. I thought I was imagining you. I thought you were... Never mind.'

I can see him in focus now. More than just the eyes and beard. They *are* reminiscent of my father, but the voice is all wrong – lighter, less gravitas – and he has better teeth. Probably got them fixed, as people do nowadays. He's younger than I am, by a couple of years at least. And he smells nice: fresh and sharp, very masculine.

'How are you feeling? Better?'

I nod.

'I think you had a panic attack, Beth. Has this happened before?'

Another nod.

'We should get you off the floor and onto a seat. There are some benches in the playground. How about—'

'No, please. I can't.'

'Sorry?'

'I can't go in there.'

'Oh. Right. Um, didn't I see the little girl you were with heading inside?'

I gulp. 'Daisy!'

'Don't worry. I'm sure she's fine.' Billy stands up to look. 'Yes, there she is. She's... Oh God, what are *they* up to?'

'Who?' I try to scramble to my feet, but my legs are jelly. I end up back in a heap, yelping as I twist my ankle in the process. 'Ow!'

'Are you all right?' He looks back at me, face scrunched up with concern.

'Never mind me. Daisy. Is she okay? What's going on?'

'There are some lads in there too with a dog. They look like they might be trouble. I thought I saw them, er... Hang on.' He turns away from me to have another look.

'Is Daisy all right?' I struggle to get up again, only to be stopped by a fresh stab of pain from my ankle. 'Please. What's happening?'

'Shit. I'd better get in there.'

He darts through the entrance of the playground just as I hear the blood-curdling sound of my daughter screaming.

Adrenaline pumps through my body and I'm on my feet – bearing the pain from my injured ankle as best I can – eyes scouring the playground for Daisy. She's right on the other side now, most of the way up the big metal and rope climbing frame, wide-eyed and ashen-faced, shrieking. Beneath her, up on its hind legs, snapping at her heels and barking ferociously, is that damn dog. The two boys are standing behind it, hoods up, shaking their fists like they're egging the mutt on. Why the bloody hell would they do that?

It's a mean-looking brown beast of an animal, even from this far away. It must be terrifying up close: all jaws and teeth and claws.

I desperately want to run in there to help my daughter.

I try to, I really do. But putting weight on my ankle is agony, plus my fear of that place is so engrained, so strong, it's like my body is repelled by it: hard-wired not to enter at any cost.

What kind of mother am I to have to put all my faith in a stranger I met a moment ago? I watch him tear through the grass surrounding the playground, slowing as he gets close.

'Help her,' I plead, hot tears of fear and frustration gushing down my cheeks. 'And be careful.'

I pray he can find a way to defuse the situation without anyone – especially Daisy, please not Daisy – getting hurt.

He's really close now. Daisy, who's still screaming and crying from her precarious perch on the climbing frame, must be able to see him. But the yobs and their feral dog have their backs to him, too busy terrorising my daughter to notice his approach. For a moment he raises his arms, palms forward, presumably to show Daisy he's friendly. Then he starts scolding the boys, gesticulating wildly with his upper body.

My heart's in my mouth. I'm terrified how this might unfold. All manner of appalling possibilities race through my doom-laden mind, scarred as it is by the brutal memories that feed my phobia.

I can see Daisy shaking from all the way over here. I will her to hold on tight, whispering: 'Whatever you do, darling, don't let go. It'll be over soon. No thanks to me.'

I'm too far away to catch more than the odd word of Billy's rebuke, especially with the road noise behind me. However, it sparks a mouthy, aggressive retort from one of the yobs, who looks ready to come to blows. I gasp. Fearing the worst, I pull out my phone, ready to dial 999. But before I do, Billy speaks again – more calmly this time – and suddenly the mood shifts. The belligerent boy stands down and his quieter pal steps forward to put the dog on its leash. A moment later, all three scarper, disappearing through a large hole in the fence on the opposite side from where I'm holding myself up, watching. Thank goodness.

I keep my eyes trained on the hole, not trusting they've really gone. Then, to my horror, I hear Daisy scream again. My head snaps back to the climbing frame, heart in mouth. At first I can't figure out what I'm seeing. Billy has her in his arms and she looks to be struggling. I fear the worst: that he's trying to abduct her. But as he puts her down and pats her on the head, turning and waving at me, the penny drops. She fell, when I wasn't even looking in the right direction. Billy caught her, potentially saving her life.

Who is this guy?

Where did he appear from, just at the right moment, like a guardian angel?

I wave back and smile like my lips won't stretch any further.

I wish I could run in there and throw my arms around the pair of them, but that'll have to wait until they get to me. Once they're both safely outside that ghastly place, which has now given me a fresh reason to hate and fear it.

TWO

'How can I ever thank you?'

Billy shrugs. 'There's no need. I'm glad I could help.'

I tighten my arms around Daisy's shoulders, giving her a squeeze. 'Have you said thank you to Billy, love?'

She nods, having barely uttered a word since he brought her back to me. She's probably in shock. Totally understandable. I know I am.

'We're both incredibly grateful,' I say. 'I was... um, you caught me at, er, a bad...'

'Listen, there's no need to explain.' Billy smiles, so calm in spite of everything that's happened. 'I did my good deed for the day. Everyone's safe and sound. End of story. Daisy was incredibly brave. What quick thinking to jump out of reach on the climbing frame. As for the boys with that dog, they were nasty little bullies.'

'How old were they?' I ask. 'What did you say to them?'

'Twelve or thirteen, at a guess. I told them to clear off. That they should be in school, not scaring little girls. One of them tried to play the big man but crumbled when I claimed to be an off-duty policeman and threatened to arrest them. I'm not police, by the way, but it had the desired effect. I doubt they'll be back in a hurry.'

'Really? Wow. Good thinking. How come they weren't in school?'

Billy shrugs. 'They claimed it was a teacher training day. Yeah, right. God knows what was going through their minds to want to scare Daisy like they did.'

'Do you know what kind of dog it was?' I ask. 'I'm not a pet person.'

'No idea, other than a vicious brown one. Some kind of cross-breed, maybe? I'm not into dogs either. Honestly, I was afraid it might go for me when I got up close. No wonder Daisy was scared. Idiotic young lads should not be in control of an animal like that in public, especially where kids play. If I knew who those boys were or where they lived, I'd be having a stern word with their parents.'

'You and me both.' I purse my lips. 'I didn't get a proper look at them. And as you can probably tell, I'm not exactly a frequent visitor to the playground, so I couldn't even narrow it down to any likely suspects.'

Turning to Daisy, I ask: 'You didn't recognise them at all, did you, love? Are they boys you've seen before?'

She shakes her head.

The taxi I called a few minutes ago, to avoid having to walk any distance on my injured ankle, pulls up.

'Here we are,' I say.

Billy nods. 'I'll be on my way. Unless there's anything else I can do for either of you. Can I give you a hand getting into the cab, or—'

'No, I'll manage, thanks. The pain has eased a bit. Please don't let us hold you up any longer than we have already... Unless, um, you want a lift somewhere.'

'No, that's fine. I'm good. I'll see you around, yeah?'

He waves, winks at Daisy and walks off, back towards

where we came from before the drama unfolded. I'm a little disappointed to see him go. It's not every day you meet a nice guy like that, and I'm in the market for nice – I think. The jury's still out on that. It's all a bit fresh. I am single for the first time in forever. Well, separated, at least. In the eyes of the law, I'm still married, but I don't see it that way. When your husband turns out to be a liar and a cheat, that's that, as far as I'm concerned: vows null and void, union over. I kicked him out. Good riddance.

And yet it's never quite so straightforward when there are kids involved. There are two in our case: Daisy and her elder brother Ethan, who's fourteen. Rory, the arsehole ex, will always be their father, so it's not like I can cut him off and never have any contact again. I would enjoy waving a younger, better-looking model in his face, though. And Billy would fit the bill nicely.

What am I thinking? After such a near miss. I need to snap myself out of it. Focus on what matters.

Once we're in the back seat of the taxi, heading to school at last, I look Daisy in the eye. 'Are you all right?'

She nods, although I can see fresh tears forming. I give her hand a squeeze. 'What exactly did those boys do? What happened?'

'They started throwing the ball at me and the dog kept chasing it, barking really loud. The ball nearly hit me and I got scared, so I ran away, towards the climbing frame. The dog ran after me. It was massive, Mummy. I was scared it was going to bite me.'

'Oh, you poor thing.'

'The mean boys were laughing and telling it to attack me. They said it was really hungry and I could be its next meal.'

I'm appalled by the sheer nastiness of this opportunist bullying – and furious at myself for letting it happen right under my nose. 'That's awful. It must have been a big shock, darling, but you're safe now. It's over. Have a good cry. Let it all out.'

After she's calmed down, I get serious. 'What made you run off like that into the playground, Daisy? You know you're not supposed to. You know I can't go in there.'

'Sorry,' she whispers.

'Why did you do it?'

She looks down at her new black school shoes. 'Don't know.'

I consider probing her further, but I don't have the heart. She's been through enough; I doubt she'll do it again. Also, I am painfully aware – not least because of the taxi driver in earshot – that it's not exactly normal for a child to be banned from entering a playground, of all places. Or for a mum not to dare to follow her in there, especially when she's at risk of being attacked. How I wish it wasn't the case. Life would be so much easier.

I froze. I wasn't there for Daisy when she needed me. That's the fact of the matter. If Billy hadn't turned up when he did, well, it doesn't bear thinking about. Daisy's a child. A well-behaved one for the most part. There's no point in me getting angry at her when the person I'm really mad at is myself.

'Please don't do it again,' I say.

'I won't.'

My mind flashes back to the dentist: the reason Daisy was out of class in the first place. 'Is your tooth all right? You didn't knock it or anything in the playground?'

'I don't think so.' She runs her tongue over it like she did earlier. 'Feels the same as before.'

'Before we went to the dentist?'

'No, after she fixed the hole.'

'Good.'

The cab pulls up outside school and, having asked the driver to wait for me, I take Daisy's hand and hobble towards the entrance.

'How are you doing?' I ask her before we step inside.

'Fine.'

'Sure?'

She nods.

I don't believe her. She looks pale and I definitely spotted a waver in her bottom lip. However, I plant a kiss on her forehead and tell her how proud I am of her. Then I hand her over to the school staff and take the taxi home.

I spend the rest of the day with an ice pack on my twisted ankle, feeling guilty about all my failings as a mother.

THREE

The following Saturday, it's time to mow the small front and back lawns of our semi before someone mistakes the place for a jungle.

I've been putting this off forever. Largely because Rory always used to do it and I don't want to take over. I can hardly ask him to continue, though, after turfing him out. Plus, I wouldn't want to give him the satisfaction of thinking I still need him for something.

The weather is perfect: a balmy throwback to the highs of July and August. I scowl at the overgrown grass from my bedroom window as the warm sun kisses my face.

'Ethan?' I call.

My fourteen-year-old's damp, freshly showered head appears around my door quicker than expected, riding on an eye-watering cloud of deodorant. 'Yes, Mum?'

'You're up and about early.'

'I'm off out.'

'Where to?'

'Playing football with my mates. I told you yesterday.'

'Did you?'

He rolls his eyes.

'So you're not interested in making a few quid?'

'What do you mean?'

'If you mow the grass for me, I'll pay you a fiver.'

He roars with laughter. 'You're all right, thanks. Ask Daisy. Perhaps she'll do it.'

'Don't be cheeky. You know she's not old enough. Big help you are.'

Ethan turns away. 'Sorry. I'm a busy guy.'

An hour later, fresh out of delaying tactics and dressed in old scruffs, I wheel the mower out of the shed, plug it into the extension cord dangling from the open lounge window and push it in the direction of the unruly front lawn.

A voice calls my name from the end of the drive. I look up, expecting to see a neighbour; to my shock, it's the guy who saved me and Daisy the other day.

'Billy? What are you doing here?'

'I was passing by, having a walk, when I spotted you in the garden. Thought I'd say hello. How funny that we live so close to each other. I'm just around the corner on Meadow Street. I moved in a few weeks back.'

'Wow.' This seems weird somehow. And yet the playground where we ran into each other *is* only a short walk away. It's not that surprising to find he lives nearby. Something had to bring him to the area. 'Good to see you again.'

He smiles, flashing those nice teeth of his. His eyes twinkle in the sun. I can't help but notice his strong shoulders and muscular arms in his tight black T-shirt.

'Glad to see you walking normally again,' he says. 'Did the ankle take long to heal?'

'No, it was worlds better by the next morning, thankfully.'

'Good stuff.' Grinning, he nods towards the lawn. 'Been putting it off? Looks a tad overdue.'

'Don't.' I flick my hair back, stand up straight and try to forget the awful outfit I'm wearing. 'It hasn't been cut for yonks.'

Yonks? Since when do I use that word? What's wrong with me? Why am I behaving so weirdly?

Billy squints at the ground near my feet. 'You're not planning to go at it straight away with the mower, are you?'

'Um, yeah, why not?'

'Don't you have a strimmer?'

'For the edges? I was going to do those at the end.'

'At that length, personally I'd strim the lot first. Not too close to the ground. Just enough to make it more manageable for the mower.' He pulls a face and takes a step back. 'Sorry, am I mansplaining? That wasn't my intention, honestly. I was trying to be helpful. You must have done this lots of times before. Please, ignore me.'

I laugh. 'Actually, I haven't done it many times at all. My husband always used to... but we're separated now.'

Part of me, I'm embarrassed to admit, hopes Billy might offer to do it for me. He pauses for a long moment, like he might be considering this, but instead he nods and says: 'Right. Anyhow, I'm sure the last thing you need is for someone like me to sweep in here offering unwanted advice. How's, um, the little one doing?'

'Daisy's fine, thanks to you. I'm still so grateful.'

He shuffles his feet on the tarmac. 'Forget about it.'

What comes out of my mouth next is unfiltered and a surprise even to me.

'I won't forget,' I say. 'In fact, ever since, I've been wishing I'd done more to show my appreciation. Now here you are again, and it turns out you live around the corner. It must be a sign. I'd love to cook you a meal to say thank you and to welcome you to the neighbourhood. How does that sound?'

'Um, yeah, sure. That sounds brilliant.'

Something about his reply makes me add: 'Of course, you're

welcome to bring along any, er, family you have too: partner, children, whatever.'

Billy chuckles. 'I wish. No, it'll be me, myself and I. A family of one.'

I fight not to smile. 'How are you fixed this evening?'

He wrinkles his nose. 'Do you know what? I'd love to, but I have plans tonight. I could do tomorrow, if that works.'

'Tomorrow?' I pull a face like I'm trying to remember if *I* have any other plans, which I don't. 'Yeah. I think I could make that work. Not too late, though, as the kids have school the next day. Would around six o'clock suit you? Sorry, that probably sounds really early, but—'

'That would be great. See you then?'

'Definitely.'

'Excellent. I'll let you get back to your lawn.'

I tell the kids about Billy's upcoming visit when we're eating together that night: pizza and chips, a typical Saturday treat.

'What?' Ethan snaps. 'Why is he coming for Sunday tea? Does Dad know?'

I take a deep breath. 'Like I just explained, Billy's new to the area and I want to thank him for helping your sister escape those nasty boys and their dog. What's the problem? And why does it matter if your father knows about it or not? It's none of his business.'

'I'm going to tell him,' Ethan says. 'He has a right to know if you start inviting boyfriends round. Is this bloke going to be staying the night?'

'Ethan!' I shout, louder than intended. 'How dare you speak to me like that? Billy is not my boyfriend, and of course he won't be staying over. He's coming to have tea with the three of us and that's that. I expect you to be on your best behaviour.'

'I'm still telling Dad.'

'You can tell your father whatever you like. It's no secret. Now eat your food and be quiet, if you don't have anything nice to say. Otherwise, you can leave the table.'

'I will.' He shovels a final piece of pizza into his mouth before thumping up the stairs to his bedroom.

'What's wrong with Ethan?' Daisy asks.

'He's a teenager.' I sigh.

'Well, *I* think it's nice that Billy is coming for tea, Mummy. He's my friend. He rescued me. Can we bake him a cake?'

'Of course. That sounds like a perfect idea.'

FOUR

I take a few minutes to spruce myself up the next day before Billy arrives. Nothing fancy. I don't want to look like I've made too much of an effort. Clean clothes – my newest jeans and a fitted top; a comb through my hair; perfume, eyeliner and some concealer to hide the ever-present bags under my eyes.

Afterwards, I look in on Ethan, who's sprawled on his bed in a creased T-shirt and joggers, playing a game on his mobile. His thick, curly ginger hair looks like it hasn't seen a brush in weeks. At least the back and sides are tidy, although I don't know why he has to have them shaved so short. Apparently the muffin-top look is all the rage.

'I hope you're going to be polite this evening,' I say.

He glances at me and grunts. Thankfully, he doesn't comment on my appearance.

'Be nice. Smile. He'll be here soon.'

He grunts again, but his eyes remain on his mobile.

I sigh, resisting the temptation to ask him to clean his room.

Daisy is downstairs, reading a book in the lounge, which is the tidiest it's been in ages, thanks to my earlier efforts. She's wearing a pretty blue dress; her medium-length wavy blonde hair is in a neat ponytail.

'You look nice,' I say.

She looks up and smiles. 'You too, Mummy. Will Billy be here soon?'

'He should be. I'm going to check on the food.'

I've made lasagne, which is already cooked and keeping warm. Nothing to check, in other words. Even the side salad is already prepared in the fridge. I only need to pop the garlic bread in the oven when he gets here and ramp up the temperature. Cake for pudding, made by Daisy.

The real reason I head to the kitchen is to catch my breath after a sudden sense of panic washes over me. When was the last time I had an adult guest over for dinner? I can't even remember. The house looks a state. *I* look a state. It's all going to go horribly wrong and I'll make a fool of myself.

What do I tell him if he asks about my job?

Worse still, what if he brings up the playground and my inability to go inside; my meltdown on the pavement? Oh God, I really couldn't handle that. The only believable explanation would be the truth: what happened all those years ago, which I try not to think about, never mind share. My darkest secret. The source of so much pain in my life – so many struggles with my mental health. No, that's the last thing I want to discuss with Billy.

I sit down at the table and hold my head in my hands.

I need to calm down.

Breathe.

Slow and steady.

Stop overthinking things.

Breathe.

Take it as it comes.

I can do this.

Cross one bridge at a time.

Breathe.

The doorbell sounds. Shit.

It's only five fifty. He's early.

I give my cheeks a light slap, take a final deep breath and stride towards the front door with feigned confidence. Fake it till you make it. That's what they say, right?

I paste on a smile as I swing open the door. It's wiped off when I see who's waiting for me on the other side: not Billy, but bloody Rory.

'Hi, Beth,' the weasel says, a sickly grin plastered across his face, like it's the most natural thing in the world for him to be on my doorstep.

'What the hell are *you* doing here?'

'Not exactly the reception I was expecting,' he says. 'I thought you'd appreciate me ringing the bell rather than using my house key.'

'What? Why are you here? You need to leave.'

His hair is gelled back; he's clean-shaven, wearing an ironed shirt and holding a bottle of wine. Like he's the man I've invited over. What the hell?

'Leave?' Rory says. 'I thought I was invited for dinner. That's what Ethan told me.'

Ah, right. Now this makes more sense.

'You didn't consider it odd that our fourteen-year-old son invited you? You didn't think to check with me first?'

'No, but I'm guessing I should have.'

'Damn right.' I'm about to call Ethan down from his room when, to my horror, Billy appears at the end of the drive, also in a smart shirt and holding a bottle of wine.

Brilliant.

What do I do now?

FIVE

I reach forward to grab a handful of Rory's shirt, pull him inside and growl: 'Go through to the lounge. Your daughter's in there. Don't come out. And don't get comfortable. You're not staying.'

I shove him past me into the hall and turn my attention to Billy as he approaches, a perplexed look on his handsome bearded face.

'Hi, Beth.' His eyes dart behind me into the house. 'How are you? Everything, um, all right? I haven't got the day or time wrong, have I?'

'No. There's been a slight misunderstanding, that's all. Nothing whatsoever to do with you. Could I explain later?'

'Sure. I can come back another time if—'

'No, please come in.'

An awkward moment follows when, as he passes me to enter the hallway, we both weigh up whether to greet each other with a kiss. We don't. Instead, he hands me the bottle of wine. 'For you.'

'Thanks. That's very kind.'

I direct him through to the kitchen, which is thankfully

closed off from the lounge, and offer him a seat at the table. 'Can I get you a drink?'

'Just water for now, please.'

'Of course.'

Handing the glass over, I say: 'Sorry. I'll need a few minutes to deal with that family situation you, er, witnessed at the front door. Could you possibly bear with me?'

Billy smiles, unfazed. 'Sure. Anything I can do to help?'

It's not clear whether he's talking about the food or the Rory issue, but the answer is no thanks either way.

I walk to the lounge, open the door and shut it behind me, glowering at the pathetic cheat of a man I no longer think of as my husband. The fact that Daisy is in the room with us, sitting next to Rory on the sofa, forces me to choose my next words carefully. 'There's been a mistake. Apparently our son's idea of a hilarious wind-up, or at least an attempt to make things awkward. Listen, I get why he's done this. It's understandable in the circumstances – even though he's got totally the wrong end of the stick about what's happening. But I can't deal with it right now. Could you please leave and take him back to your place for the night?'

Rory sighs. 'I suppose so. But could you at least tell me who the man in the kitchen is who will be sitting down to a meal with my wife and daughter?'

'It's Billy,' Daisy says. 'The nice man who rescued me when I was in trouble.'

'I'm sorry, what?' Rory asks, messing his gelled hair with one hand. 'What nice man? What trouble?'

I sigh. 'I was going to tell you when I next saw you. Can it wait? I think the least you owe me is the benefit of the doubt here.'

The weary, testy look that accompanies my words has the desired effect.

'Fine,' Rory says. 'Where is Ethan?'

'In his bedroom. He'll need an overnight bag, including his school uniform. And let yourselves out, please. No need to make this any more awkward than it is already.'

Rory nods, although he's clearly not best pleased.

'Great. Daisy, say goodbye to your father. You can come back to the kitchen with me and make Billy feel welcome.'

Ten minutes or so later, as I'm checking on the garlic bread in the oven – kitchen door closed – I hear the front door slam and breathe a sigh of relief. They've gone.

The meal goes smoothly after that. Billy has seconds and still leaves a clean plate. He and I enjoy a couple of glasses of wine. And the conversation flows. He's great at involving Daisy, asking her questions about herself, then giving her space to respond, unlike a lot of adults. He's really complimentary about her cake, which tickles her pink.

'You made this? Seriously?'

She nods several times, eyes like saucers. 'Mummy helped a bit. Do you like it?'

'I love it. Delicious. Perhaps you should consider becoming a baker or a chef one day. I think you'd be superb.'

Cheeks flushing, she adds: 'I made it specially for you. To thank you for rescuing me.'

'You did?' Billy throws me a subtle grin. 'Wow. Well, it's very much appreciated. Rescuing you was an honour, Daisy.'

I put some filter coffee on after the cake, sending Daisy up for a shower.

'Do I have to?'

'Yes, love. School in the morning. You can pop down again afterwards, if you're quick. Don't brush your teeth until right before bed. We'll do that together again.'

'Has she said much about what happened with the boys and their dog?' Billy asks once she's out of earshot.

'Not really. I've noticed her flinch a couple of times walking past other big dogs. But the experience doesn't seem to have scarred her too badly, thank goodness.'

'What about you?' He strokes his thick beard, which is dark brown with flecks of auburn. The gesture reminds me of my father.

'I'm fine, thanks,' I reply, stifling a yawn. 'Sorry... Long day.'

'I should get out of your hair,' he says.

'Oh, I didn't mean it that way. You've not even had your coffee yet.'

I should probably add that every day feels like a long one when you don't sleep well, but I resist. Billy must already think I'm a mess after what he witnessed outside the playground. No need to divulge any further flaws.

'Sorry about earlier,' I say now that Daisy is no longer around. 'My son, Ethan. He's a teenager and, well, not particularly loving the fact that his parents no longer live together. Unbeknown to me, he decided to tell his dad, Rory, that he was the one invited for dinner. Hence why he also turned up.'

To my surprise, Billy chuckles. 'Sounds like the sort of stunt I'd have pulled when I was a lad. Where is he? Upstairs?'

'No, I asked Rory to take him back to his flat for the night.' Smiling, I add: 'It was pretty funny, I suppose. Little rascal.'

'How long have you been, er, separated? If you don't mind talking about it.'

'It's still pretty fresh. Only a few months since he moved out.'

'Do you think you might get back together one day?'

'No chance. That door's closed.'

Billy nods. Poker face. 'Fair enough. I'll stop prying.'

'What about you, Billy? What is it that brings you to the area? How are you settling in?'

SIX

Billy

He's ready for the personal questions when, inevitably, they come.

He tells Beth that he moved here purely for work. IT contracting for various clients in the city. The kind of role that tends not to lead to many follow-up questions.

He also tells her he's recently turned thirty years old, putting them in roughly the same age bracket. She accepts this without question. The beard definitely adds a few years – a good pay-off for the annoying itchiness.

'I didn't fancy living in the city centre,' he says. 'Too close to work. Too many people. Generally too hectic. I had enough of that down in London. That's one of the reasons I escaped back to the north, looking for more chilled vibes. Here's ideal. Fifteen minutes in and out on the tram; a more relaxed, village-type feel, plus plenty of bars, restaurants and takeaways.'

'Hmm,' Beth says. 'Sounds like you don't cook much.'

He suppresses a laugh. 'Busted. Sit me behind a computer and I'm dynamite. In front of a hob or oven, not so much. That's why this has been so nice here tonight. Such a delicious home-cooked meal. Thank you for having me.'

'You're welcome. And your house. How's that?'

He clears his throat. 'Good. It's a two-up, two-down terrace, so nothing that exciting, but perfect for me. The guy I bought it from renovated and modernised it: stripped floorboards, ethernet plugs, new kitchen and bathroom. That kind of thing. Nothing for me to do other than move in, really. The neighbours seem nice.' He winks. 'Especially the ones around the corner.'

She offers him more coffee.

'No thanks. I've got work in the morning and I'll be up all night, wired, if I have another.'

'Too strong?'

He laughs. 'No, perfect. I know my limits, that's all.'

'Anything else? Another glass of wine? Water?'

'No, I really should be making tracks.'

On the way out, after he's said goodbye to Daisy, Beth mentions the fact that her laptop has been playing up. 'I don't suppose you could have a quick glance sometime, could you? I've no idea what to do with the thing; I'd love to get your professional opinion.'

This is good news. She trusts him already. And she's looking for a way to keep in contact. Billy plays it cool rather than snapping her hand off. 'Um, sure. I'm a bit tired now, but maybe next time?'

'Oh, sorry. I didn't mean now. It's not important. I—'

'How about I pop over sometime during the week, when I get a spare minute?'

'Only if it's not too much trouble.'

'It's not. Thanks again for the lovely dinner.' He darts forward and plants a quick kiss on her cheek, which turns pink in response. 'See you later.'

He allows himself to look back once and wave. And then he

strides off in the direction of his new house. The one he doesn't actually own at all but is renting. Why did he say otherwise? Everything else went so well. According to plan. Why tell an unnecessary lie that he could easily get caught out on? He got carried away. Sloppy. None of that next time. He needs to stick to the script.

Anyway, at least the next time is already laid out for him, thanks to Beth and her gift of a dodgy computer. All he needs to do now is sit tight and wait. A little longer than she's expecting. Playing it cool is definitely the right thing to do. The last thing he wants is to risk scaring her off.

SEVEN

THEN

Beth

It was early July in the mid-noughties, before people had seriously started calling it that. I was a happy fourteen-year-old. Barely a care in the world. Blissfully ignorant of the horrific ordeal that was waiting for me around the corner, ready to knock my world off its axis.

I was particularly happy at that moment because I was close to the end of my third year at high school. I'd been handed my end-of-year report earlier and, thankfully, it was good. I was actually looking forward to showing Mum and Dad when I got home.

It wasn't quite summer holiday time yet, but that sprawling six-week period of freedom and fun was within spitting distance. Friday today – meaning the start of the weekend – and only a fortnight to go until we broke up. In the meantime, school wouldn't really be school. Based on previous years, I was expecting the next two weeks of classes mainly to consist of quizzes, card games and snacks; the odd movie perhaps – and very little work.

The hard part was out of the way. Everyone was ready for a break, including the teachers. Some lucky kids would be absent: aka off on cheap early holidays with their parents. Mum and Dad wouldn't dream of taking me and my younger brother, Sean, out of school early. They frowned on those who did, no matter how much I told them it didn't matter.

Anyway, I knew I'd enjoy twiddling my thumbs and gossiping with my friends about what we were going to get up to in the holidays. Plus, I had a week in sun-soaked Greece to look forward to at the end of August – on an island called Skiathos – which Mum and Dad had booked ages ago. As it turned out, a vacation we'd never actually go on. But I didn't know that back then.

I was walking home just after 3.30 p.m. with my two best friends, Sara and Lou.

'Right now,' I said to them, 'this is my favourite time of year.'

'But we haven't even started the summer holidays yet,' Lou replied.

'Exactly,' I said. 'It's all still ahead of us – and the next couple of weeks at school are going to be a breeze. Lots of time to daydream about what we'll get up to. As soon as the holidays start, it's the beginning of the end. Next thing you know, it'll be September and we'll be back in class.'

Sara put her arm around my waist. 'I love you, Beth, but I reckon that's a bit screwed up.'

'Why?'

'Well, you're basically saying things are best before they happen. I'm not sure that's true.'

I threw a playful punch at her shoulder. 'Not everything, obviously. I'm only talking about the summer holidays. Six weeks always sounds like such a long stretch at the start. Then you blink and it's gone.'

'Hey, look.' Lou nudged me. 'Isn't that the lad you fancy up ahead?'

Mind refocused, I looked forward to see who she was talking about. It wasn't obvious purely from what she'd said, since I had my eye on quite a few boys. Not that I'd ever had an actual boyfriend or even kissed anyone at that point. However, I had a feeling that was about to change. I'd recently become aware of lads, and even some creepy men, looking at me in a certain way. Let's just say I was developing curves in all the right places and I wasn't doing a lot to hide the fact.

Other than the pervy older guys, I'll admit I enjoyed the attention. It made me feel seen, confident, powerful even. Especially after spending most of primary school being considered a swotty wallflower. Sara and Lou weren't quite on the same page yet, but I figured they'd catch up eventually.

Lou was right. Dreamy Dean from the year above was up ahead with a small group of other lads, all but one in school uniform. I'd only spoken to him a couple of times so far, but I'd thought about his floppy fair hair, pale green eyes and athletic frame on many occasions.

'That's Dean, right?' Lou said.

I nodded, hissing at them both to slow down so we didn't reach him too soon.

'Does he know who *you* are?' Sara asked.

'I'm not sure. We have chatted, but only briefly.'

'When?'

Lowering my voice, I said: 'Remember when I helped out at that parents' evening, directing people to the right classrooms? He was doing it too. We bumped into each other a couple of times.'

Sara deliberately bumped into me, nudging me into Lou. 'Are you going to say hi?'

'Maybe,' I said. 'If he doesn't say it to me first.'

'Loving the confidence,' Lou said.

'Play it cool,' I whispered before we got within earshot. Then I looked firmly in the direction of the lads: Dean plus four others. They were definitely watching *us* now. I employed a coy smile, well practised in front of the mirror, which I hoped would invite them – Dean in particular – to make conversation as we passed.

Sure enough, once we were a couple of metres away, the one not in school uniform stepped forward. 'Hello, ladies.' A cocky older lad in shorts and a T-shirt, with a buzz cut and bad acne, he was chewing gum, a cigarette tucked behind one ear. After brazenly looking each of us up and down, he focused his gaze on me, asking: 'Going anywhere nice?'

In your dreams, ugly boy, I thought. What I said was: 'Hi. We're just heading home.' Then I turned towards Dean, who was standing to my left, smiled sweetly and asked him how he was doing.

Dean's cheeks flushed as he shuffled his feet. 'Um, hi. I'm good, thanks. How are you? It's, er, Beth, right?'

'Yes,' I said, chuffed that he remembered but determined not to show it. Turning back to the non-uniform guy, who looked around seventeen or eighteen, I said: 'What are you boys up to?'

'We're heading to the park for a bit. Gonna have a few tins, smoke a couple of spliffs. You three want to join us? We'll look after you, won't we, lads?'

The others murmured their agreement.

I glanced at Sara and Lou. I could tell from their eyes, plus the fact that neither of them had said a word during this exchange, that they weren't into this one bit.

'Thanks for the offer, but we can't. We've got plans later. Maybe next time?'

'Shame. I'll look forward to that, though. I'm Mac.' He insisted on shaking each of our hands, before standing aside to let us past. 'Have a good one, ladies. See you soon.'

As we walked away, I made a point of turning back and, with a flutter of my eyelashes, saying: 'See you, Dean.'

'Yeah, um. Bye, Beth.' A moment later, I heard him getting ribbed by his pals, which made me smile.

The other two weren't so amused, particularly Sara.

'What the hell was that?' she asked me once we were a decent distance away. 'That Mac guy was gross. Were you actually considering going to the park to do drugs with him and his horrible clammy hands?'

'No,' I said. 'I only spoke to him to try to make Dean jealous.'

'Does Dean drink and smoke weed?' Sara asked.

I let out a long sigh. 'How would I know? Loads of lads are into that stuff. He's totally fit. Do you reckon he's into me?'

'Well, he remembered your name,' Lou said.

I nodded. 'He did, didn't he?'

EIGHT

NOW

Ethan

Well, that backfired. Now he has to spend the night at Dad's poxy flat. He likes to call it an apartment – his father, that is – which makes it sound like somewhere rich New Yorkers live in movies. Dad's place isn't anything like that. No uniformed doorman. No shiny gold elevator. Definitely no iconic views of Central Park.

It's a tiny ground-floor flat with two small bedrooms: one with a double, where Dad sleeps, and the other with two singles, a metre apart. Ethan usually shares this with Daisy. Far from ideal. The carpets are manky. It smells of damp. And it's far too close to the tram line for comfort. You can literally feel the vibrations whenever a tram passes.

At least he has the bedroom to himself tonight. And there's Wi-Fi, even if it isn't as fast or reliable as at home.

'Shall we order pizza?' Dad asks after tapping on the bedroom door and peering around it.

Ethan, who's lying on the bed staring at his mobile, doesn't care that he also had pizza yesterday. 'Sounds good.'

'Shall we share a large pepperoni? Garlic bread on the side?'

'Sure.'

'What are you up to?'

'Nothing.'

'Come through to the lounge. We can watch something together.'

On your rubbish small TV, Ethan thinks. 'Fine.'

He knows Dad will eventually want to talk about what he did. He's surprised he hasn't mentioned it already, like when they had to frigging walk back here, since Dad hadn't brought the car.

Sure enough, once the pizza arrives and they're both scoffing away, some TV quiz show on in the background, the question comes: 'So what was that all about then, mate, inviting me over at the same time as that other bloke?'

Ethan stares at the telly. 'Dunno.'

'Come on. You can do better than that.'

'I thought it would be funny.'

'Right.' Dad nibbles a slice of pizza. 'Well, it wasn't very nice of you, Ethan. You wasted my time, for one, and you really embarrassed your mum in front of her, um, guest. Apologise to her tomorrow, please.'

'I thought I was doing you a favour. Don't you want to make things up with Mum and move back home?'

Dad looks taken aback. He turns the TV volume down. 'It's complicated, mate. I messed up. I've explained to you what happened. It's my own fault that I'm here. You shouldn't be pulling pranks that upset your mum. She can invite whoever she likes for dinner.'

'So that's it? You and Mum are done for good? You're going to get a divorce? You're going to keep on living *here*?'

'I don't know. We'll have to see how things go. Your mum needs time and space. It's not that bad here, is it, at least for now?'

Ethan resists the urge to shout that it's bloody awful here. That he doesn't want to be a kid from a broken home, living between two places. Having to deal with step-parents one day. Maybe even step-siblings. His best mate, Liam, has an elder stepbrother, Marty, who's always picking on him, nicking his stuff and making fun of him. Punching him to give him a dead arm. He once spat in his hair gel and put some of his pubes in there. Freak. Liam's been talking about getting his hands on a blade so he can defend himself. Give the prick a bit of a scare.

Sometimes Ethan hates Dad for what he did. Hooking up with someone else behind Mum's back. What was he thinking? Why would he do that? He almost wishes he didn't know, like Daisy, who is apparently 'too young to understand'.

Other times, he feels sorry for Dad, having to live here on his own most of the time. Pretending it's nice when anyone can see that it's crap. This makes Ethan mad at Mum. Did she do something to push Dad away? And why won't she give him another chance? It's obvious he's sorry. Couldn't she at least try to forgive him?

Not that he'd ever say any of this to Mum. He'd be too worried about upsetting her. He knows how fragile she can be, despite her attempts to hide it. She's been better since stopping work, at least, but he does worry about her, especially with Dad not living at home.

As for this bloke coming over for his tea today, that got Ethan in a bit of a panic, thinking how Mum might start dating him. How he might end up moving in, closing the door on any chance of Dad coming home. So Ethan did what he did, which actually made matters worse, as it stopped him being there to keep an eye on them. To make sure Billy – stupid name – knew his place. Bollocks.

'It's not that bad here, is it?' Dad asks again, his eyes sad and pathetic.

'It's fine. Please could you turn the telly back up? I can't hear it.'

'Sure, but it helps to talk about things sometimes, you know. Bottling up your emotions is never good.'

Ethan grabs another slice of pizza and stares at the TV, pretending he's really into this boring quiz show. He wonders how long he needs to stay here to keep Dad happy before he can return to his makeshift bedroom with his phone and get some peace and quiet.

NINE

Beth

Monday mornings. I used to really dread them. Far worse than the usual back-to-work gloom that most people get after a nice weekend away from the office.

That's what happens when you grow to hate your job. When you've got a selfish, cloth-eared bastard for a boss who doesn't appreciate you and keeps piling on the pressure, ignoring your pleas for help, until you reach breaking point. Until you're disappearing to the loo at frequent intervals to get away from your desk and have a cry. Especially when you're always so tired, because sleeping has been a problem forever.

It sounds absurd now, but I didn't realise I was suffering from workplace stress until my GP said so. I thought it was my fault that I couldn't cope, because of all the stuff from my past and, recently, the break-up with Rory. I guess I hoped there might be a magic pill they could prescribe to take the pain away and allow me to keep on working like a robot. Instead, I got signed off with stress and prescribed some books and CDs from the library about mindfulness and meditation. I'm on a waiting list to see someone in person, so I can talk about it, although I'm not holding my breath for that to happen any time soon.

All of this makes it sound like I have a high-powered, dynamic career. I don't. It's an office job, answering phones and keying meaningless crap into sluggish computer systems so dated that we don't even have the capacity to work from home. I used to be able to do what was required of me with my eyes closed. But then came the management changes and the countless cutbacks, which I somehow survived.

My workload massively increased while my salary stagnated.

Something had to give.

I'll have to return there at some point. I can't keep getting signed off forever. But for now, at least, work isn't something I have to worry about. I can't tell you what a relief that is, particularly on Sunday nights and Monday mornings like this, when I'm shattered. Typically, I woke from one of my bad dreams at 4.22 a.m., night sweats and all. I barely slept after that. It's hard to nod off again when you've imagined yourself, in vivid detail, being chased through a park by a faceless, bloodthirsty monster.

I've not long returned home from dropping Daisy off at school. Now I'm wondering what to do with myself for the rest of the day. I refuse to go down the daytime TV rabbit hole.

Perhaps I should read some of those prescribed books. I could even have a go at meditating.

But no, I don't feel like any of that. I'll probably do some housework instead. The place is a mess, as usual.

I start in my own bedroom, because that's the least untidy.

As I'm dusting the top of the large oak-effect chest of drawers Rory and I once chose together, I lift my laptop out of the way. It's been there ever since I dug it out for Billy to hopefully look at, following the meal I cooked for him just over a week ago. I've not heard from him since then.

I'm not bothered about the laptop. I only mentioned it as a

somewhat pathetic excuse to see him again, having really enjoyed his company that night. Why didn't I give him my phone number or ask for his? I've been out of this game for too long. I considered walking past his house a few times last week, in the hope of bumping into him, but at least I managed to talk myself out of that.

If he's interested, he'll come back. If he doesn't, so be it.

Similar thoughts occupy my mind as I sweep through the house on my cleaning mission. By the time I'm done, having a shower to freshen myself up, I'm firmly convinced I'll never see Billy again unless we bump into each other by chance.

Eating a sandwich for lunch, it occurs to me that maybe, if I do want a new relationship, I should try online dating. That's what people do these days, right? It's all websites and apps. Funnily enough, until Billy came along, I hadn't realised I was interested. I guess I thought I was past all that. But why should I be? Rory's had his fun, shattering our marriage in the process. Why can't I do the same?

I am only thirty-three. That's hardly old, is it? I'm still arguably in my prime, even if I rarely feel it.

That said, it's way too close for my liking to thirty-four: a particular milestone I've never looked forward to reaching. An age that will always have negative connotations for me, forever fused to horrific memories. But I'm not thinking about that now. Thankfully, my birthday isn't until February. I'll cross that terrifying bridge when I come to it.

People often assume I'm older – charming – because of the age of the kids. What can I say? I had them young, like my parents before me. Many people these days seem to wait as long as they can, putting their careers first. Each to their own, but that's not my bag.

Rory and I settled down early. I thought he was the one. That we'd be together our whole lives. So much for that. Still, I stand by having the children when we did. At least we won't be knocking on sixty when they hit adulthood.

No sooner have I cleared away my lunch than the doorbell sounds.

I expect the postman to greet me with a parcel as I swing open the front door, but it's not him.

It's Billy.

'You're in,' he says, eyes twinkling. 'I hoped I'd catch you. How are things?'

'Good.' Hopefully I look less shocked than I feel. 'Would you like to, um, come in?'

'Sure. I thought it was about time I came to have a look at that laptop of yours. I meant to do it last week, but work was ridiculous. I'm off today. You too?'

'Uh-huh,' I reply, nice and vague, since I haven't told him yet about being off with stress. 'Brew?'

'Cup of tea would be lovely. Milk, no sugar, please.'

I shut the door and lead him through to the kitchen.

'Your hair looks nice,' he says. 'Have you done something different with it?'

I feel my cheeks flush. Is he flirting with me? It sure sounds like it. Unless I've missed a trick and he's actually... gay? No, that can't be it. Can it?

'I washed it,' I say, self-consciously flipping the ends back over my shoulders. 'It's not dry yet, so the curls are looser than usual, which makes it look longer.'

'Well, whatever it is, it definitely suits you.'

TEN

Billy has been looking at my laptop for a good ten minutes. I've no idea what he's doing, but he seems to know his way around, as you'd expect of an IT contractor.

'Another drink?' I ask him across the kitchen table.

'No thanks. I can't stop long. I need to get to the gym.'

'How's it looking?"

'You could do with more memory. I'd also recommend defragmenting the hard drive and installing better antivirus software.'

'Right. Is that a big job? Should I book it in somewhere? I'm not in a rush. I rarely used it even before it started playing up. But it would be nice to have a reliable alternative to my phone.'

'I can fix it, if you like,' he says, shutting the lid and looking me in the eye. 'I'd have to take it away for a few days, though.'

'Really? That's so nice of you. Are you sure you have time?'

'Yeah, no problem.'

'Thanks so much. I'll pay the going rate, obviously. Should we swap phone numbers?'

'Good idea.'

Once Billy's gone, I can't stop thinking about him. What's

wrong with me? I'm like a love-struck teenager. He's so capable and, well, handsome. My eyes kept lingering on his biceps, his strong shoulders and the smooth, tanned skin at the top of his chest as he looked at my laptop. I hope he didn't notice me ogling him. How embarrassing would that be? Especially if he turns out to be gay.

I don't think he is. I don't get that vibe from him. Does that mean he's into me too, in light of the compliment about my hair? Perhaps. I'm so out of practice.

Next I wonder whether handing my computer over to him was a good idea. It's not like I know him well, is it? And I didn't ask him for a receipt, because that would have been weird. What if he never comes back with it? Rory would say it was a bad idea. He worries about security, scams and so on, more than I do. But it's not like I don't know where Billy lives, roughly at least. I've got his phone number too now. And the laptop probably isn't worth much. It's pretty old.

Shit. Is there private stuff on there? I rack my brains, but no, I can't think of anything. Rory and I didn't have the kind of relationship where we made sex tapes. There was a time when we couldn't keep our hands off each other and were quite adventurous, but that was years ago, back when we first got together. We barely had sex at all those last few years, mainly down to me not being in the mood. No, it's more private documents or financial information I'm concerned about, but I still can't think of anything significant. There's no active email client on the laptop and I can't ever remember using it for online banking. Rory used to do all the money stuff on his own computer. These days, I use mobile apps for everything.

Why am I fretting about this? Billy is a lovely bloke, so kind and generous with his time, who's given me no cause whatsoever to suspect him of anything untoward.

· · ·

Later that day, after picking Daisy up from school, I get the feeling something's not right.

'What's up, love?' I ask once we get through the front door. 'You've barely said a word.'

Daisy shrugs. 'Nothing.'

'Are you sure? Did something happen at school?'

'I don't want to talk about it.'

'Why not, love? Did you have an argument with one of your friends? Was the teacher cross with you? Come on, please tell me. A problem shared is a problem halved, remember.'

It takes a fair bit more coaxing, but eventually, tears in her eyes, Daisy opens up. 'It was Lori.' She snivels. 'When we did PE, I tied my hair back and she said my ears stick out. She laughed at me and called me Dumbo, like the elephant. Some of the others were laughing too.'

'That's really mean.' I give her a hug. 'And it's not even true. Your ears are perfect. They don't stick out at all.'

'They do a bit,' Daisy says, mouth curling down at the sides. 'I had a look in the mirror in the toilets when no one else was there. I'm not tying my hair up any more.'

I kneel in front of my daughter, gently tuck her hair behind both ears, even though she resists, and make a point of looking at them in great detail.

'What are you doing, Mummy?'

'Bear with me a minute... Right, I'm done.'

'What do you mean?'

'I've given your ears a thorough examination and I can confirm that they are one hundred per cent perfect. Not big. Not sticky-out. Not in any way whatsoever. They're lovely ears, rather like mine, in fact, of which I'm rather proud. This Lori is clearly a stupid idiot who should get her eyes checked out.'

Too much? Maybe I shouldn't have called Lori names. Not exactly setting a good example. However, I'm furious. I know exactly who she is. I remember her from one of Daisy's birthday parties, and she was a pain in the neck then: tiny with a big mouth. She was always asking for something she couldn't have and bossing the other children around. I've a good mind to speak to her mother or father at the school gates tomorrow, or maybe even to have a word with the teacher.

'Where was Mrs Williams when Lori was mean to you?'

'Not sure.'

'Does she know about it?'

Daisy shakes her head.

'Would you like me to speak to her?'

'No. No way! Please don't, Mummy. I wish I hadn't told you now. It was nothing, honestly. I'm not even that upset.'

I'm thrown by the fervour of her reaction. Is this because she's so afraid of Lori?

'What's the problem? Why don't you want me to tell your teacher?'

'Because everyone will think I'm a telltale and no one will want to play with me.'

That kind of makes sense, I guess. 'What *do* you want me to do about it, then, love?'

'Nothing.'

'Are you going to do something about it instead?'

'Like what?'

'Stand up to her. Tell her to stop being nasty. And definitely don't stop wearing your hair tied back.'

'Maybe.'

'It sounds to me like she's a bully, Daisy. And bullies usually crumble when you challenge them. You're bigger than her, right?'

Daisy nods.

'She's probably jealous of you.'

'Why would she be jealous of *me*? She's really popular.'

'Hmm. I bet you're not the first person she's been mean to, are you?'

'No.'

'There you go. All the others she's picked on probably don't like her much at all.'

'Can we stop talking about this now, please, Mummy?'

I don't want to, but equally I don't want Daisy to think twice about telling me such things in future. I'll drop it for now, but I'll be keeping my eye on the situation. 'Okay. Would you like a drink and a biscuit?'

'Yes please. Can I watch some TV?'

'Fine, but only for half an hour. Do you have any homework?'

'Reading.'

'Don't forget to do that.'

'I won't.'

Fifteen minutes later, Ethan gets home. He lets himself in with his key and I hear him heading straight upstairs.

'Are you not going to say hello?' I ask, walking from the kitchen to the hallway.

'Hi, Mum,' he calls from upstairs.

'How was school?'

'Fine.'

'And your English test?'

'It was okay.'

'Think you passed it?'

'We'll see. Can I go now?'

'Sure.'

I return to the kitchen, peering in on the lounge en route. Daisy is sitting on a cushion on the floor right in front of the TV, glued to whatever garish cartoon it is she's watching.

Ethan and I have moved past his little prank of inviting his father for dinner at the same time as Billy. We talked it through when he got home the next day and he apologised.

'He's not your boyfriend, is he?' he asked.

'Of course not,' I replied. 'He's a nice man who I wanted to thank for helping your sister.'

'Good.'

'Is that what you were worried about? Is that why you did it?'

'Dunno.'

Goodness knows what he'd be like if I did end up dating someone. Not that I'm going to let that put me off doing what's best for me. In truth, I often feel lonely. I need adult company. I notice that more and more since Rory left and I went off work with stress.

I mean, look at me now: both my kids are home and neither is even in the same room as me. Something needs to change. Surely I deserve to be happy. Especially after all the bad stuff I've been through in my life so far. I might look okay on the outside, but my soul is a patchwork quilt of scars.

ELEVEN

Ethan

He's doing homework. Boring physics homework that he barely understands. He's been putting it off for days, but it's due in first thing tomorrow, so he needs to get it finished.

The doorbell rings. Who's that at half past five on a Thursday afternoon? Probably a delivery driver with something Mum's ordered online.

She calls up from the kitchen. 'Ethan, could you get that?'

'Why can't you? I'm doing homework.'

'Please, love. I'm in the middle of something tricky here.'

When Ethan was downstairs earlier, she was preparing some weird healthy vegetarian recipe she'd found in a magazine. Part of him would rather let that go wrong so they have to order takeaway instead.

The bell sounds for a second time.

'Ethan! Now, or I'll have to dock your pocket money.'

'Fine. Give me a second.'

He gets up off his bed and puts his physics exercise book

and question sheet to one side. Then he stamps downstairs and opens the door.

Shit. It's Billy – that bearded bloke Mum had round for dinner after he helped Daisy escape from some bullies with a dog. Boys who Ethan, as a big brother, would love to get his hands on to scare them back. If only someone had actually managed to get a good look at them. Two lads a bit younger than him in hooded tracksuits with a brown dog. Not much to go on.

Ethan got sent to Dad's for the night without meeting this supposed hero dude. But prior to that, he'd watched from his bedroom window, seeing him and Dad arrive at almost the same time, much to his amusement.

What the hell does Billy No-Mates want now?

'Hello? Can I help you?'

'Ah, you must be Ethan. Nice to meet you. I'm your mum's friend, Billy.' Flashing an annoying smile, he extends his right arm, apparently looking for a handshake.

Ethan stands there, rigid, saying nothing. He deliberately leaves Billy hanging. But when the hand doesn't get withdrawn and the vibe turns awkward, he takes it. He tries to give it some oomph, but Billy's hand doesn't flinch or flex. Like it's made of stone. Like he could crush Ethan's much smaller, weaker hand in an instant. Dickhead.

'Is your mum home?'

Ethan nods.

'Could I maybe come in, then? I have something for her.' Billy lifts up his left hand, holding a plain white plastic bag.

'Hang on. I'll check.'

Ethan shuts the front door in Billy's face, leaving him outside. He walks through to the kitchen, where Mum is in the process of moving a vegetable-filled tray into the oven.

'Who was it?'

'Um, that guy, Billy.'

Mum's eyes light up, much to his annoyance. 'Oh, really? What did he want?'

'To see if you were home.'

'And? What did you say? You didn't send him away, did you? Oh, for goodness' sake, Ethan.'

'Chill out. I didn't send him away.'

'So where is he?'

'Waiting outside the front door. He asked if he could come in. I said I'd check.'

'That's plain rude. Let him in right now, Ethan. Show him through.'

'Fine.'

Ethan trudges back to the front door and swings it open.

He spots the tail end of a frown on Billy's face.

'Mum is in the kitchen. You know the way, right?'

'Yes, thanks.'

'Good.'

He returns upstairs without looking back, leaving Billy to it, and shuts his bedroom door. Knowing Mum will be occupied for a while with her visitor, and with Daisy safely out of the way at Dad's, he takes the opportunity to have a look at his recent purchase, which he's stashed away in an old shoebox behind a load of junk under his bed. He lies on the floor and rummages around until he finds it and pulls it out: his first ever knife.

It feels nice in his hand, that weighty mix of metal and wood. He opens the five-inch blade and enjoys the solid clunk as it locks into place at the back. Then, with the dark wood and brass handle in the grip of his right hand, he runs his left thumb and forefinger up and down along the smooth sides of the stainless-steel blade. He carefully feels the spike on the end and then, even more cautiously, rubs the tip of his finger across the cutting edge, which is nice and sharp to his gentle touch.

This lock knife is big enough to land him in serious trouble, should he ever get caught with it. So why did he buy it?

He's not entirely sure. One minute he was agreeing to accompany Liam when he went to buy a knife to scare his horrible stepbrother, Marty. The next, he was buying one too. Partly because he liked the look of it. Partly because of what the lad who sold it to them said. Connor, a scary Year 13, able to source a variety of contraband via his twenty-something elder brother, met them in a park after school. He showed up with several knives in a backpack and started chatting about how it was important that they could defend themselves.

'Everyone's carrying a blade on the streets these days,' he said. 'I'm not saying that's a good thing. It ain't. It's a worry, truth be told. Things can get serious out of nowhere. But you don't want to be the lad who's not prepared. Know what I mean? Fingers crossed you'll never have to use it. It's all about the deterrent, innit?'

After swearing never to reveal where they got them, they both ended up buying one. So far, neither has been put to use, other than in private moments like this.

'Are you going to actually pull it on Marty?' Ethan asked Liam when they were walking home from school earlier today.

'Yeah, if I have to. That's why I got it. He hasn't been bothering me so much the last few days, though. He's been busy with other stuff. We'll see what happens.'

'You'll need to be careful, whatever,' Ethan said. 'You don't want to end up stabbing him. And you definitely don't want him getting hold of it and turning it on you.'

'Yeah, I'm not stupid, dude. I have thought about this stuff.'

In his bedroom, Ethan stands in front of the mirror and holds the open knife next to his face, pulling his best psycho sneer.

Then Mum calls his name, so he folds it shut and shoves it in his pocket. 'Yes?' he calls back, opening his bedroom door a crack.

'Tea will be ready soon, love. Could you come down and lay the table, please?'

'In a minute.'

He dives back under the bed, returning the knife to its secret hiding place, where it will hopefully never be discovered. Imagine what Mum would do if she did find it. He'd be in so much trouble. She'd probably march him to the nearest police station and make him hand it in, before grounding him for the rest of his life.

These thoughts make Ethan wonder whether he did the right thing buying it. He already knows the answer: of course not. Maybe he should chuck it away or sell it to someone else. Perhaps he'd be better stashing it at Dad's place. Where, though? His flat is so small.

Relax, he tells himself. It'll be fine where it is for now.

He trudges downstairs to lay the table, hoping bloody Billy has already left.

TWELVE

Beth

'There you are,' I say to Ethan when he finally appears to lay the table. 'Could you set three places, please? It'll be ready in five or ten minutes.'

'Isn't Daisy staying at Dad's tonight?'

'That's right. I've invited Billy to join us. I've made far too much.'

Ethan glances at Billy, who's seated at the kitchen table, and scowls.

'Problem?' I say.

'Um, no.' His cheeks redden. He lays the table in silence before making to leave.

'Where are you going?'

'My room. I've got loads of homework, remember.'

'Well, as I said, the food will be ready very soon.'

'Can't you call me?'

'Fine. But don't take ages to come back down when I do.'

'Sorry about him and his attitude,' I say to Billy once Ethan's gone. 'Teenagers.'

'Don't worry. He probably sees me as some kind of threat. He's being territorial, that's all. Typical behaviour for a young lad. I'd have been the same at his age.'

'Leaving you waiting outside, though, after you've been good enough to fix my laptop and bring it back.' I roll my eyes. 'How much do I owe you, by the way?'

He waves away the question. 'Nothing. On the house. It didn't take long and you do keep feeding me lovely food.'

'You haven't tried this yet. It's a bit of an experiment.'

'If it tastes as good as it smells, I'll be happy.'

'What about the extra memory? Come on, that must have cost something. Let me pay for that at least.'

'No, as luck would have it, I had some lying around that fitted. Perk of the job.'

When I call Ethan back down, he's every bit as unfriendly to Billy as I feared he would be, verging on hostile.

I try. Billy tries. We ask him all sorts between us, but all he gives in return are monosyllabic answers.

'Are you into football?' Billy asks at one point.

'I play a bit.'

'What team do you support?'

'Why?'

I clear my throat to get Ethan's attention and frown at him, nudging his leg under the table.

'United.' He doesn't look up from the plate of food he's barely touched.

'Nice one,' Billy says. 'You must have been pleased with the score at the weekend.'

'Hmm.'

'Eat up,' I say. 'Moving it around the plate won't land it in your stomach.'

'I don't really like it, Mum. It doesn't taste of anything. It needs meat. Can we never have this again, please?'

Billy throws me a supportive look. 'Well, I think it's delicious. I only wish I could cook this well. Then I wouldn't have to rely on microwave meals and takeaways.'

'Who wants dessert?' I ask once the main course has been cleared away. 'I've got yoghurt, chocolate mousse or ice cream.'

'No thanks,' Ethan says without missing a beat. 'Can I get back to my homework?'

'This is a first. No afters, and keen to do your homework? Are you actually my son or has he been replaced by a doppelgänger?'

Ethan pulls a face. 'What does that even mean?'

'Never mind.' I don't have the energy to challenge his non-compliance any further. 'Fine, you're excused.'

He's up from the table and off in a flash.

'That was fun, wasn't it?' I say in hushed tones to a chuckling Billy. 'Bet you can't wait to come back and have some more scintillating conversations with my chatterbox son.'

'It's no problem. I have a thick skin. That said, I do prefer to wear gloves when I wash up.'

'Sorry?'

'That was my roundabout way of insisting on doing the dishes.'

He won't take no for an answer, so he ends up washing while I dry. We make a good team.

Later, over coffee, he invites me for dinner at his place, which takes me by surprise. 'Oh, right. Um, okay, thank you. That would be nice.'

'Have I put you off with the tales of my bad cooking? I can't promise anything fancy. It might even be takeaway, but I can't very well keep coming here for food without reciprocating, can I? That would be plain rude.'

'It's not necessary or expected,' I say. 'Especially after you fixed my laptop.'

'Still, I want to.'

'That's very kind of you, then. I'd love to. To be clear, is it an invite for me only or the kids too?'

'Up to you. Whatever suits.'

Sensing a chance to enjoy some adult alone time with Billy – to see if he's actually interested in me like I'm interested in him – I say: 'I'll leave the kids behind. Give us some peace and quiet. They're due to spend the night at Rory's on Saturday, if you don't already have plans, of course.'

'No, I'm free. Sounds good. Shall we say around eight o'clock?'

My first thought, being used to kids' eating times, is that this sounds late. But I don't say so, for fear of coming across like a mumsy fuddy-duddy. Instead, I reply: 'Perfect. It's a date.'

The last bit slips out automatically, leaving me embarrassed. 'Um, would you like me to bring anything?' I add, avoiding Billy's eye. A desperate attempt to cover up the obvious.

'No, just yourself.' He makes no reference to my date comment, thank goodness, so I try to pretend it never happened.

After Billy's gone home, Mum video-calls me.

'Hi, love. How are you?' She smiles from my phone screen with a sparkling set of perfect pearly whites that I've never seen before.

'Hi. Not as good as you, by the looks of things. Have you had your teeth done? They look amazing.'

She roars with laughter. 'I wondered if you'd notice. Yes, I decided to upgrade my smile to keep up with the Joneses, so to speak. You like?'

'Definitely. Wow, I bet that cost a bit.'

'Hopefully worth every penny. I can be a standard-bearer for the English in Canada now, to prove that we don't all have awful teeth. And I'll look much better in photos with Roger. It used to drive me crazy how yellow my teeth looked compared to his. Now I can give him a run for his money.'

Mum emigrated to Toronto about eighteen months ago after a whirlwind romance with a Canadian chap ten years her junior who she met on a cruise and married a few months later. I miss her a lot, but I'm also delighted she's happy at last. Roger is kind and he's clearly madly in love with her. She deserves that.

I knew she'd call today, as it's my brother's birthday. It would have been, anyway, if he was still with us. Sean was killed in a motorbike crash around six and a half years ago. I miss him even more than Mum. At least I can still talk to her. He's gone for good. Taken from us far too early.

He's been in the back of my mind all day. He's the reason I made that veggie meal at which Ethan turned his nose up. It was meant as a kind of tribute to my brother, because he was a vegetarian. However, to be fair to Ethan, I never told him this. He does at least remember his uncle, unlike Daisy, but I'm not sure exactly how much he recalls.

After small talk about the weather and the time difference between here and Canada, plus the usual questions about how everyone in the family is getting on, I take the bull by the horns. 'Sean would have been twenty-eight today, God rest his soul.'

Mum nods. 'I know. I had a little cry earlier, wishing he was still with us.'

'Me too. It never gets any easier, does it, living without them?'

'No. At least we still have each other, even if we can't be together as often as we'd like any more.'

'Yeah.' I wish I could give her a hug. Nothing beats actual human contact.

'Where are my gorgeous grandkids?' she asks eventually. 'Can I speak to them?'

'Daisy is with Rory tonight,' I say. 'Ethan's home, but he's being a real teenager at the moment. He's got loads of home-work, so he says, and I don't have the energy to try to lure him out of his bedroom. Sorry. You can always try him directly on his phone, if you like.'

'I understand, love. How are you? You look tired.'

'I'm fine.' I say this more out of habit than because it's the truth. I do feel shattered, but what's new? It's more or less my permanent state of being.

'How are things with Rory?'

'Hmm. He's doing his bit with the kids, for the most part. Things are fairly amicable. I'd rather not have to see him at all, since it's impossible to do so without remembering what he did. But hey ho. He's Ethan and Daisy's dad.'

'Is there really no hope of you giving him another chance? You could always try marriage counselling, or—'

'Mum, we've been through this so many times before. You know the answer. Nothing's changed.'

'Okay, I'll stop. What about work? How's that going?'

'Fine,' I lie. 'Busy.'

I haven't told her about being off with stress. I know I should have, but I don't want to worry her on top of everything else. Plus, I can't face all the questions I know she'd ask. It's not worth the hassle. The slight danger is that she'll find out from talking to one of the children, although it's not something I've spoken to them about in great detail, as I equally don't want them to fret. I've said I'm having a break to focus on other things, spinning it along the lines of a sabbatical. It's not like kids tend to be very interested in their parents' work, anyway.

I consider mentioning Billy to Mum, despite it all being so new and fragile, since there's not really anyone else with whom I can discuss such matters. Ultimately, though, I say nothing, partly not to jinx it and partly because I don't want to have to explain the unfortunate circumstances of how we met. Maybe next time we speak I'll tell her, once I've had the chance to test the waters alone with Billy at his house.

I ask after Roger, who I am genuinely fond of, and she says he's doing great. She goes on to regale me with various stories of what they've been up to in and around Toronto, before asking when we're coming to visit. 'Soon, hopefully,' I say to appease her, even though I can't see how we'd realistically afford it.

'I hope so,' she says. 'I miss you all so much. You'd love it here.'

When we eventually hang up the call, I realise we barely spoke about Sean. Feeling bad, I dig out some photos of him, making myself cry again, wishing he was still around. My late father too, of course. I miss them both every single day. But on certain special days, like this one – my baby brother's birthday – the pain is particularly acute.

Mum and I are the lucky ones, supposedly: the survivors. But it never feels that way. What's lucky about having your dad and brother taken from you, years before their time?

THIRTEEN

THEN

'I'm so sorry. I can't believe I did that. What a klutz I am.'

I looked up, pretending to be surprised it was Dean's lunch tray I'd knocked over, having 'accidentally' bumped into him while racing past.

'Oh, it's you,' I said. 'Hi, Dean. I was in such a rush, I didn't notice anyone was standing there. Did it spill on you or is it mainly on the floor?'

Dazed, he stared down at the fresh mess close to his feet in the school canteen, slowly shaking his head. 'Um. No, I think I'm all clear.' He reached down and wiped a blob of tuna from his shoe with one finger. 'I am now.'

'Don't worry about the mess.' I was already kneeling down to pick it up. 'I'll sort it. It's the least I can do. And then I'll buy you another lunch.'

He knelt too and started helping me. 'It's fine, Beth. You don't need to do that.'

If this was a high school rom-com, our eyes would have met and we'd have almost kissed. That didn't happen. But I did insist on buying him lunch afresh. And we did end up sitting together to eat. Bingo.

It was the Friday after we'd seen each other with our friends. I'd spotted Dean around school a few times since, but only from afar. I'd been looking for the perfect opportunity to run into him. Having spotted my chance at last – both of us on our own, so no one else to get in the way – I'd done literally that.

Chatting with him at the lunch table, it was a struggle not to grin from ear to ear. I couldn't believe my spur-of-the-moment ploy had worked. And it had only cost me the price of an extra lunch.

'Looking forward to the holidays?' I asked.

'Yeah, can't wait,' he said in his deep, sexy voice, running a hand through his gorgeous hair and smiling like a god. I couldn't tear my eyes away from him. I hadn't stopped thinking about him for days, particularly with so little else happening at school.

'Going away anywhere nice?'

'Yeah, to Greece with my parents, but not until the end of August.'

'No way,' I said. 'Me too. Whereabouts are you going? One of the islands?'

For a moment, I imagined us ending up at the same resort in Skiathos at the same time, having the most perfect holiday romance. Then he broke the spell by revealing he was going to Crete, which is miles away. I looked it up as soon as I got home.

Anyway, on the bright side, because we were both due to go away around the same time, that hopefully meant there would be plenty of opportunities to meet up locally beforehand.

'Who was that Mac guy you were with the other day?' I asked later in the conversation. 'I've not seen him around before. He's older, right?'

'Yeah, he's seventeen. He's training to be a plasterer.'

'How do you know him? Did he used to go to school here?'

'No, he only moved to the area a few months ago. He's the cousin of one of the other lads we were with last week – Sam. Do you know him? He's in my year.'

I shook my head. 'I don't think so. Not by name, anyway. What does he look like?'

Dean described Sam to me, but it didn't ring any bells. Other than cocky Mac, who I couldn't help but notice, I'd not really paid attention to the others. I'd only had eyes for Dean.

'Why are you so interested in Mac?' he asked. 'Are you into him? I, er, think he likes you. He kept going on about you after you left.'

'Really?' I couldn't help feeling flattered by this, but equally I didn't want anything getting in the way of my pursuit of Dean. Imagine if he friend-zoned me rather than stepping on his mate's toes. 'No, I'm not into Mac. Definitely not. He's not my type at all. You can tell him that, if you like. I wouldn't want anyone to get the wrong idea.'

I monitored Dean's expression as I told him this. He wore a pretty good poker face, but I thought – or maybe hoped – I spotted a glimpse of glee. It would have been interesting if he'd then asked me to describe my type, but that didn't happen.

What did happen was that we continued to talk for ages after we'd finished eating, about all sorts. It was our first proper conversation and we had plenty to say to each other.

The big breakthrough came after the bell sounded to mark the end of lunch.

'Wow, where's the time gone?' Dean said.

'I know, right?' I twirled my hair and used that coy smile again while holding his gaze.

Please ask me out, I thought. I willed myself to somehow broadcast this message to him on a subliminal level.

Miraculously, it worked. The next words he uttered were music to my ears.

'Would you, er, like to hang out sometime, Beth?'

'How do you mean?' I asked, already growing in confidence now I could tell at last that he was interested in me. 'In a group with our friends, or just the two of us?'

'Whatever you, er, prefer.'

'What do *you* prefer, Dean?' I raised an eyebrow and bit my lower lip, imagining myself as a sultry seductress from a film noir.

'Yeah, um, probably the two of us, like now. This has been fun.'

'Apart from when I spilled your lunch all over the place.'

He smiled. 'You more than made up for that.'

'Good. I've enjoyed our chat too. Just to be clear: you're asking me on a date?'

He scratched his head. 'Yes, I guess I am.'

'Cool. I'd like that. Let me know when and where.'

I walked away calmly, like it was the most normal thing in the world to have been asked out by the boy of my dreams. Once Dean was no longer nearby, I let out a scream of joy and punched the air. Then I sought out Sara and Lou to tell them the exciting news.

FOURTEEN

NOW

Rory

He slumps on the sofa after finishing cleaning the apartment. How on earth did it get such a mess? It's only him here a lot of the time. Apparently, without Beth to keep him in check, Rory's not as tidy as he thought he was. He did his bit for all the years they were together, though, didn't he?

Okay, maybe he didn't do as much housework as his wife back then, but he was never like one of those old-fashioned guys who do nothing. He cooked. He cleaned. Sometimes. Should he have done more? Probably. However, in his role as a conveyancing solicitor, he was working longer hours than Beth and earning the bigger salary.

Mind you, Beth was always the one looking after the children, ensuring they were where they needed to be on time with everything they required; teaching them the basics like how to tie their shoelaces and read an analogue clock.

How did she end up being the one to do all of that? It's not like it was something they ever discussed. It just ended up that way. Beth was a natural mother from the word go. Rory had to learn how to be a dad on the job, making lots of mistakes along the way. How would he have managed without her in the early days?

Now, he has to, as well as doing all his own cooking and cleaning in this rental place, which is definitely no replacement for the family home he misses every day.

With hindsight, he should definitely have done more around the house and with the kids. If he had, perhaps Beth might have given him a chance to make things up to her, rather than simply turfing him out. Maybe she'd have considered forgiving him for his betrayal.

Now, although he hasn't entirely given up hope of a future reconciliation, it's not looking good. He and Beth hardly speak, other than to discuss arrangements for Ethan and Daisy. And when they are in each other's company, however briefly, the way she looks at him: there's no sign of love there any more. Not that he can see.

As for Rory, he loves Beth more than ever, as ironic as that might sound in light of his cheating. Take someone important away from a person who takes them for granted and they'll soon realise how much they want them back.

He was so chuffed when Ethan told him he was invited for dinner. He dared to hope it might lead to a breakthrough. But instead, it was a fiasco.

It also opened Rory's eyes to the dismal scenario of Beth starting to date other men. Something he hadn't really considered beforehand, like an idiot; another potentially huge barrier to block their path to reconciliation.

Why wouldn't Beth start dating again? She's a charming, clever, beautiful woman, still in her early thirties. She has her issues, sure, but who doesn't? There will be no shortage of guys wanting to get to know her. Most of them creeps, probably, only after one thing. Like he can talk, having been led astray so easily by his own libido.

Anyway, the immediate threat – for now – is one man in particular: Billy. The guy with whom he's spent time under the same roof but never actually met. The man who was invited for dinner when Rory wasn't.

He did catch a glimpse of him. He has the kind of thick beard Beth likes and Rory has never been able to grow. He looked younger and in far better shape than him, like someone who regularly goes to the gym. Oh yeah, and he happened to have rescued Daisy from two yobs and their savage dog that could have seriously hurt her. Something Beth eventually got around to telling Rory about, which happened in the playground, of all places: her no-go zone.

He's thankful to Billy for saving Daisy when Beth couldn't. Of course he is. Who knows what might have unfolded otherwise? But equally, Rory doesn't want his wife spending lots of time with this mysterious bloke, who apparently lives around the corner from the house. Having appeared out of nowhere, Billy now seems to be ever present. Ethan said he was around for dinner again on Thursday. And tonight, while Rory has the kids, Beth is going for a meal at Billy's place. Not that she's told him that. This latest info is courtesy of Ethan again, who at least has the good sense to be sceptical about his mum's new 'friend'.

Will tonight be the night their friendship moves to the next level? Jeez, he truly hopes not. That thought will be eating away at him all evening now.

Rory looks at his watch: 5.46 p.m. Nearly time to pick up the kids. He'll have to take the car if he wants to be punctual, which he does. The last thing he needs is another reason for Beth to be annoyed at him. No, he'll be knocking on the front door at six o'clock on the dot, holding up his side of the deal. Showing her that he can be reliable even when it involves clearing her evening ahead of a date.

That sounds utterly pathetic, but what else can he do? He only has himself to blame for being in this mess.

FIFTEEN

Beth

I watch through the window as Rory pulls up outside. Bang on six o'clock. Wow.

'Your dad's here,' I call to Ethan and Daisy. 'I hope you're both ready.'

Ethan's first down the stairs, backpack on one shoulder. 'Yes,' he says, punching the air. 'He's in the car. No walking.'

'Lazy lump.' I ruffle his hair and straighten the collar on his polo shirt, despite his defiant wriggling.

'What time's your date?' he asks, curling up his top lip as he says that last word.

'It's not a date. Billy's just a friend. We're having takeaway, I think. Nothing fancy.'

'Hmm.'

'Daisy, are you coming?' I call again. 'Your dad's here.'

'I'm having a poo,' she replies, a slight echo to her voice as it reaches me from the bathroom. Perfect.

'Hurry up then, please.'

'I will. Nearly done, but it's a bit of a hard one.'

'Too much information.' Ethan pulls a face while slipping on his jacket.

I open the door to reveal Rory's surprisingly cheery face. 'Hello,' he says. 'How are you?'

'Fine. You?'

'Good. Looking forward to having some company in the apartment tonight.' He looks over at Ethan. 'Hi, mate.'

I hate it when he calls him that. I want to say something – *he's not your mate, he's your son* – but it no longer feels like my place to do so. At least he doesn't use that word with Daisy. I think it's some kind of attempt to bond with Ethan on a blokey level. It sounds stupid to me.

'Daisy's on the toilet,' I explain. 'She'll be down soon, hopefully.'

An awkward silence descends on the three of us as we wait, Ethan sitting on the bottom stair; Rory and I standing in the hallway, twiddling our thumbs.

I wonder if Rory might ask what I'm doing tonight, but he doesn't. He probably already knows, thanks to the spy in our midst. So be it. A part of me hopes he does know and feels a pang of jealousy. He deserves that. He might look like the doting father now, but he wasn't thinking about Ethan and Daisy when he was cheating; riding a wrecking ball into our family unit for the sake of getting his rocks off. Mr Sleaze. Every time I think about him with *her*, I picture it in my mind. It makes me sick to my stomach.

'What's for tea tonight, Dad?' Ethan asks.

'I thought we could get a burger. Use a drive-thru.'

'Nice one.'

I bite my tongue. The last thing they need is more junk food. Rory seems to feed them crap whenever they're at his flat. He might not be the best cook in the world, but I'm sure he could rustle up something a little bit healthy. How hard is it to prep and boil a vegetable or two? I will have to say something if he keeps on this way, but not yet and never in front of the kids. We must try to continue presenting a united front as parents. It would be chaos otherwise, plus totally unfair to put them in that piggy-in-the-middle position.

'I'm wiping my bottom now,' Daisy shouts, making all three of us crack up.

'Don't forget to wash your hands properly,' I call back.

'I won't.'

Finally she comes down the stairs, dragging her pink holdall behind her.

'Have you got everything you need?' She insisted on packing her bag herself. It certainly looks full.

'Yep.' She nods vigorously.

'Is it okay if I have a peek inside to check?'

'Yep.'

I unzip the holdall, which isn't especially heavy, and find it stuffed full of soft toys. Luckily, there is also a change of clothes, fresh underwear and a wash bag. 'Good job,' I say, smiling to myself.

'Thanks.'

I give her and Ethan a kiss and a squeeze, nod at Rory, let them all out of the door and wave goodbye. Finally I'm home alone.

With nearly two hours to spare before my 'date', I take the opportunity to enjoy a hot, uninterrupted bubble bath. Once I've opened the window and cleared the air, that is, as well as cleaning the tub.

Sinking into the delightful, soothing warmth is bliss.

After a few welcome minutes of rest, eyes closed and brain muted, my mind wanders. Could things get physical tonight? Is that likely? Is Billy really interested in me romantically? And is that definitely what *I* want, or am I jumping in, head first, without thinking it through?

A sense of panic rises in my chest. It's years and years since I've done so much as kiss anyone other than Rory. I, for one, took our marriage vows seriously when we were still together.

'Relax,' I tell myself. I say it out loud in the hope it will drive the message home. 'Calm down. You don't have to do anything you don't want to do. You're in the driving seat. Go out and enjoy yourself. Don't overthink it.'

I lie back and focus on how the warm water and the bubbles feel on my body. I take slow, deep breaths and fight to clear my mind of everything other than the lovely sensation of sinking deeper and deeper into the heat and the foam.

A while later, I wake with a start, the water far cooler; the skin on my fingers and toes wrinkled like prunes.

Crap. How long was I asleep? I look up at the waterproof kids' clock, bright orange, with suckers holding it onto the tiles at the side of the bath, and see that it's already after seven thirty, which doesn't leave me long at all.

Brilliant. What an idiot. The one upside is that I didn't wash my hair, opting to tie it out of the way instead, tucked inside a shower cap.

I pull the plug, leap out of the water and grab my towel. Still busy drying myself, I hop into my bedroom and quickly choose an outfit: a black pencil skirt with a crisp white blouse. Smart, like I've made an effort, but hopefully not too much. It'll go nicely with my knee-high black leather boots. Rory could never get enough of them.

There's no time to apply a lot of make-up or do anything fancy with my hair. Not that I was planning to go overboard. I do what I can, and as I get to the point of applying some lipstick, I pick a deep red colour Rory always used to say suited me.

Wait. Why the hell am I still considering what *he* likes as part of my decision-making process? That's totally messed up, like I've been conditioned to please him.

If I wasn't running late, I'd wipe it off and pick another colour. However, I do decide not to wear the black leather boots after all, opting instead for a demure pair of comfortable slip-ons. Part of me regrets this as I walk the short distance to Billy's house. There's something about those boots that makes me feel super-sexy and confident: a boost I could do with right now. At least I'm not dressing to impress the memory of my ex, though.

I arrive at his front door and check my watch: almost quarter past eight. Oops. I take a breath and press the bell. He answers in a flash, wearing a warm smile, a smart pair of black jeans and a pressed navy shirt. 'Hello, how are you? Please, come in.'

We greet each other with a kiss on both cheeks.

'Sorry I'm late,' I say. 'I won't bore you with the details.'

'Oh, don't worry. You look lovely.'

'Thank you. You too.'

'Can I take your coat?'

Dammit. I haven't brought the bottle of expensive white wine I've had chilling in the fridge since yesterday. In the rush to get here, I omitted to pick it up. Now I feel terrible for arriving empty-handed.

'Everything all right?' Billy asks, a puzzled look on his face.

'Um, I forgot to bring the bottle of wine I bought specially. I might nip back for it.'

'Don't be silly. I have plenty of wine.' He grabs my hand and gives it a gentle squeeze; our eyes lock, to the point where I wonder if we're about to kiss. However, he breaks the moment, adding: 'Give me your coat and relax, please. You're my guest.'

A few minutes later, I'm perched on the edge of his tan leather sofa, sipping Prosecco, watching through the open glass doors that lead to the kitchen as he cooks. Some kind of instrumental jazz is playing at low volume from an expensive-looking speaker on the dining table between us. The house is pretty much how he described it: exposed polished floorboards and everything recently renovated. It makes me think of my own house as tired and dated.

Looking around, eyes scanning every visible nook and cranny while I'm alone here in the lounge, I'm impressed how clean and tidy he keeps the place. Or at least how clean and tidy he's made it look today, perhaps for my benefit. There's little of a personal nature. No posters, pictures, books or photos on display. Just a large wall-hung television, that fancy speaker, a couple of computer magazines, a well-thumbed TV guide and a cheese plant, which looks healthy enough. Typical bachelor pad, I suppose. Plus, to be fair, he hasn't been here long.

To my pleasant surprise, he's actually making the effort to prepare our meal himself, despite his comments about not being able to cook.

'How's it going? Anything I can do to help?'

'No thanks,' he calls back. 'Sorry to leave you alone while I do this, but I'm having to concentrate pretty hard to get it right.'

'Not at all. I'm impressed. I wasn't expecting this.'

He chuckles. 'Don't get ahead of yourself. Wait until you've tried it first. And if it's awful, blame the online cookery video I watched about a hundred times.'

I'll enjoy it however it tastes, thanks to all the effort he's put in to make it for me. And it certainly smells delicious from where I'm sitting.

'How's the laptop? Behaving itself, I hope.'

'Yes, perfect,' I reply. 'Thanks again for fixing it.'

I'm sure it is working well, but the embarrassing truth is I haven't even opened the thing since Billy returned it. I've grown so used to doing everything on my mobile, I have no real need for it. Oops.

. . .

'This is gorgeous,' I tell him when I bite into the main course: tagliatelle in a creamy sauce with ham, cheese, mushrooms and peas. The starter of buffalo mozzarella with beef tomatoes and avocado was lovely too. 'Someone has clearly been playing down their skills in the kitchen.'

Billy smiles. 'You're very kind, but honestly, I wasn't. This did not come easily. There were even a couple of trial runs, I'm embarrassed to admit, but I'm delighted you like it.'

'I really do, and I very much appreciate the effort. What a lovely surprise.'

'I won't try to pretend I made this,' he says later as he serves me a delicious-looking slice of chocolate and toffee cheesecake for dessert. 'It's shop-bought, but hopefully as good as it looks.'

It absolutely is, as I tell him in between mouthfuls.

Next thing, we're sitting together on the sofa, drinking coffee and then more wine. I feel tipsy. Before I know it, inhibitions put to one side, I'm twirling my fingers in my hair and batting my eyelashes like a lusty teenager. I'm making physical contact, touching his arm or leg at every opportunity. Gradually shuffling close enough to him on the couch that I can smell the warm, woody scent of his aftershave. I'm laughing at every little jokey thing he says, like he's the most hilarious person I've ever met. And I'm throwing so much eye contact his way, he may as well have a spotlight tracing his every move.

I don't get much back in return, though. He's chatty enough, but he's not flirting like I am. Nor does he seem to be as affected by the alcohol.

'I really like you, Billy,' I say, speaking slowly to avoid slurring my words.

'That's nice to know. I really like you too.'

'Do you?' I shake my head. 'I can't read you very well. One minute I think we're on the same page; the next, I'm not sure. Honestly, I haven't spent time one-on-one with a man since

Rory; he and I were together from a young age. But I'm pretty sure you and I nearly kissed earlier. What was that all about, if you're not interested?'

Billy shuffles in his seat, eyes avoiding me. 'Um, I'm not sure exactly what you want me to say. What, er, page do you think we're on?'

The wisest thing to do at this moment – knockback incoming – would be to pretend I'm joking. I've clearly got the wrong end of the stick. He's *not* into me. So what do I do? Dig myself deeper, naturally.

'Cards on the table,' I say, heart racing. 'I was under the impression that something more than friendship might be developing between us. Apparently, I was wrong, which is fine. But from my perspective, you've been giving out mixed messages. Why go to all this effort to impress me tonight? I'm confused. Are you put off by the fact that I'm older than you? I thought guys were into that: cougars and so on. Besides, we're only talking a couple of years. Unless you prefer your women young, without any baggage. Am I right? Is that it?'

He looks dazed by my words. 'I, er, I don't know. Um... I'm not sure what to say.'

'Helpful.' I rise to my feet. 'I think it's time for me to leave.'

'What? No, please don't. I—'

'Seriously, I'm going home. Thanks for the meal, but this is uncomfortable now. Please could I have my coat?'

Billy also stands, face scrunched up. 'Listen, I can explain.'

'Not today. I'm done. Coat, please?'

My mind is made up; my determination fuelled and locked into place by the mixture of alcohol and adrenaline racing through my veins.

'Let me walk you home, at least.'

'No need. I'm right around the corner.'

With a heavy sigh, Billy goes through to the hallway and returns, at last, with my coat.

'Thank you.' I grab it and head for the front door. I add a curt goodnight before disappearing into the darkness, mortified, tears quick to flow, feet clip-clopping on the pavement as I rush home.

How I wish I'd never come here tonight.

SIXTEEN

Billy

There's a text on his phone from Beth when he wakes up on Sunday morning. He reads it while still in bed, blinking to clear the sleep from his eyes:

> *Apologies for my behaviour last night. I'm mortified. Don't know what came over me, other than too much wine. Thanks for making all that effort. So sorry for ruining things.*

He's surprised to hear back from her so soon, especially with an apology. He feared he'd have to be the one to give ground; thinking it over with a stiff whisky after she left yesterday, he couldn't decide on the best way to play that.

This is a good result after a particularly bad night when all his hard work nearly blew up in his face. He hadn't expected her to declare her feelings so soon. He's known for some time that she's interested in him romantically. She's easy to read in that regard. However, he figured she'd wait for him to make the first move, at least for the time being. Quite the miscalculation on his part.

He probably shouldn't have plied her with so much alcohol. She did that to herself really, though. Yes, he made plenty available, but that was mainly him being a good host. She was the one doing most of the pouring and asking for more.

She was so drunk, she didn't even notice him slip out after her when she left. He followed her all the way home as she weaved her slow, winding route along the pavement. He kept a good distance so she didn't see or hear him, although he could have probably stayed much closer and still not been spotted. Only once she was inside the house, having struggled for ages with the key to open the door, did he remove himself from the shadows and return to his own home. Well, his home for the time being.

What now?

He weighs up the options and decides not to reply to her message straight away. He will do eventually, probably later today, by which time she'll no doubt be super-glad to hear from him.

As for how to take things forward now that she's brought romance into the picture, he's not sure. He'll have to tread carefully. The last thing he wants is to push her away after making so much progress. But is she ready to hear what he has to tell her yet?

Tricky.

SEVENTEEN

Ethan

'Have you pulled the blade on Marty yet?' he asks Liam when they're vaping behind the sports hall on Monday lunchtime.

Liam shakes his head. 'Nah, not yet. I haven't seen much of him lately. I think he might have snagged a girlfriend. He's been out a lot and he's on his phone more than normal. Can you imagine anyone wanting to get off with that loser? I bet she's hanging.'

Ethan nods his head in agreement while exhaling a big vape cloud. He only got into vaping recently. He shamelessly jumped on the bandwagon after loads of his mates started doing it. Now he's hooked. Mum and Dad wouldn't be happy if they found out, but there's no reason they should unless they caught him in the act. Vapes don't leave a smell on you like cigs, which he tried once and found rancid. Plus, he's not sure his parents would even know what a vape was if they found one. Same goes for Daisy, who doesn't know he's into it either.

He's not old enough to legally buy a vape, but getting hold of one is easy. There's always some kid selling them at school, and if you know the right shops to use – the small ones where they don't care about the law – you can buy them there too.

'How was your weekend?' Liam asks.

'Fine. Spent Saturday night at Dad's. Didn't do much other than watching telly.' It pains him to add: 'My mum was on a date.'

'Really? Who with?'

'That supposed friend of hers who rescued Daisy from the lads with a dog. The dickheads I've never managed to track down.'

'Right. He's floating about a lot.'

'Tell me about it.'

'What's he like?'

'Dunno. Not interested.'

'He doesn't have any kids of his own, does he?'

'Apparently not.'

'Bonus.'

'Hmm. I'm hoping he'll get yeeted soon. Mum wasn't in a great mood yesterday. Fingers crossed it didn't go well.'

'Oh yeah,' Liam says as they head back into school, 'I forgot to tell you, mate: Connor pulled me for a chat at break.'

'As in blade Connor?'

'Yep.'

'What did he want?'

'It was a bit weird. First of all, he asked how I was finding "the steel".'

'He called it that?'

'Uh-huh. He was dead secretive. Whispering and shit. Walls have ears and all that.'

'Right. What did you say?'

'I said it was all good. Then he lowered his voice even more and asked if I was interested in earning some cash doing a few little jobs for him.'

'Shit. What did you say?'

'I said I was all right, but then he gave me this look, like he was fuming, and I shat myself. You know what he's like.'

'So what did you say?'

'That I'd think about it.'

'Mate, that's not good. Who knows what he might want you doing?'

'Don't. I reckon I'll try to avoid him for a bit and hope he forgets. Anyway, I thought I'd best give you a heads-up in case he pulls you too.'

Ethan grimaces. 'Do you reckon he will?'

'Honestly, I dunno, dude. I wasn't expecting him to pull me, was I?'

This thought haunts Ethan for the rest of the day. Every time he walks down the corridor, from classroom to classroom – later as he heads home – he fears bumping into Connor. Fortunately, he doesn't, but that doesn't stop him worrying about it.

It was one thing buying a knife off a scary sixth-former he barely knew. But since then, Ethan's heard rumours about Connor's elder brother being a gang member involved in drugs and all sorts. If he'd been aware of that in advance – as he suspects Liam was, although he denies it – Ethan wouldn't have agreed to meet him in the first place, never mind buy a knife from him.

What the hell have they got themselves into?

EIGHTEEN

Beth

I can't get Billy out of my head. What's wrong with me?

I sent him an apology text yesterday, soon after waking up on my sofa at around 5.30 a.m. I was still in my outfit from the previous night and shaken by my latest nightmare, in which I'd been forced back to work only to find the office deserted apart from a shadowy figure who crept up on me and attacked me at my desk.

It took Billy forever to respond to my message. It was something like eight o'clock in the evening when my phone finally pinged. His reply read:

Don't worry. No harm done. Catch up soon.

What does that even mean? It sounds like he's not offended, but where do we go from here? Can we seriously still be friends? I want that, I guess, if I can get past the embarrassment. We do get along really well and I've appreciated having an adult to talk to in person other than Rory.

Until I know people well, I struggle to come out of my shell with them. It happened far quicker than usual with Billy. Probably because of the dramatic way we were thrown together when we met, plus the fact he saw me at my most vulnerable and didn't pass judgement.

Saying that, perhaps he did judge me unfit to be girlfriend material. Based on the way I fell to pieces in a crisis, unable to save my own child, who could blame him for writing me off as damaged goods?

I do have more than my fair share of hang-ups. That's why I'm usually so introverted and cautious around strangers: unless I'm riled enough about something to speak my mind, when anger overtakes reticence.

I wasn't always like this. There was a time, growing up, when I considered myself an extrovert. When I wasn't afraid to let people in; when I made new friends without even thinking about it. But that all changed at a certain point. Extreme trauma will do that to you.

Sometimes it almost feels like the hell I experienced at such a young age rewrote my DNA. It certainly shattered my innocence, my hopes and dreams, my everything, way beyond repair. There was no going back to my old self – my old life. I had to start again and carve out a new path forward. We all did as a family. Some of us more successfully than others.

The place where I grew up isn't a million miles away from where I live now. But it may as well be. I cut all ties long ago; left and didn't look back. It was the same for each of us. A family decision. I could hop in my car and be back there in no time. I could easily look up people from that past life. It would only take a few taps and swipes on my phone, but why would I put myself through that?

As for my work, there's no one there I would really consider a friend. Some of them are nice enough, but they're just colleagues. What would I say to them without work issues to discuss? I've never socialised with any of them outside the office. I thought I had everything I needed at home until Rory destroyed that.

Now that I'm off with stress, the last thing I want to do is think or talk about work with anyone. At first, a few colleagues did send me messages, wishing me well, but they soon stopped when I didn't reply.

As for the parents at the school gates, there are some I smile at and say hello to, maybe even make a bit of small talk with, but again, none I consider friends. I could probably turn that around with a bit of work, particularly in terms of parents of children Daisy sees at parties, play dates and so on. Unlike Ethan, she's still young enough to require some parental involvement in such scenarios. I'd have to change their perception of me, though. Right now, depending on our interactions so far, they probably either consider me aloof or a timid mouse. Over a period of time, I'd need to convince them that I'm actually approachable and sociable: a prospect that fills me with dread.

So back to Billy. I keep thinking about him and what happened on Saturday night. I keep almost sending him another text or calling him, but something stops me. I'm afraid of making things worse; of saying the wrong thing. However, I need to do something, because I can't go on like this. I've been sitting here in the kitchen going over the same stuff in my head, drinking brew after brew, ever since the Monday morning school run.

I either need to do something decisive about Billy or put him out of my mind, at least for now.

Easier said than done.

Is part of me hoping that if we do stay friends, we might still end up together? Probably, if I'm totally honest, but I really ought to let go of that.

One thing bugging me is that he's not given a reason why

he's not interested in me romantically. That surely rules out him being gay. If he was, he'd have said so, wouldn't he?

'Sorry, babes, I think you're gorgeous, but I'm afraid I prefer a bit of sausage.' Wink, wink. Nudge, nudge. That would have done it, no problem. And we'd have spent the rest of the night laughing about it, gossiping about men, best pals.

Maybe he already has a girlfriend. But if that's the case, why refer to himself as 'a family of one' when I first invited him over? Unless he was planning on cheating, only to feel too guilty at the last minute. That explanation could work, at a push, but it's more likely he simply doesn't fancy me and never has. I probably imagined the flirting because it was what I wanted to happen.

That's a bitter pill to swallow for a woman recently cheated on by her husband. Another knock to my self-confidence. Also, don't they say that men can never truly be friends with women, as they always want to sleep with them? Well, not in my case. Brilliant.

Dammit. I'm getting nowhere. Chasing my tail. Wildly speculating without getting close to any answers.

I need a change of scenery. It's dry outside, even if the sun isn't out. Hopefully a walk will clear my head.

NINETEEN

THEN

Dean took me on our first date on the first official day of the summer holidays: a Saturday. I was over the moon and had been looking forward to it ever since the previous Monday, when he'd approached me by my locker at break time.

'Do you like bowling?' he'd asked, looking every bit as fit as usual.

'Um, yeah,' I'd replied, smiling, hoping lots of people saw us chatting. 'You mean tenpin bowling, right? As opposed to the other kind, you know, that you play on grass.'

Dean looked at me like I'd asked him the weirdest question in the world. I suppose it was strange. It's not as though you see many teenagers playing lawn bowls. But since I'd played both sports in the past and neither recently, it felt like a normal query in the moment.

'Yeah, tenpin bowling.' He leaned on the locker next to mine.

'I do like it, yes, although I'm pretty rubbish. I've only been a couple of times and not for ages.'

'That doesn't matter. Fancy going with me on Saturday afternoon?'

'This Saturday?'

'Yeah, if you're free.'

'Sure. That would be great.'

Dad dropped me off at the bowling alley. 'Sorry, what's the name of this chap you're meeting again?' he asked before I got out of the car.

'Dean.'

'And he's from the year above at school?'

'That's right. He's really nice.'

'Good. Well, I hope you and Dean have a great time. Do you need a lift back, or...'

'I'm not sure yet. Can I give you a call if I do?'

'No problem.'

My younger brother, Sean, who'd come along for the ride for no obvious reason other than to annoy me, started energetically snogging his hand, tongue and all, on the back seat.

'Gross,' I said. 'Dad, can you tell Sean to grow up? He's being weird.'

He looked in the rear-view mirror and frowned. 'Ignore him, Beth. Sean, don't wind up your sister.'

'Have a great date,' Sean whined, regardless, emphasising and elongating the last word in a way that made me want to wring his annoying neck.

'Bye, Dad.' I gave him a hug. 'Thanks for the lift.'

I didn't say anything to my stupid brother. When I glanced back, I saw he'd pressed his lips to the window, still not giving up on his puerile teasing. Idiot.

My belly a flutter of nerves, I walked inside, looking for the main reception desk, where Dean and I had agreed to meet.

He was there already. He greeted me with a wave and a smile, followed by a very brief and unexpected peck on my lips when I drew close.

'Hi, Beth. How are you?'

'Good.' I tried not to look flustered by the kiss, but it was difficult, because I *was* flustered.

'You look nice,' he said. Just as well. It had taken me long enough to fix my make-up and settle on the right skirt and top.

I smiled. 'Thanks. You too.'

He was wearing denim shorts and a polo shirt; he definitely did look great, as always.

He'd already booked us a lane and paid for it. He refused to take any money towards it, which I thought was really nice. Once we'd both changed into a pair of those clown shoes they make you wear, I insisted on getting in the soft drinks and a bag of sweets to share.

Having eventually entered our names on the lane's confusing computer system, we were about to start bowling when Dean caught sight of something in the distance and let out a groan. 'Oh no. You have to be kidding.'

'What?'

'Some of my mates have turned up.'

'Oh, right,' I said, my heart sinking. 'How come? To play with us?'

'No way. I didn't invite them. They probably want to take the piss. Don't look over. Let's hope they don't spot us.'

That seemed unlikely, but I went along with it. Dean put on a brave face, full of encouragement as I bowled my first two balls straight into the gutter. Then he took his turn, narrowly missing on the first delivery and knocking down five pins on the second.

'Well done,' I said.

'Hmm.'

We had a couple more turns each. I managed to knock down a few pins, but nothing to write home about. Dean got a spare and then a strike.

'That's more like it,' he said.

I high-fived him. 'Nice. Do you do this a lot?'

'Now and again.'

He hadn't mentioned his mates for a few minutes, but I could tell they were on his mind. I caught him looking out for them several times, although he did at least try to be discreet.

Then they showed up at our booth and there was no more pretending. The three of them arrived while I was up bowling. Mac announced himself by wolf-whistling as I bent over to throw my second ball, which did at least connect, giving me a score of six.

'Nice pins,' he said, which I ignored.

'Hello.' I looked at one of the others, who I recognised from Dean's earlier description as Sam, Mac's cousin. I smiled like it was normal for them to have turned up. 'How are you all doing?'

'Not as well as Dean,' Mac said. 'How come you're out on a date with him when you could be with me instead? I thought you and I had a connection.'

Dean got to his feet. 'Come on. There's no need for that, mate. Why are you being aggro?'

Mac shuffled closer to him and the pair faced off, neither speaking for a long moment, eyeballing each other. I feared they were about to have a scrap and I wasn't sure whether I ought to say something or try to intervene. I looked back at Sam and the other guy to see their reaction; they were both smirking, like this was what they'd wanted or at least expected to happen.

I didn't recognise the other guy. He looked significantly older than the rest of us – early twenties, at a guess; well built, like he spent a lot of time lifting weights; dark hair, slicked back. A man rather than a boy. So why wasn't he behaving like it?

I was on the cusp of pulling Dean and Mac apart myself when Mac's expression changed from a scowl to a wide grin, breaking the tense mood. 'Ah, come on with you,' he said, landing a playful punch on Dean's shoulder. 'I'm winding you up, buddy.'

Dean nodded. 'Fair enough. You got me there, Mac.'

He looked relieved but still on edge, wide-eyed, like he hadn't fully calmed down yet.

'Oh, Deano.' Mac ruffled his hair, making him stiffen again. 'Relax, honestly. It's fine. We're good, yeah?'

'Sure. All good.'

Mac turned to me and, in a seemingly friendly tone of voice, which I still didn't trust, said: 'Sorry, love. I was having a bit of fun. Banter and all that between mates. You know how it is. No offence, yeah?'

'It's fine.' I avoided his eye.

'We'll get out of your hair now,' he added. 'We have a lane of our own booked. You lovebirds can get on with your courting. Don't do anything I wouldn't do.'

'Are you okay?' Dean asked once they'd gone. 'I'm sorry about that. Mac can be a real dick sometimes, especially when his elder brother is around. If you don't want to stay, I'll understand. We can go somewhere else. Whatever you want.'

'No, let's carry on,' I said. 'They've gone now.' That wasn't quite true. I could still see and hear them as they noisily settled into their own lane. However, it wasn't too close by, thankfully.

I gave Dean's hand a squeeze. 'Was he really winding you up? It seemed a bit too real to me.'

'He definitely fancies you, so he probably *is* cheesed off about me taking you out. As for the rest, who knows?'

'So that older guy is Mac's brother?'

Dean nodded. 'Yep, Lenny. He's twenty-two. I don't, um, know him very well. He's a bit... er, never mind. Let's talk about something else. We should try to forget they're here.'

I looked over at them as he said this. Mac and Sam were larking about near the ball rack, trying to get each other in a headlock; Lenny was heading towards the bar. The poor couple playing in the next lane to them didn't look at all amused.

We continued with our game, and for a while it felt like

things were returning to normal. Yes, it was hard not to feel like we were being watched, because Mac was forever looking our way and trying to get our attention with a thumbs-up, a wink or a nod. Meanwhile, he and Sam were messing around non-stop, annoying everyone around them, while Lenny watched, supping on a pint. However, we both did our best to ignore them, and I did start to relax again and enjoy myself.

What I really wanted was for Dean to wrap his strong arms around me at the foul line, in the pretence of showing me how to bowl better, like I'd seen in so many cheesy movies. But he was never going to do that with Mac and co. watching. So I had to settle for enjoying his company and being as tactile with him as I possibly could, without making things weird. I was hoping for a snog at the end, once we were properly alone.

I was picturing this in my mind's eye, while admiring the view from behind of Dean bowling one of his final balls, when the sound of a loud, sweary argument erupted. I knew before I even looked where it would be coming from – and sure enough, I was right. Although not about the person involved. I'd expected it to be Mac. Instead, there was his brother, hand clasped around the throat of the bald chap in the next-door lane, calling him every name under the sun and threatening to 'end' him.

I later learned that the bald dude had complained to Lenny about the disruptive, boisterous behaviour of his brother and cousin. He'd probably assumed that since he was the oldest of the group, he would respond like a reasonable adult and tell the others to calm down.

Unfortunately, despite his quiet, seemingly calm demeanour up until that point, Lenny was anything but reasonable.

'Bloody hell,' Dean said under his breath as he sat down next to me. 'What now? There are kids around. Why's he kicking off?'

'I've no idea. Is he often like this?'

Dean didn't give me a verbal reply, but his eyes seemed to be screaming: 'He's a psycho!'

'Why do you hang out with him?' I asked.

'I don't. Not often, anyway. Sometimes he turns up with Mac.'

'He's not much better. Why do you hang out with *him*?'

Dean rubbed his chin. 'I dunno. He's a mate.'

Dump him, I thought.

He started to stand up. 'I should see if I can calm things down.'

I grabbed his arm. 'No, please don't. Look, some staff members are going over. Leave them to sort it. They'll probably kick them all out.'

That was exactly what happened, but only after Lenny had poured the remains of his beer over the bald guy's head, spat in the face of the manager and made the kind of nasty, foul-mouthed scene that no one present would forget in a hurry. Sam kept quiet as it all unfolded, but Mac, unsurprisingly, had plenty to say. None of it reasonable or pleasant.

It was a huge relief when they'd finally gone, after more shouting while swapping their shoes and then again on the way out of the door. Everyone was looking at each other, like: who the hell are these guys?

I was thankful they hadn't involved us in any way while they were getting turfed out. That would have been mortifying. Still, the whole experience did put a dampener on the date.

We hung around for a while after our bowling game, which I lost, obviously. We had fun playing pool and air hockey. Dean was much more relaxed by that point.

And – drum roll – we snogged. Not once, but twice, in fact. The first was a short but very welcome moment of lip-locking delight after he pulled me into a quiet spot next to a fruit machine. It was unexpected, so I didn't have time to overthink it. I loved every moment and Dean couldn't stop grinning afterwards either. We only broke off because this old dude started playing the fruit machine. As for the second occasion, which couldn't come soon enough, that was in a ginnel near the end of my road before we parted ways after taking the bus home. We kissed for ages, and by the end, I was so drunk with lust I could barely walk in a straight line.

I feared it was written all over my face when I bumped into Dad mowing the front lawn, but if he did notice anything different about me, he didn't let on.

'Ah, you're home,' he said. 'Did you have a nice time?'

'It was good, thanks.'

He leaned forward against the handle of the mower. 'And? Did you win?'

'Sorry?'

'The bowling. Did you beat Dean?'

'No, I was useless.'

'But you had fun?'

'Yep.'

He winked. 'That's my girl. Feel free to make your old dad a brew if you happen to pass the kettle. I'm parched.'

TWENTY

NOW

Why have I ended up here?

I'm at the entrance to the playground. The one where Billy rescued Daisy.

It's quiet, which is unsurprising, considering most kids are at school, but there are a handful of toddlers on the smaller equipment, supervised by a similar number of adults.

I watch them from the safety of the pavement, daring myself to enter, but my body goes rigid at the mere thought.

This is what always happens. I've challenged myself to go in so many times, but it never works. My entire being is programmed to steer clear, come what may. I've never managed to put so much as a toe across the entrance.

It's the same with all playgrounds. Never once have I pushed either of my children on a swing or helped them down a slide. As much as I'd love to be able to get over this debilitating phobia, I can't.

It's exasperating.

An impenetrable wall.

I understand how weird and incomprehensible it must seem

to anyone not in the know, but they've not been through what I have. They've got no idea.

They've not experienced the sheer horror, fear and devastation that still haunts me every single day; that feeds my nightmares from a bottomless, torturous pit of misery.

So why am I punishing myself like this now? Why am I trying to do the impossible?

A large part of it is down to what happened to Daisy. I failed her when she needed me most and had to rely on the kindness of a stranger. A stranger who went on to become a friend, until I ruined it.

I'm on my own as an adult. That's what the current situation with Billy has reminded me. Yes, Rory's still around, but I can't rely on him like I once did. I need to be self-sufficient. I can't be held back by wounds from the past.

And yet here I am, unable to place one foot inside the playground.

I need help, but from where? Nothing I've tried over the years has worked. And if I can't get beyond some prescribed books and a waiting list for my work-related stress, why would this be any different? It's not like I could afford to seek private treatment either, even if I thought it might be useful.

'Hello, Beth,' a friendly voice says, snapping me out of my introspection and back into the moment.

Standing in front of me is a woman I vaguely recognise. She has a little girl in tow, who I'd guess to be around two years old. This must be the mum of one of Daisy's classmates, but I'm struggling to place her.

'Hello.' I give her my warmest smile, hoping it might go some way to making up for the fact I don't know her name. I consider asking how she is, in a further attempt to hide my cluelessness, but nothing comes out of my mouth.

'Annette, Liam's mum,' she says, helpfully.

That's it. Of course. She has shorter hair now than I recall. I can't even remember the last time we saw each other, even though Liam's been round to the house plenty of times with Ethan.

'Sorry,' I say. 'You caught me in a daydream. Gosh, how long's it been? How are you? And this must be... Chloe, right?' I blow a kiss at the little girl and wave, which seems odd as soon as I've done it.

Liam's parents split a while ago, while the boys were still at primary school. Chloe was the result of Annette's new relationship with... the name escapes me. There's an elder stepbrother too; Liam's not keen on him.

'Yes, we're good, thanks. I'm taking Chloe for a quick go on the swings because she's been a very good girl this morning. Haven't you, love? How are you, Beth? I was sorry to hear from Liam about you and Rory splitting up. I know what a strain that can be.'

'Thank you,' I say. 'No, it's not been easy, but we're getting there. Gradually settling into the new world order.'

'It gets better, I promise. My life is so much happier now, but it took a while to get here. If you ever need anyone to talk to, you know where I am.'

'Thank you,' I say with a catch in my throat. I fear I might start to cry, but I just about hold it together.

She reaches out and touches my arm. 'I mean it, truly. It must still be very raw.'

I nod, not yet trusting myself with any more words.

'Anyway,' Annette says, ruffling her daughter's hair, 'I'd better get this one on the swings. Lovely to see you, Beth. Hopefully we can catch up again properly soon. Chin up.'

'Bye,' I say, forcing a smile onto my face.

They walk past me into the playground and I remain for a few minutes watching them. Chloe's little face is a picture once she gets on the swing and her mum starts pushing her. She's smiling and giggling, loving every minute of it. The sight both warms my heart and makes me sad.

Overall, bumping into Annette has a positive impact on me. It's a timely reminder that I am at least capable of being friendly with other mums.

When I go to pick Daisy up from school later, I make an effort to smile at everyone I even vaguely recognise. I say hello to a handful of waiting parents; I have a brief discussion about the weather with the aunt of a boy in Daisy's class who I think might be called Thomas.

Not exactly revolutionary behaviour, but it feels like a good start.

Then Daisy emerges with a sullen look on her face and a redness about her eyes. She might not be crying now, but she definitely has been.

'Hello, darling,' I say, keeping a cheery tone to my voice. 'How are you?'

She grabs hold of my hand and, without saying a word, leads me away.

'What's up?' I ask once we're a little way down the road.

'Nothing.'

Yeah, right.

I wait a minute or two before adding: 'Are you sure there's nothing the matter, love? You seem upset.'

'I'll tell you at home.' She remains silent for the rest of the walk.

I stay quiet too, for the most part, although my mind's racing, wondering what on earth has got her so upset. If it's that Lori again with her horrid Dumbo comments, I'm going to have to do something this time, no matter what Daisy says.

At home, I get her a drink and a biscuit and sit her down in the kitchen. Her face is like thunder.

'Are you going to tell me what's the matter now?'

'It's Lori again.'

I knew it. What's that nasty girl been saying now? I claw my fingers into my knees. 'What's she done: called you names again?'

Daisy shakes her head. 'She didn't invite me to her birthday party.'

As soon as she's got this out, she bursts into a crying fit. I pull her into my arms and give her the biggest of hugs.

'Oh, honeypot. I know that must feel terrible right now, but it's not the end of the world, honestly. You don't even like her. Why would you want to go to her silly party?'

'Because every other girl in class was invited. Even some of the boys.'

'Did Lori say anything mean to you about it?'

She shakes her head again. 'No, she just didn't give me an invite when she handed them out at break.'

Wow. That is nasty. What a bitch. What can I reasonably do about it, though? It's not for me to say who Lori can and can't invite to her birthday. I mean, I could have a word with her parents and point out that Daisy feels very left out, but would that be a good idea? Ironically, I almost wish that she *had* called her names again, because that would have given me proper grounds to kick off.

'I had to cry a few times,' Daisy continues, 'but I went to the toilet and tried not to let anyone see.'

Picturing this breaks my heart. I feel her pain like my own – arguably worse. 'Oh, you poor thing. Didn't your teacher notice something was wrong?'

'I said I was fine. I didn't want Lori to know I was upset. I think she guessed, though. Why does she hate me so much? I didn't do anything to her.'

'She doesn't hate you.'

'How do you know?'

'She's a silly girl who's jealous of you. You come across

people like this from time to time in life. It's hard, I know, but it blows over.'

I wonder about telling Daisy that she could always do the same thing to Lori when her own birthday comes around. But that doesn't feel like good parental guidance.

'When is the party?' I ask.

'I don't know.'

'Right, well, whenever it is, we'll do something really nice that day. The two of us. Whatever you fancy. How does that sound?'

Daisy peers at me through fresh tears. She does something with her mouth that looks a little bit like a smile and there's a hint of a nod. Then she starts full-on sobbing again, so I pull her into another giant hug.

'You are amazing,' I tell her. 'You're the best daughter a mother could ever wish for and I love you so very much. We'll get through this. One day you'll look back and think: why was I so upset by not going to silly Lori's even sillier party?'

'She's having a magician,' Daisy says in between sniffs and sobs. 'And I love magic tricks.'

I hear the front door swing open and slam shut, followed by the sound of footsteps – presumably Ethan's – running up the stairs.

'Hello!' I call. 'Is that an intruder or my son?'

'Hi, Mum. I'll be down in a minute.'

Why is it that he always runs to his room first when he gets in nowadays? He never used to do that. Maybe I ought to have a rummage around in there to see if he's hiding something. Are girlie magazines still a thing? Surely not. It's all on the Internet these days, isn't it? I don't even want to think about that.

If I do have a snoop around his room – I can't yet decide whether I should or not – it'll have to be when he's at school or staying at his dad's. I'll have to be careful to cover my tracks too. Otherwise, he definitely won't trust me in future.

By the time he appears in the kitchen, Daisy has stopped crying, but still the first thing Ethan says to her is: 'What's up with you?'

'Don't mither your sister. It's school stuff. How was your day?'

'Fine. What is there to eat?'

'The usual. Have a look in the cupboard. But don't spoil your appetite.'

'Why, what's for tea?'

'Spaghetti bolognese.'

'Again?'

'Unless you have something you'd rather prepare instead.'

'Right. Very funny.'

'What's funny about that? You should be learning to cook and helping more around the house as you get older. I'm not your slave.'

Ignoring my comment, Ethan grabs himself a drink of squash and raids the biscuit tin.

'You can make me a cup of tea, if you like,' I say, to which he replies that he has loads of homework.

'I saw Annette today: Liam's mum.'

A flash of what looks like panic crosses his face, which is odd.

'How come? Where? What did she want?'

'I bumped into her while I was having a walk. We said hello and had a quick chat. I can't even remember the last time we saw each other before that.'

'Right.'

'She was with Liam's younger sister, Chloe. She seems cute.'

'Half-sister,' Ethan replies.

'No need to split hairs. How is Liam, anyway? You should have him round after school sometime. He could stay for tea.'

'Yeah, maybe.'

'Everything all right between you two? You haven't fallen out or anything, have you?'

He scrunches up his face. 'Why would you say that?'

'Well, you seemed a bit weird when I mentioned Annette.'

'I don't know what you're on about.' He's full-on scowling now.

'Hmm,' is my only response, wishing to avoid an argument in front of Daisy.

Moments later, Ethan has disappeared back upstairs.

'How are you feeling now?' I ask Daisy.

'Okay,' she says, unconvincingly.

'The best thing you can do, love, is get on with something else and put it out of your mind. The two of us could go for a walk, if you like. Fresh air is always good.'

'We already walked home from school,' she says, monotone. 'I'm tired. Could I watch telly for a bit?'

I don't have the heart to say no, even though I'd rather she didn't. 'Sure. Not for too long, though. And don't sit too close to the screen, please. It's bad for your eyes.'

TWENTY-ONE

Billy

Tuesday night and there's been no more communication with Beth since the message he sent her more than forty-eight hours ago.

Billy is surprised. He thought she'd have replied to that pretty quickly, even though he made her wait all day for his response to her apology text.

Perhaps he was too curt. He picks up his phone and looks again at what he wrote:

Don't worry. No harm done. Catch up soon.

Hmm. Perhaps the last bit was where he messed up. It could be interpreted as a brush-off.

Dammit. What next, then?

He checks to see if she's on her laptop, but of course she's not. She never uses the stupid thing. Why did she bother getting him to fix it? What a waste of his skills that's turned out to be.

After pacing up and down in the lounge, he gets his navy waterproof jacket and heads out of the door. He's going to have a walk around the block, passing Beth's house in the process. He doesn't really have a plan, but he's hoping either something will occur to him along the way or maybe he'll bump into her when he walks past. Admittedly, the latter is not very likely after nine o'clock on a dark, drizzly school night. At best, he might get a glimpse of her through the window. What will that achieve?

He could always knock on the door unannounced, but that doesn't feel like a good idea. Daisy will probably be asleep. Plus it would be strange – creepy even – and that's definitely not the vibe he's going for.

Unless the kids are at their dad's place tonight. That might be possible. Billy hasn't yet got his head around the intricacies of how Beth and Rory share parenting duties. They seem to organise things on an ad hoc basis, as far as he can gather.

Once outside, he reaches behind his neck with both hands and removes the rollaway hood from where it's zipped inside the collar of his jacket. He pulls it over his head, reassured by the anonymity it affords.

To begin with, he walks at a brisk pace. However, once he gets close to Beth's house, opting to take the pavement on the opposite side of the road, he slows right down and scans the property in detail.

There are various lights on. *That* he can see. But each window visible from the road is covered by curtains or blinds. Beth's small red Fiesta is parked in the drive as always. She barely seems to use it, other than for odd trips to the super-market and such. She usually walks everywhere locally. He doesn't know her well enough yet to ascertain whether this is for cost-cutting, exercise or environmental reasons; he'd wager it's a mix of all three.

The car gives him an idea, but he needs to think it through, so he continues on past the house, turning his attention to the neighbouring and opposite properties to check for open curtains and any CCTV cameras he hasn't spotted previously.

The coast is clear, as far as he can tell. Excellent.

He speeds up and completes the loop around the block, returning to his own house before popping to the gym to distract himself by pumping iron.

A couple of hours later, he grabs a different coat – a long, dark, nondescript cagoule with a roomy hood – pulls on a pair of thin leather gloves and goes out into the wet and blustery night.

He starts his loop the opposite way this time, so it takes a little longer to get to Beth's house. When he arrives, everything is much the same as earlier, albeit darker. Lots of folk have gone to bed already. In Beth's house, there's still a light on somewhere, probably the upstairs landing, but all the front-facing rooms are now shrouded in darkness, as he'd hoped would be the case.

Taking a deep breath and a final three-sixty sweep of his surroundings, he darts across the road, hunched inside his raincoat, hood pulled tight around his head, and ducks down the drive. Staying in a crouched position, he approaches the rear driver's-side tyre of Beth's car, which is facing away from the house and sheltered from the next-door neighbours' view by a low fence.

A vehicle passes by on the road, its lights briefly illuminating the area, but not far enough to reach the shadowy spot where he's chosen to squat. He reaches forward, kneeling now, and runs his hand around the tyre rim until he finds the valve. He removes the cap, which is a bit fiddly in gloves, and then presses the protruding end of his house key into the core.

The ensuing gush of escaping air sounds very noisy close up, but Billy's confident the bad weather will stop the noise travelling. He keeps going as long as he dares, which feels like forever but must only be a minute or so. Eventually, satisfied by the now squidgy, deflated dark rubber, he screws the cap back in place, somehow managing not to drop it. Shifting from his sodden knees to his haunches, he checks there's still no sign of anyone around before rising and calmly walking back to the road.

Another car passes, its headlights illuminating the driving rain bouncing off the road, but he's no longer bothered about being spotted. He's already well past Beth's drive. An anonymous dark figure walking along the pavement.

All the same, he takes a detour home. He only passes one other pedestrian en route: someone walking a soggy dog on the opposite side of the road. He doesn't meet their eye or say hello.

When he finally gets back to the house, he strips off his wet clothes and has a hot shower. His mind is ticking away, planning the details of his next move, which he's hopeful will set his plan back on track. Fingers crossed.

TWENTY-TWO

Beth

I'm weighing up what to have for lunch when the doorbell goes. Probably Daisy's new wellies, which are due to be delivered today. Great. I was worried they might turn up when I was on the school run later.

'Oh, hello,' I say, unable to hide my surprise on opening the front door. 'Billy... How are you?'

Even with the wind outside blowing fresh air towards me, I feel my cheeks flush.

I'm not dressed for company – especially not Billy – in today's cleaning attire of bleach-stained grey joggers and an unflattering baggy white T-shirt. My hair is a loosely tied bird's nest.

'Hi,' he says, my fashion antithesis in crisp jeans, tan brogues, a smart grey shirt and a black corduroy blazer, with a leather satchel over his right shoulder. 'I'm good. How are you?'

'Um, yeah. I'm okay, thanks. I'm doing some, er, housework, as you might be able to tell from my lovely outfit.' I pause before adding, more out of obligation than genuine desire: 'Would you like to come in?'

He smiles. 'I will, but I can't stop. I'm heading into the city. Business stuff. I thought I might get away with working from home all day today, but no such luck. I've been summoned in person.'

'Fun.' I resist the temptation to say that he looks nice as I let him inside and we continue chatting in the hallway.

His eyes are sparkling. He seems in a great mood, surprisingly, considering how our last in-person chat ended.

'So, what's going on?' I ask.

'I, er, felt like I should call by and say hello. I wanted to make it crystal clear that I'm really not bothered or offended in any way about how Saturday night ended. You should hear some of the things I've said over the years after one too many shandies. I'd love us to stay in touch and keep seeing each other, Beth, truly. You're the first real friend I've met since moving here and I really enjoy our chats.'

'I do too,' I say, feeling teary but fighting not to show it.

'Also,' he goes on, 'I wanted to clarify my position. To explain why I didn't respond to your, um...'

'Advances?'

'Yeah.'

'There's no need, honestly. I'm a grown woman. Now that I've had time to reflect, I can see it was wrong to accuse you of leading me on. Very presumptuous on my part. You were nice to me – a real gentleman – and I read that all wrong. Probably a lot to do with me being out of the game for so long.'

'I don't want you thinking it's anything to do with you,' he says. 'You're gorgeous. Anyone can see that. I'm incredibly flattered by what you said to me. In normal circumstances, I wouldn't hesitate. But I'm not in the right place to have a relationship now. Simple as that. It's on me. There's a good reason, which I will share with you at some point, when I'm ready, but I can't find the right words at the moment. Sorry.'

He gives me puppy eyes that melt my heart. I pull him into a hug – the friendly kind – and tell him it's fine. That I'd love to stay friends and keep meeting up. I mean it too. He's clearly had his heart broken, probably fairly recently. Okay, that's not exactly what he said, but I'm definitely getting those vibes, and I can't help but feel sorry for him as a result. If anything, it brings me closer to him, in light of what Rory's put me through.

Does it also leave me with some hope for the future? Yes, I think so. Lots of great relationships start out as friendships. Perhaps I simply made my move too soon.

And if we remain friends, then so be it. A friend is exactly what I need at the moment. The fact he happens to look great is an added bonus.

'Right, I do need to get going now,' he says, already reaching for the latch. 'Let's do something together very soon, yeah? We should go out somewhere, perhaps. Wherever you fancy. Have a think and let me know.'

'I will. Thanks for calling round. I appreciate it.'

'Of course.'

I'm still in the hall, having let him out and said goodbye a moment earlier, when the doorbell sounds. I expect it probably will be the parcel this time, but no, it's Billy again.

'Back already?'

He flashes a grin. 'Yeah, I couldn't stay away.' Then his face twists into an altogether different look, troubled, like something's wrong. 'You're not planning to go anywhere in the car today, are you?'

'No, why?'

'You have a flat tyre. I noticed it on my way out.'

'Oh no. You're kidding. Seriously? Could you show me?'

'Of course.'

I bob out in my slippers, despite the ground still being wet from last night's rain. He's right: one of the back tyres is flat as a pancake. 'Brilliant. Thanks for letting me know. I definitely wouldn't want to drive it like that.' I sigh. 'I'll have to get it fixed, I guess. You don't happen to know a mobile tyre repair firm, do you?'

'Have you got a spare?' he asks. 'Or one of those cans of gunk?'

'Um, I'm not a hundred per cent sure. I *think* there's a spare, but I've never had a puncture before, so it's not something I've ever really looked into.'

'Have you got the key?'

'Hang on.' I nip inside to get it.

'If you unlock the boot, I can have a look.'

I press the relevant button on the key fob and Billy swings the boot open as I watch. He lifts out a bulging hessian bag, which contains numerous other reusable shopping bags I've accumulated, and hands it to me, together with an umbrella, a can of antifreeze and an empty water bottle. Next, he lifts up the carpet to reveal a tyre.

'Yep, you've got one. Lucky. Most cars don't nowadays. It's a space saver, rather than a full-size tyre, but it could certainly get you to a garage, if needs be. If you've never had a puncture, though, I'm guessing you haven't changed a tyre before.'

'That would be correct. But I could always give it a go. How hard can it be? There must be instruction videos online, right?'

'Yeah, I'm sure there are,' Billy says, 'but I'll be honest, I wouldn't fancy doing it for the first time alone, based on watching a video clip. Don't you have breakdown cover?'

I grimace. 'It felt like a waste of money, considering how little I use the car, so I cancelled it.'

'Right. I'll tell you what: if you can wait until later today, how about I come back after work and we do it together? I'm no expert, but I have at least changed a tyre a couple of times. I'm sure we could muddle through together.'

'No,' I say, 'you don't need to do that. You've done enough for me already. I'm sure I can call a local garage and ask them to come out.'

'They'll charge you a fortune. Come on, let me help, Beth. That's what friends do, right?'

'I don't want to put you out again.'

'You're not, seriously. I enjoy a challenge.'

He wears me down and eventually I accept his kind offer.

TWENTY-THREE

That evening, at around half past six, Billy returns. He's changed into a much older-looking pair of jeans and a scruffy jumper, and is carrying a small black bag in one hand.

'I'm back,' he says. 'In my scruffs. Not interrupting teatime, am I?'

'No, we've just finished. Well, the kids have. I'm going to grab something later. What's in the bag? Have you brought along some fancy tools?'

'It's a portable air compressor,' he says. 'Runs off the cigarette lighter in the car. After I left you, I remembered seeing my neighbour use one the other day, so when I got home, I asked him if I could borrow it. I figured before we started exerting ourselves using wrenches and jacks, it might be worth trying to put some air into the tyre and see if it holds for a bit. It might be a slow puncture or, as my neighbour pointed out, some kid might have let it down as a prank. It's happened round here before, apparently.'

With some teamwork – me plugging in the device and locating the correct pressure; Billy connecting it and turning it on – we make swift progress. A minute or two later, he declares: 'Right. That's it. Feels solid as a rock, at least for now.'

I lean over his shoulder to have a gander. 'Already?'

'Yep, look.' He presses his thumb against the sidewall and invites me to do the same. 'All we can really do is wait and see. If it's a serious puncture, it'll be flat again in no time. If it's a slow one, it could take a while longer.'

'What do you recommend I do?'

'I'm no car expert,' he says. 'I don't even own one at the moment. But if it was me, I'd keep an eye on it for a few days; if it still looks solid by that point, I'd forget about it. I've had a good feel around the tyre and I didn't come across any screws or nails. You'd have to move it to be entirely sure, but I reckon you might be all right.'

I grin. 'And there was me looking forward to learning how to put the spare on.'

Rising to his feet, Billy chuckles. 'We can still swap them over, if you'd rather take this tyre to a garage and get it checked out. It's not too big a job, assuming I don't mess something up.'

I nod. 'How about you talk me through the theory instead?'

'Sure.'

So he does, in a refreshingly good-humoured, clear and concise way, answering my countless questions without a hint of impatience. I can't imagine Rory being so accommodating.

He also shows me how to check and adjust the pressures of the rest of the tyres, including the spare.

Afterwards, I invite him inside for a cup of tea, which turns into omelettes and wine. Only the one glass.

Daisy is happy to see him again, but Ethan barely says a word, skulking off from the lounge to his bedroom as soon as we come inside.

Later, when the two of us are alone in the kitchen, I find myself opening up to Billy about all sorts: being off work with stress; Daisy's upset over nasty Lori's party; Ethan's secretive behaviour.

He's a great listener. He doesn't try to offer forced solutions to everything, like some people do; he sympathises, asks pertinent questions and generally makes me feel better. Like I'm not alone and it's normal to be anxious about such matters.

With the Ethan situation in particular, which I'm yet to discuss with Rory, it's useful to get some male input. 'Were you like that at his age?' I ask.

'I was definitely a bit of a caveman, grunting and snarling a lot. And yeah, hiding away in my bedroom most of the time. He'll be going through all kinds of physical and emotional changes and I doubt he'll want to talk about them, particularly with his mum. Also, I'd be surprised if he wasn't looking at, um, porn pretty frequently. Sorry, too much information?'

'No, it's fine. I appreciate your honesty – and for what it's worth, you're probably right. Not that I particularly want to think about such things. But better that than drugs.'

TWENTY-FOUR

Ethan

He's flicking through video clips on his phone, looking for something to make him laugh and to take his mind off the fact that Billy's hanging out with Mum again downstairs. Then a message comes through from Liam.

L: *What's up?*

E: *Nothing much. You?*

L: *Freaking out.*

E: *How come? What's happening? Marty's not being a dick again, is he?*

L: *No, he's out.*

E: *So?*

L: *Connor collared me on the way home.*

E: *What? When? I was with you most of the way.*

L: *Yeah, it was after we split. Around the corner from my place. Like he was waiting for me.*

E: *Shit. What did he want?*

L: *Same as before. He said I'd had plenty of time to think about his offer and he needed an answer.*

E: *You said no, right?*

L: *Not exactly.*

E: *Mate, wtf! Why?*

L: *You weren't there, dude. You didn't see the mad eyes he was throwing at me when he asked. If I'd said no, I reckon he'd have either bashed me on the spot or majorly screwed with me somehow. It wasn't really a question. It was an order.*

E: *So what does that mean? You work for him now?*

L: *I guess so.*

E: *Doing what?*

L: *No idea. He didn't go into specifics. He told me he'd be in touch soon. He gave me a phone – one of those dead basic ones that only does calls and texts. He said to always keep it on me. And he told me not to worry. That I wouldn't have to do anything hard, but the money would be good.*

E: *All above board, then? Yeah, right.*

L: *I'm shitting it, mate. I honestly don't know what to do. I probably shouldn't have messaged you about it. Can you delete all this when we're done?*

E: *Yeah, okay. You're being paranoid, though.*

L: *Still. You'll do it, right? Promise?*

E: *I already said I would.*

L: *Thanks. Sorry, I'm losing the plot. What if he gets me involved in drugs or something?*

E: *That's why you shouldn't have said yes.*

L: *Mate, we've been through that. Oh bollocks.*

E: *What now?*

L: *Bloody Marty's back. By the way he just slammed his bedroom door, it sounds like he's in a bad mood.*

E: *He probably got dumped by that ugly girlfriend of his, if she ever existed in the first place. I still can't imagine anyone wanting to be with him.*

L: *Don't. I can't handle his bs tonight. Not on top of everything else. Gotta go. Laters.*

E: *No sweat. See you tomorrow.*

TWENTY-FIVE

Billy

That went well. Couldn't have gone better, really. Letting down the tyre was a genius move. Worked like a charm. Walking back after food and wine at Beth's, air compressor in one hand, Billy's happy now that things between them are back on track.

They're friends again, to the point where she's confiding in him about personal stuff. He's not entirely convinced that she's given up on the idea of them becoming romantically involved, based on the lusty way she was eyeing him up when she thought he wasn't paying attention. But that ball has at least been kicked into the long grass.

It was particularly interesting that she told him her concerns about Ethan being secretive with her. He's the one member of the family – other than Rory, naturally – that he's not managed to get on side so far. Perhaps he could use what she told him to try to find common ground with the kid.

The problem is that Ethan sees him as a threat. He's clearly holding out hope that his parents will eventually get back together. And Billy looks like an obstacle to that goal. Hence why Ethan invited his dad over that first time Billy came round for dinner. His mum can tell him they're just friends as much as she likes; he'll never buy it, not as things stand.

However, there is one guaranteed way that he could change Ethan's perspective once and for all, allowing him to view Billy in an entirely different light. No longer a threat.

Before today's success, Billy was almost ready to play that card, but only because he felt boxed into a corner. Now his gut's telling him it's not yet the right time. Okay, it'll never be the perfect time to make such a massive revelation. When he does so – and he can't realistically hold out much longer – it will have to be handled delicately. He has no idea how Beth, in particular, will react. However, delaying it a tiny bit longer gives him the chance to strengthen the foundations of their rapport, hopefully increasing the likelihood that she'll accept what he has to tell her, rather than flat-out rejecting him. It's trickier than that, though. Each extra day he waits to tell her is risky too.

On reaching his house, Billy lets himself in and, so he doesn't forget, pops immediately upstairs to the loft hatch and tucks the air compressor away inside. He didn't actually borrow it from a neighbour. He bought it earlier from a car shop in town. He didn't want to tell Beth that, fearing it would sound suspicious, as would already owning an electric tyre pump without having a car. Would it really, though? Would she have given it a second thought? The fib was arguably not required. An unnecessary potential tripwire, like when he previously lied to her about owning this house rather than renting it.

The problem is, once you get used to lying, it becomes habitual. Mental note: wind it in a bit. The fewer lies the better.

He puts on the kettle and, while waiting for it to boil, checks his phone. There's an unread message from Beth, which he opens:

Hi. Wanted to say thanks again for your help with my car today. I so appreciate it. You're a star and a great friend. I won't mess things up again, I promise. X

Billy smiles. Perfect. He fires off an immediate reply:

You're welcome. Really happy we've smoothed things out. See you soon. X

Cup of tea made, he takes it through to the lounge, flicks on the telly and sprawls out on the couch.

Finally time to relax after a busy, productive day.

Unfortunately, someone else has other ideas. His phone starts to vibrate with an incoming call from a withheld number.

Part of him doesn't want to answer. It's probably a scammer or salesperson trying to flog him something. But equally, he knows it could be a call he needs to take.

He answers it and raises the phone to his ear. 'Hello?'

'It's me.' The voice on the other end of the line is instantly recognisable. 'Can you talk?'

Billy sits up in his seat. Clears his throat. 'Hi. Yeah, I'm alone. How are you?'

'Fine. Let's keep it brief. Where are you up to? Is everything going to plan?'

TWENTY-SIX

THEN

Beth

Two weeks into the summer holidays, Dean asked me to be his girlfriend.

We'd met up on several occasions since that first date at the bowling alley. That was the beauty of us getting to know each other outside term time: no school to get in the way of having fun.

We'd both been round to each other's houses. He'd briefly met my parents, who'd thankfully not said anything too awkward or embarrassing. Unlike stupid Sean, who'd made constant kissing and farting sounds outside my bedroom door, giggling like he was hilarious. As for Dean's parents, I'd had lunch with them one day and they'd been really welcoming. Nice and relaxed. Even better, there were no annoying siblings to wind us up, since Dean was an only child.

The rest of that first fortnight, we'd mainly got together outside, as the weather had been great. Most of the time it had been just the two of us. We'd gone to the cinema with Sara and

Lou once; they weren't interested in getting to know any of Dean's mates after the last time.

I'd met with Dean and 'the lads' on two occasions in the park. There had been some drinking and smoking going on, but nothing too bad and not involving Dean, at least when I was there. Lenny hadn't been present on either occasion, thankfully, but Mac had. He'd been crude, repeatedly calling me Bubble Butt, for instance – despite Dean telling him to shut up – and blatantly ogling me, especially after boozing and puffing on a joint.

'Come and have a suck on this,' he'd said to me, out of Dean's earshot, before holding a spliff in my direction.

'No thanks. I'm fine.'

'Your loss, darling.' He'd grabbed his crotch, sniggering and winking at one of the others. 'You'd love it, trust me.'

Yeah, right. Loser.

Anyway, the girlfriend thing happened on the third Saturday of the holidays. Part of me had been hoping Dean would ask, considering how well things had been going. And yet I also wondered if he might hold back, in light of our upcoming separate holidays to Greece at the end of the month. In case he wanted to have a holiday romance. I certainly didn't. I was smitten. Totally focused on him. But he was a boy and, well, I knew what they could be like, at least from what I'd read in magazines and heard from other girls.

So when we were lying together on the grass in his back garden – mid-afternoon sun beaming down, the place to ourselves since his parents were out shopping – I was shocked when he suddenly leaned over, looking serious.

My initial thought – ever the optimist – was that he might be about to dump me.

'I've been thinking,' he said.

'Oh. What about?'

'You and me.'

'Right. I see.'

'I've really enjoyed these last two weeks, spending so much time together.'

'Me too.' I was expecting a *but* to follow.

'I think we should make it official. Will you go out with me – be my girlfriend?'

'Oh, right,' I said, a rush of relief and happiness washing over me. 'Thanks very much.'

Strange answer, I know. I was so delighted, I temporarily lost control of the filter between my brain and my mouth.

'Is that, um, a yes?' he asked, scratching his head.

'Sorry,' I replied.

'So it's a no?'

'No! I mean yes. It's a yes. Absolutely. Yes please.'

I got there in the end, just about.

There was lots of snogging and rolling around in the grass after that. And the first thing I did once I left Dean's house was run round to Sara's, a few streets away. Her mum let me in, saying that Sara and Lou were upstairs.

I burst into her bedroom, where they were both sitting on the bed, chatting over a bag of popcorn. 'Hi. How's it going?'

'Good,' they replied in sync.

'You're never going to believe what happened to me today. It's the best news ever.'

They glanced at each other before looking at me with expectant faces.

'What was that?'

'What was what?' Sara replied.

'That look you gave each other. Like you've talked about this before, when I wasn't here, and you can guess what I'm about to say.'

They looked at each other again.

'Why not just tell us your news?' Lou said.

'You've spoiled it now.'

Sara let out a sigh. 'Oh, come on. We haven't even said anything. You've been spending a lot of time with Dean recently. That's all. We're assuming it's to do with him.'

'Well, yes, it is.'

'And?' Lou said. 'Are you going to tell us, or what?'

I did – and they were good enough to at least feign surprise before giving me hugs and congratulating me.

'We're really happy for you,' Lou said. 'But does this mean we'll never see you any more? We've already missed having you around so far this holiday. It's not been the same without you.'

Sara nodded. 'You will make time for us, won't you?'

'Of course. Always.' I knew they were right, and I felt bad. 'Sorry about the last couple of weeks. It's been a whirlwind. I'll definitely make more time for you both, I promise.'

This seemed to be enough to reassure them.

'I still can't believe Dean is my boyfriend,' I said later. 'He's such a good kisser. I mean, I've nothing to compare it to, but I honestly can't imagine how anyone else could do it better.'

Sara and Lou giggled.

'I could always set you two up with Mac and his brother,' I said for fun. 'Who knows? They might be amazing kissers too.'

'No thanks,' they replied as one.

Lou made a retching sound so loud and dramatic it had us all in stitches.

If I'd known then what I do now, I'd never have made such a joke. No way. But I was still so innocent at that moment, I didn't see the harm. I thought life was wonderful. I was in a chilled, happy place, not realising it was the calm before the storm.

I had no clue of the darkness that was coming.

TWENTY-SEVEN

NOW

Rory

It's raining but not especially cold when he drives round to the house on Thursday lunchtime. What he still thinks of as his home, even though it isn't any more, in practical terms, and probably never will be again. It's Beth and the kids' home now.

Yes, Ethan and Daisy also spend time at his apartment every week, but he knows they don't think of it as their own. How could they when he doesn't either? It's a rental. What he sometimes considers, at low moments, to be his private purgatory. He hopes it's temporary, but a part of him fears he'll still be there in several years. He's already become acclimatised to the musty smell and the noise and vibrations from passing trams, which he barely notices unless something or someone – usually Ethan – draws his attention to them.

It can get lonely. At times, he even feels that way when the kids are visiting, particularly if they're busy doing their own stuff on phones or tablets. On their last visit, he found himself watching them from across the room, imagining them gradually fading away, like ghosts of his old life. Ethan was so engrossed in his mobile that evening, he barely came up for air.

Rory hides the melancholic feelings whenever they emerge, often behind a joke or a smile. He'd never want to trouble the kids with them and he isn't Beth's problem any more. He's hyperaware that he brought the current state of affairs on himself. At least he doesn't always feel so down. His mood ebbs and flows like the tide. What he does need to watch is the self-medicating – the drinking alone to lift his spirits – which is a more regular thing now than ever before.

Perhaps he should follow Beth's example and start dating. He could sign up for one of those apps and hook up with all sorts of new women. Sow his wild oats, so to speak. The irony is, despite fantasising about that sort of thing all the time when he and Beth were together – particularly once the sex dried up – he doesn't want to do so now. That's not to say he won't ever, but for the time being, he'd rather focus on other things. Part of this is about proving a point to Beth: showing her he's not the philanderer she thinks, despite what he put her through. It's almost certainly too late to make any difference. She's moved on. He probably has to accept that. But it's also for the kids and himself. He doesn't want to feel like the bad guy any more. He wants to be sure he's learned from his mistake and is now fully in control of his urges.

It's a cliché, but what happened meant nothing. It was drunken sex. Once. With a former colleague he ran into while staying away at a business conference. If he'd kept quiet, he'd almost certainly have got away with it, not least because his 'partner in crime' moved down south years back. But the guilt ate away at him, so he came clean, praying Beth might under-stand and give him another chance. But she didn't. And the fact that she knew the woman involved – had met and liked her back when she and Rory had worked together – only seemed to make matters worse.

As he understands it, Beth is still seeing this mysterious Billy. They're officially 'just friends', according to Ethan, but Rory thinks that's probably bullshit for the kids' benefit.

When he first caught a glimpse of Billy, that time they were both at the house, something about him looked familiar. However, he couldn't put his finger on what it was until later, when it dawned on him that, weirdly, Billy looked a little like Beth's father. Not that Rory had ever met him. But based on photos, there was a definite similarity. Unless it was just the thick dark beard. It wasn't like he got a really good look at the guy, so that could be it.

And yet there is a school of thought that says women have a tendency to fall for men who look like their fathers. That's what's been niggling at him. The idea of Beth falling for anyone but him makes his skin itch. He knows he's lost the right to feel that way, but he does, nonetheless.

Rory pulls up in front of the drive. Is anyone home? Beth's car is there, but that doesn't mean much. She barely uses it. An upstairs window is open, which could be a good sign.

Beth answers the door after a few seconds. Seeing it's him, a frown appears on her forehead. Brilliant. What a great effect he has on her these days.

'Oh, it's you.'

'I'm afraid so.'

'Is there a problem?'

'No.'

'You're still on for having the kids tomorrow night?'

'Of course.'

She rubs her chin with her forefinger. 'Right. So what can I do for you? How come you're not at work?'

'I'm on my way back to the office from a meeting. I was passing. Thought I'd call in.'

'You want to talk to me about something?'

'I do.'

'You'd better come in, then.'

Wow. He hadn't expected it to be this hard to get through the front door.

She offers him a seat in the kitchen, and a cup of tea, which he accepts.

'You're not ill, are you?' she asks out of nowhere. 'You're not about to tell me you've got some terrible disease or something?'

'What? Why would you say that? No, of course not. I'm fine. Fighting fit.'

'Good. What is it you wanted to talk about, then?'

Straight down to business. 'The kids.'

'Right.' She looks relieved. 'Couldn't it have waited until—'

'No, I thought it was about time we had a word together in private, when they're not standing right next to us. I'm a little concerned about, um, both of them, really.'

TWENTY-EIGHT

Beth

It's Friday night and I'm excited. I'm going out. To an actual bar/restaurant. It occurred to me yesterday that I hadn't been properly out in forever. So as the kids are at Rory's tonight, I asked Billy if he fancied joining me for a night on the tiles. Well, that's maybe overselling things. We're not heading into the city centre. One step at a time. We're staying local; going to a new gastro pub-type place within walking distance.

It's ridiculous how much I'm looking forward to this. I've put on a little black dress and everything. I even thought about wearing heels, although common sense kicked in when I considered the walk there and back.

The doorbell goes. That'll be Billy. He's five minutes early, but it's no problem. I've had plenty of time to preen, with no kids to organise or feed. I'm raring to go.

'Hello,' I say, swinging open the door and greeting him with a kiss. 'How are you?'

He beams a lovely smile at me, his teeth looking superwhite in contrast to his dark beard, which is sleek and shiny, like he's been grooming it with beard oil.

'You look fantastic,' he says.

'Thanks, you too.'

At least it's not only me who's made an effort. Billy smells amazing and looks so dashing in chinos, smart brown boots and a light-blue designer shirt.

I have to remind myself that he's not on the menu.

We arrive at the bustling venue early, and the friendly, attentive greeter asks if we'd like a drink in the bar before he shows us to our table.

'Yes please,' Billy says after checking with me first. He carries himself with such an appealing confidence. Self-assured without being arrogant. He might be a little younger than I am, but it doesn't feel that way. Why am I still so attracted to this man?

I can't go down this road again. I need to stop. I have to focus on our friendship. Enjoy this for what it is, end of story.

'What are you drinking?' he asks me at the bar.

'Hmm. Maybe a cocktail. You?'

'Gin and tonic.' He hands me the laminated menu and I pick a porn star martini. I haven't had one for ages, but when it arrives, I know I made the right decision. Delicious.

'How's everything with Ethan and Daisy?' Billy asks as we're sipping our drinks, sitting next to each other on bar stools.

'Same, pretty much.'

'No breakthroughs in the past couple of days, then?'

'Nope. Daisy remains uninvited to that stupid bloody birthday party tomorrow and Ethan's still giving off shifty vibes. Rory actually popped over during the day yesterday to talk to me about them.'

Billy raises an eyebrow. 'Really?'

'Yeah. I didn't know what was going on when he turned up out of the blue, but he said he was concerned. He already knew about Lori upsetting Daisy and he also thought Ethan was being secretive. It was the first time we'd spoken one-on-one in ages, and you know what, it was kind of nice. There was a good co-parenting vibe. Apparently, he's more engaged with his kids than I gave him credit for.'

'Right,' Billy says. 'Have you tried speaking to Ethan about what's going on with him?'

'Not directly. It's never felt like the right moment. He can be quite offhand. Typical teenager. I might have to resort to having a proper nosy around his room next time I'm cleaning there. I've been holding off, not wanting to intrude on his privacy. But Rory reckons I should go ahead and do it.'

Billy strokes his beard.

'Do you disagree?' I ask.

He shrugs. 'What do I know? I'm not a parent.'

'You were a teenager once.'

'So were you. What were you like at fourteen?'

This catches me unawares. 'I... um. That's not an easy question to answer, actually.'

'Sorry, have I touched a raw nerve? I didn't mean—'

'No, no. It's complicated, that's all. Another time.'

The greeter reappears to show us to our table, which is tucked away in a quiet corner. Well, as quiet as it gets on a busy Friday, which is perfect: we can hear each other talk and yet there's a nice vibrant feel to the place.

'Lovely here, isn't it?' I say. 'I've wanted to check it out for a while. Glad it doesn't disappoint.'

Billy winces. 'Easy, tiger. Don't jinx it. We've not tried the food yet.'

'Ah, I'm sure it'll be great,' I say.

And it is. We both have crayfish and prawn salad to start. For mains, I have a perfectly cooked medium-rare fillet steak, while Billy has crispy pork belly. Lastly, it's a crème brûlée for me and Billy goes for the cheeseboard, which is so big I have to help him.

'I'm so full,' I say afterwards, sipping on a black coffee.

'Me too, but it was all delicious, wasn't it?'

'Absolutely.'

We shared a bottle of red with the meal, but I was careful not to overdo it, especially after that initial cocktail, which packed a punch. I didn't want to end up so drunk that I ruined things again.

Heading home, I can't resist fishing for more information about Billy's romantic past. He drank quite a bit more than I did, including an Irish coffee, so I hope he might divulge more than usual.

'Come on,' I say as we walk side by side. 'What's the story with you, Billy? I'm guessing you've had your heart broken recently. Am I right? Was it a tough break-up that brought you here, looking for a new start?'

He groans. 'I don't think now's the time to go into all that, Beth.'

'You're such a closed book. What's that all about? I thought we were friends. I tell you all sorts about me and my family, but what do I know about you? I'm not even sure exactly what you do for work, other than something computer-related. Have you ever been married or in a long-term relationship? Have you got brothers or sisters; nieces or nephews? I've literally no idea. You could be a spy for all I know. Come on, give me something.'

He stops walking, and when I do the same, he takes my hand. Looks me in the eye, deadly serious. Takes a deep breath. 'Are you sure you want to do this right here, right now?'

I have a nervous feeling in the pit of my stomach. 'What's going on, Billy? You're starting to freak me out.'

He pauses. Stares into the distance. 'We're not far from my place,' he says eventually. 'How about we head back there and then we'll have this conversation? Unless you'd rather we go to your house. That's fine too. It's only a little further.'

'No, your place is fine.' I try to keep my voice steady while my mind and stomach do somersaults. What on earth is going on? What can of worms have I opened? It seems I'm about to find out. But do I want to?

TWENTY-NINE

The rest of the walk back to Billy's house must only take five minutes, but it feels like an hour. Neither of us says a word as we continue alongside each other on the pavement. It's so strange. I open my mouth to make small talk a couple of times, but nothing comes out.

I'm racking my brains for clues about what he's going to tell me, but it's fruitless. All I know is that I sparked this by asking him to be more open with me.

It can't be as simple as a bad break-up. That suggestion got this ball rolling, but it has to be way more serious or convoluted for him to have reacted so dramatically.

When we finally reach his front door, still in silence, my heart is thumping. What if he's a serial killer and he's about to murder me? No, stop it. That's absurd. This is the guy who rescued my daughter not so long ago. A good man who's repeatedly come to my aid. I'm not having one of my nightmares now.

How bad can it be?

Shit. It couldn't be somehow linked to the playground, could it? What happened when I was just a teenager. The secret from my past that I haven't even shared with my own children yet. Please, no. Please don't let it be that. It's shattered my life enough already. He could have found out – that is feasible – but I desperately hope not.

'Cup of tea?' he offers after hanging up my coat and showing me through to the lounge.

I figure I might need it. 'Yes please.'

'No sugar, dash of milk, quite strong?'

'Well remembered.'

Is it me or is his face really pale when he returns with two steaming cups?

'Right,' he says once we're both sitting down, facing each other. 'Sorry for dragging this out, but what I have to tell you is, er, delicate.'

'I'll have to take your word for that, Billy. I have no idea what's going on.'

'Yes, I get that. Sorry.' He places a hand over his forehead, using a finger and thumb to massage his temples. 'It's hard to know where to begin. We should have had this conversation sooner, but it never felt like the right time until now.'

His Adam's apple bobs up and down in his throat as he swallows. 'Hmm. Where to begin? There is a reason I haven't told you much about me and my background. It, um, wasn't entirely an accident that I was there to help you and Daisy when we first met at the playground.'

'What are you talking about?'

'It's, er, hard to say this without sounding creepy. I'd been watching you. Not in a stalkerish way, though. I—'

'Watching me? Both of us? When? For how long?'

'On and off for a couple of weeks prior to that. Just you, unless one of the kids happened to be with you, like Daisy was that day. I've never followed her or Ethan by themselves.'

'Oh, that's all right, then.' I claw my hands into the sofa cushion. Part of me wants to get up and leave immediately, yet I'm equally curious to get to the bottom of this chilling revelation. 'Why the hell would you do that, Billy, unless you were a stalker?'

'Because *you're* the reason I moved here, Beth. I wanted to meet you and I was looking for a way to do so. I was getting to know you while I waited for the right moment to introduce myself in a natural way.'

'Yeah, because that's really natural – following someone without them realising. Hang on, did you set up the whole thing with the boys and the dog in the park? Did you deliberately put Daisy at risk to—'

'No, of course not. They were nothing to do with me, but I was happy to help get rid of them. You've said yourself that if I hadn't been there, things could have taken a far more sinister turn.'

'Oh, this is *all* sounding very sinister right now,' I say. 'You need to explain yourself, pronto. Otherwise, I'm out of here, calling the police, reporting you for harassment. Why would I be the reason you moved here? We were total strangers before all of this. It makes zero sense.'

Billy clears his throat. 'You're probably asking yourself why you're still here, letting me talk, aren't you? I bet part of you is screaming inside to get as far away from me as possible. But you haven't. Why? Because you've got to know me and, on some level, despite all of this, you trust me. If I wanted to harm you, Beth, I've had plenty of opportunities already. You know that. You also know I'm telling you this of my own volition. I waited until now because I know it's a lot to take in. If you hadn't got to know me first, I doubt you'd have even heard me out.'

'So explain. Now. Why would you move here because of me?'

Billy takes a deep breath. Then he says something that floors me. That I could never have seen coming in a million years.

'Because you're my sister.'

THIRTY

Billy

There, he's said it. He's dropped the bomb at last. He didn't head out thinking tonight would be the night. He'd intended to wait. But then things reached a point where he felt like he could no longer hold back.

It's a huge weight off his shoulders. That's his initial feeling.

Now it's time to see how Beth responds.

He watches her as his words sink in. He expects her expression to reflect waves of shock, horror, confusion and various emotions in between. He anticipates countless questions.

But these things don't happen. Instead, her face turns to stone. For what feels like forever, she says nothing. Nor does she look at him. Her eyes are glazed over, staring at the wall.

Billy wants to say something to break the silence, but he daren't.

Eventually, in a tiny voice, Beth says: 'I had a brother once. He's dead.'

'I know. Sean, right? You told me he was killed in a motor-bike crash.'

'I was *his* sister. No one else's. I have no other brothers.'

Carefully, calmly, Billy replies: 'I understand what you're saying. But I'm also your brother. Half-brother, to be accurate. Your father had—'

'Don't you talk about him. You don't know anything about *my* father.'

'I'm sorry, Beth, but I can't explain this otherwise.'

She closes her eyes and lets out a sharp sigh. However, she doesn't repeat her instruction not to continue.

'I never met him,' Billy says. 'He had no idea I even existed. That was Mum's choice after she fell pregnant. It was a brief relationship they had, but she told me she loved him. He chose his family. That was that.'

'Why now?' Beth's voice is devoid of emotion. She won't even look at him. 'Why would you come to me with this now, if it's even true? Why not years ago?'

'I didn't know until recently. I grew up with no clue of my father's identity. I wasn't interested. I thought he was a lowlife who abandoned us. Mum only told me the truth right before she died.'

She finally meets his eye again. 'Your mother is dead?'

'Yes, just gone six months. Cancer.'

'What kind?'

'Breast. That's where it was first discovered, anyway. But it was super-aggressive. Spread really quickly. Her whole body was riddled with it by the end.' There's a catch in his throat as he says this. It's the first time he's spoken about his mum in a while. It never gets any easier.

'I'm sorry for your loss.'

'Thank you.'

After a pause, Beth adds: 'You decided to seek me out after she died?'

'Yes.'

'Any siblings?'

'No.' Cautiously, he continues: 'Apart from you. That's why I came here. You're the closest family I have left. I couldn't stay away, but equally I didn't feel I could walk up to your front door out of the blue and make these claims. Does that make any sense?'

She doesn't reply.

'I mean, with hindsight, I could have found a better approach. But grief is hard. It's affected me in all kinds of ways I didn't see coming. I've been struggling to think straight a lot of the time. I was so desperate not to mess things up with you. I did what I did. I can't change that now. I'm sorry.'

Beth looks at him with an ice-cold expression he's never seen cross her face before. She speaks in a slow, detached monotone that almost sounds like a different person. 'So, to be clear, all this time, right from when I first met you outside the playground, you've been feeding me a pack of lies, pretending to be someone you're not. And prior to that, you covertly watched me and my family. Now you have the audacity to sully my late dad's good name by claiming he cheated on my mum while I was a toddler, fathering you in the process.'

He doesn't respond straight away. Partly because it's unclear whether she's finished; partly because he's unsure how best to answer. Eventually, as she continues to stare at him, eyebrows raised, he forces himself to speak.

'I, er, can't dispute any of that. I know it's a lot. I know you'll need time to let it all sink in. Have I handled everything perfectly? No. I've already admitted that. But now at least I can say I've told you everything. The truth. Any other details you want to know about my life prior to coming here, ask and I'll tell you. If, on the other hand, you never want to see me again or have anything to do with me, that's your choice, and I'll respect it. I'll be gutted, though, I'm not going to lie. I've so enjoyed getting to know you and your family, like you wouldn't believe. It's the first time I've really felt anything since I lost Mum.'

He lowers his eyes and pauses to catch his breath. When he looks back up, Beth is on her feet. 'You're leaving?'

She nods.

'I understand.' He gets up to retrieve her coat. She's already holding the front door handle.

'Here.'

She nods again. Takes it. Opens the door before she even puts it on.

'I'll give you some space,' he says. 'No rush, no pressure. You know where I am. I'll be waiting. Feel free to contact me any time, day or night. Anything you might want to ask.'

She throws him one last lingering look and then she's gone.

THIRTY-ONE

Beth

As soon as I get inside, I pour myself a large glass of wine. My mind is reeling. What the hell just happened?

In the space of one conversation, Billy flipped my whole life on its head. Or at least that's what he tried to do. How much I allow that to happen depends on what I choose to believe. I could simply ignore him and try to forget we ever met. He did say he'd respect my decision if I wanted nothing more to do with him. And yet how can I trust that he'll stick to this pledge now he's outed himself as a stalker and a serial liar?

How am I supposed to process all of this? It's mind-blowing enough that he spied on me and my children. He then notched up the deception several levels by developing a deceitful relationship with me – and Daisy to a degree. He successfully manipulated both of us into liking him, coming across as such an all-round nice guy. Only Ethan had the good sense to resist his charms. And as if that wasn't enough, now Billy is claiming to be my long-lost brother, dragging Dad's good name through the mud in a desperate attempt to explain his outrageous actions. Where does this guy get off? He must think I'm stupid. Why would I ever believe such an absurd, desperate claim?

I pick up the wine glass, drain the rest of its contents and immediately refill it. The answers to my many questions aren't to be found here, I know that. But it doesn't stop me wanting to drink myself into oblivion. It's just as well I'm home alone tonight. I wouldn't want either of the kids seeing me like this; even less how I intend to end up.

For now, my brain is still whirring: no peace or numbness in sight. And the questions keep on coming. They won't leave me alone.

What's Billy's endgame?

Why has he told me all of this now?

Why did he really stalk and befriend us if he's lying about being my brother?

It's certainly not because he wants to have any kind of romantic relationship with me. I've already served him that on a plate and he wasn't interested.

So why, then? Money? If he thinks I've got any going spare, he's not been paying attention.

None of this makes any damn sense.

I drink some more wine, finally starting to feel anaesthetised as it tops up what I had at the restaurant.

I need to speak to someone – and only one person will do. She might be thousands of miles away in a different time zone, but thanks to the joys of technology, contacting my mother is as easy as a few taps and swipes on my phone, even in my current inebriated, bewildered state.

She answers on the fourth ring. Like me, she's in her kitchen, I see as her image pops up on my screen. She's wearing a thick blue and white stripy jumper and drinking what looks like a mug of coffee.

'Hello, darling,' she says with a calm smile. 'This is a nice surprise. Say hello to Roger. He's heading out.'

My heart sinks. As fond as I am of my stepfather, it's not him I need to talk to at this moment.

'Hello, Roger,' I say as Mum flips the camera so he's in shot, standing by the back door in a thick, fleecy coat.

He waves and grins, flashing me those perfect pearly whites that inspired Mum's new teeth. 'Hi there, Beth. I'm running late for a meeting, so I can't stop and chat. But it's as lovely as ever to see your face. Catch up soon, yeah?'

'Of course.' I force my lips into a smile, hiding my wine from view.

I hear Mum say goodbye to him and then her face reappears on the screen wearing a concerned frown. 'What's going on? Is everything okay?'

I start weeping uncontrollably. I try to say a few words to explain, in between sobs, but judging by the perplexed look on her face, she can't understand any of them.

'Darling, you're breaking my heart. Please take a deep breath and tell me what's the matter. Has something happened to one of the children?'

This final question pulls me back to my senses. Grants me some perspective. 'No, no. Don't worry. Ethan and Daisy are fine. It's nothing to do with them.'

'Good. I'm glad to hear *that*. Something has clearly got you all worked up, though. Please tell me what's going on, love. How can I help? Is anyone with you? If I was there in person, I'd be giving you a big hug and calming you down.'

'The kids are both at Rory's tonight.' I take a piece of kitchen towel to dab my eyes and cheeks. 'I, um, went out for a meal. I only got home a few minutes ago.'

'Who with, Beth?'

I haven't got around to mentioning Billy to my mother yet. Somehow it's never felt like the right moment. 'It's, er, a bit of a long story, Mum.'

'It's as well I have nothing important planned, then. Fire away.'

'You're sure it's not too much?'

'Of course I'm sure.' Mum takes a sip from her mug and looks at the camera.

I take a deep breath, put my wine glass to one side for now, and start at the beginning.

THIRTY-TWO

'So Billy is claiming to be my brother. Well, half-brother. Dad's long-lost illegitimate son, supposedly. Ridiculous, right? Dad would never have done that to you – to us – would he? I can't believe I'm even telling you all this. It's so stupid. I can't work out why he'd say such things. He must have some other agenda. But I'm scratching my head and I've no idea what that might be.'

I stop talking. Look at Mum's image on my phone screen and wait for her to say something. But she doesn't. Not right away, anyhow. She is looking at the camera, but her eyes are distant, like her thoughts are elsewhere.

'Mum? Is everything all right?'

She runs the palm of one hand across her face. Blinks several times. 'Sorry, love. I got lost in my thoughts. That's, um, quite some story. I don't know what I was expecting when you started, but it definitely wasn't that. No wonder you're so upset.'

'Yeah, but it's clearly nonsense, isn't it? There's no way he could actually be my brother. Right, Mum?'

She closes her eyes and lets out a long sigh. 'Honestly, darling, I don't know. I'd love nothing more than to be able to tell you categorically that there's no way it could be true. But that would be a lie. There are things about your father that I've, er, never spoken of to you.'

I can't believe what I'm hearing. 'Sorry, what are you talking about, Mum? What does that mean?'

Her eyes look away from the camera as she continues. 'You and Sean were so young when your father died. It was such an awful time for all of us, but particularly the pair of you. To lose a parent like you did at such a tender age – I can't even imagine what that must have been like for you. All you had left were your memories of him: your amazing, loving father, who was stolen from you way before his time. How could I tarnish those memories by telling you he wasn't always perfect? Why would a mother do that unless she had to? As a parent, you protect your children from pain wherever possible, right?'

'Mum, you're talking in riddles.' I reach for my wine glass again, sensing I'm about to need a crutch. 'What are you trying to tell me: that Billy *is* my brother? That you've always known about him but hidden it from me for—'

'No! I've never heard of Billy before in my life, Beth. I have no idea whether he's your half-brother or not.'

'What *are* you saying, then? I'm confused. What do you mean by the fact that Dad wasn't perfect?'

'He was a wonderful father to you and Sean. Nothing will ever take that away. He adored you both, as you rightly remember. He just, um, wasn't always quite such a good husband. He had an eye for the ladies. There were several indiscretions.'

'He cheated on you? More than once? What? Are you serious? Dad? But you two were mad about each other. He was always buying you gifts and—'

'There were a lot of apologies, love. And probably several more incidents, affairs, whatever you want to call them, than the ones I found out about. Did I love him? Yes. I couldn't help myself. He was magnetic. Such a big, warm, charismatic man.

He had a knack for making people feel special whenever he shone his light on them. That was his gift and also his curse. He broke my heart over and over. Somehow made me believe each time that it would never happen again, which of course it did. With hindsight, now that I know the truth of a loving, respectful marriage, I was a fool. But he had me under his spell.'

'Why would you stay with him if he did that to you?' I can feel a fresh river of warm tears coursing down each of my cheeks as I take a gulp of wine.

'Do you need any more of that, love?' Mum asks. 'You might be better putting on the kettle.'

'I asked you a question.'

She swallows. 'I felt like I had to do my best to keep our family together. I feared that if I kicked him out, he might end up moving away – and I didn't want to deprive you kids of your dad. Honestly, I also feared the harsh realities of being a single parent. Little did I know that it would happen regardless.'

'Billy *could* be my brother, then?'

'It's possible. I never asked for any specifics of your dad's affairs. I preferred not to know. It was easier to stomach that way, I'm embarrassed to admit. I always wondered if something like this would emerge one day: if someone would come forward saying he was their father. This Billy. Does he, er, look anything like him?'

I flash back to the first time I met Billy, when he stopped me from keeling over outside the playground and his brown eyes and beard made me think for a moment, in my panic-stricken state, that he *was* my father.

'Maybe. A bit.' I'm unwilling to concede any more than this. There have been too many revelations tonight: about Billy and now my father. I'm not ready to accept any of them yet. I need time to process. I need a clear head.

'So what now, Mum?'

'That's up to you, darling,' she says in a gentle voice. 'Even if he is your brother, you don't have to welcome him into your life if you're not ready for that. You need to do what feels right for you and your family. You're not responsible for the consequences of your father's actions. That said, if you do want to continue to get to know Billy, please don't hold back on my account. I'm in a really good place now, with a husband who loves and respects me. It's not something I'd have a problem with at all. You and I know the value of family more than most, based on the people we've lost far too young. My advice? Sleep on this. Consider it again tomorrow with a sober mind and for as long as you need. Then go with your gut. Do whatever feels right. I'm always here to talk.'

'Thanks, Mum, I appreciate that. What about the way Billy stalked me, though, getting to know me and the kids under false pretences?'

Mum shakes her head. 'It does sound weird, but it's not like he did you any harm. On the contrary, if he hadn't been there for you and Daisy at the playground, things could have ended up far worse. Perhaps he deserves some leeway in light of his mother's death. Grief makes us behave in all kinds of irrational ways, remember that.'

'I'll try. I think I ought to go to bed now. I'm shattered.'

'Good idea. I love you, Beth. Sleep well. Speak soon.'

THIRTY-THREE

THEN

'Who's looking forward to our holiday?' Dad asked at the dinner table. 'Not long now until we'll be lounging on the beach and swimming in the sea.'

'Me!' Sean replied with predictable enthusiasm. He was still only eight, or 'almost nine', as he liked to tell everyone, meaning family holidays were the pinnacle of his summer.

I, on the other hand, was madly in love. Well, so I thought. I was certainly in lust. And that meant the prospect of being away from my gorgeous new boyfriend for any amount of time was unpalatable. Particularly as he'd be relaxing on a different Greek island, surrounded by other girls in bikinis.

'Sure,' I said when Dad threw me an expectant glance.

He chuckled. 'Now don't go overboard with the enthusiasm, Beth. What's the problem? Worried you'll miss Dean too much?'

I felt Mum kicking him under the table.

'I'm sure we're all looking forward to the holiday in our own way,' she said.

'Will they have jet-skiing?' Sean asked. Seemingly, my brother had grown bored of winding me up about having a boyfriend, which was a relief. All those fake smooching noises and gestures at the start had been infuriating.

'Possibly,' Dad replied, stroking his beard. 'But I think you might be too young for that.'

Sean frowned. 'This boy in my class, Rocky, did it last year in Spain. He said it was unreal.'

'Yeah, that's because he made it up,' I said.

'He did not.'

'Whatever.'

'Come on, you two,' Dad said. 'No need for that. There will be plenty of other exciting stuff to do, like those inflatable banana things they pull along on the back of a speedboat.'

Sean's face lit up. 'They're cool. And water-skiing. Rocky did that too.'

'Of course he did,' I replied. 'Did he also go deep-sea diving and then for a few bungee jumps? I assume he's a heavyweight boxer too, based on his name.'

Sean stuck his tongue out at me. 'I know what you'll do all holiday: read soppy stories and cry because you miss your boyfriend.' He mimed being sick.

'Stop quarrelling, you two,' Mum said. 'It's exhausting.'

Dad changed the subject. 'Anyone fancy a family stroll after tea? It's a lovely evening.'

'I will, if we can go to the playground,' Sean said. 'I want to see if I can beat my record at long jump.'

My brother had recently decided that he wanted to be an Olympian when he grew up. He was working his way through various athletic events to find out what he was best at, long jump being the latest; the large sandpit in the playground at the park was ideal for practising, apparently. I suspected that by the time he reached an actual beach, full of sand, he'd have moved on to a different event.

'What about you, Beth?' Dad asked.

'I'll walk some of the way with you, as long as we go soon. I'm meeting Dean in the park in about forty-five minutes.'

'Perfect.' He turned to Mum. 'What about you, love?'

'I have an overdue date with a pile of ironing, I'm afraid, but don't let that stop you. I'll enjoy the peace.'

'Charming.' Dad rolled his eyes playfully and then leaned over to give her a kiss on the cheek. 'We'll miss you.'

We left the house fifteen minutes later. 'So what's this Rocky's real name?' I asked Sean, mainly to annoy him.

'Richard. We call him Rocky because his pet dog's a boxer.'

'Right. Does he make a lot of stuff up? Let me guess, his dad's a millionaire.'

'No. But he did used to be a spy.'

'Who, Rocky or his dad?'

'His dad, of course.'

'Naturally. Oh, come on, Sean. Don't be so gullible. He's full of it.'

'How do you know? You've never even met him.'

Dad stepped in at this point and told me to drop it, for Pete's sake. I was tempted to be a smart alec and ask who Pete was. However, knowing I was vulnerable to being embarrassed in front of Dean, I bit my tongue.

As luck would have it, I saw Dean in the distance, walking towards us on the opposite side of the road, so I said goodbye and ran over to meet him, avoiding any awkwardness. Well, Dad did wave and shout hello, but it could have been worse.

Dean asked if I minded hanging out with his friends for a bit. Not wanting to come across as clingy, I agreed. 'Who's out?'

'The usual. I arranged to meet them near the playground.'

'Really?' I pulled a face. 'That's where my dad and brother are heading. The boys aren't going to be drinking or smoking weed, are they?'

Dean shoved his hands into his pockets. 'You know what they're like.'

'My dad will flip if he sees any of that. He'll probably stop me seeing you. Could we go somewhere else, just this once?'

A conflicted look flashed across Dean's face. 'I promised them I'd be there tonight. We've seen loads of each other recently. I, er, need to see my mates sometimes too.'

'Has one of them said something? Let me guess: Mac? What's he told you?'

Dean looked down at his Doc Martens.

'He's a prick,' I continued. 'I can't believe you don't see it. You should hear the way he talks to me behind your back. You think he's your mate? He'd steal me away from you in a second, given half the chance. Lucky for you, I can't stand him.'

'How would you like it if I slagged off your friends?'

'Go ahead. They're nothing but nice, though: to your face and behind your back. They're not angry psychos like Mac and Lenny. I don't even want to know what Mac says about me when I'm not around, but I bet it's not flattering. It's bad enough when I'm there: constant pervy references. I can't believe how you let him disrespect me.'

'That's not fair. I've told him to shut his mouth loads of times.'

'Hmm.' But you haven't actually shut it for him, I thought.

'Listen, are you coming or not, Beth?'

'Whatever. You go. I'll do something else.'

I turned on my heel and walked away from him; away from the park. I wanted him to come after me, but he didn't. All I got was: 'Beth, don't be like that.' Then, after a short pause: 'Fine. Your choice. I'll see you later.'

Was that it? No effort to convince me to stay?

As I continued walking, my feet moving faster and faster, I went through a series of emotions: anger, disbelief, disappointment and, finally, frustration with myself for handling the situation badly.

I was so into Dean – so obsessed with remaining his girlfriend – I started to rethink everything I'd told him. Started to fear he might dump me, particularly if he sought the counsel of his moronic mates.

I know. Pathetic. What can I say? I was fourteen. He'd been my crush for ages and now he was my first ever boyfriend.

Do I wish now that I'd acted differently? Hell, yes. Like you wouldn't believe. A day hasn't passed since when I haven't asked myself why I turned back and went after him, tail between my legs.

I had no idea how consequential that one bad decision would prove to be, starting a cataclysmic chain of events that would devastate my entire family. Creating a spider's web of fractures through each of our lives; changing us forever.

It's only in recent times, after so many years of soul-searching, that I can even contemplate the possibility that what happened later might not have been my fault. And yet still, as my manifold wounds continue to reject the healing process, I never stop wondering how different the world would look today if I'd simply ignored the pangs of my teenage heart and kept walking away.

THIRTY-FOUR

NOW

Ethan

He meets Liam on Saturday morning, as arranged, in the autumnal leaf-strewn park. It's the same place – a secluded spot under a large oak tree – where Connor sold them their knives. That was when this nightmare began.

'All right?' Ethan says, approaching the bench where Liam is already sitting down.

'Hi, mate,' Liam replies in a quiet, shaky voice. 'Thanks for coming.'

'No sweat,' Ethan says, like being here isn't a big deal. But that's not true. It's a huge deal. Something that kept him awake into the early hours of this morning, staying over at Dad's stupid flat, having to share that tiny room with Daisy again. He almost said something to Dad at breakfast. Almost asked for his advice. But he couldn't get the words out.

He doesn't have to be here. So far Connor hasn't approached him like he has Liam. But it's probably only a matter of time. And Liam's in trouble *now*. He's scared. What kind of mate would Ethan be if he didn't help?

'Have you got it?'

Liam nods, gesturing towards the backpack next to him on the bench.

'And the knife?'

'Yeah, that too. You?'

'Uh-huh. Where did you keep the package at school yesterday after he gave it to you? You didn't carry it around the whole time, did you?'

'No, I stashed it in my locker. I was crapping my pants about it all day.'

'I'm not surprised.'

Ethan was terrified enough taking his knife to his dad's place yesterday, where there weren't many locations to hide it, particularly with Daisy breathing down his neck. He ended up wearing his joggers with zip pockets and keeping it on his person most of the time, then under his mattress at night.

'What about when you got home?' he asks Liam. 'Did you open it?'

'It's tightly wrapped up with some kind of heavy-duty tape. I didn't dare to mess with it. I hid it at the back of my wardrobe. I was terrified about Mum finding it, or worse still, Marty.'

'What do you think it is?'

'Drugs at a guess. Maybe cash, I suppose, but I doubt they'd seal money up like that.'

'Does it smell of anything?'

'No, but it's probably in vacuum bags. Also, if it's not weed, I'm not sure it would smell, would it? It might be coke or pills or whatever. Nothing I want to get busted with, that's for sure. The sooner I get rid of it, the better.'

Ethan sighs. 'There's going to be more, though, isn't there?'

Liam's face drains of what little colour it had. He jams his shaking hands into his jacket pockets. 'I can't think about that now.'

Ethan's as nervous as he's ever felt in his life, but he does his utmost to hide the fact, for Liam's sake. His friend looks ready to fall apart, but he needs him to hold it together. 'Where do we take it?'

'I don't know.'

'What?'

'Connor hasn't told me yet.'

'I don't get it. What are we doing here now, then?'

'It needs to be delivered at midday on the dot. That's all he told me. He said to be ready in plenty of time and he'd message me the address this morning on that burner phone.'

'When did you last check it?'

'Right before you arrived.'

'Check it again.'

Liam pulls the mobile out of his jacket pocket and squints at the tiny screen before shaking his head.

'Looks like something from the dark ages,' Ethan says. 'I'm surprised it's up to receiving texts. How do you even type on it?'

'You have to use the buttons. Each number does several different letters. I tried to get my head around it the other day in case I ever need to reply. It's proper fiddly.'

'So what now?'

'We wait.'

'Brilliant.'

Ethan puffs on his vape, sparking Liam to do the same.

'So we drop it off and that's that? Or do you get something in return?'

'Shit,' Liam says, eyes like saucers. 'I don't know. I bloody hope not. What would I have to do with that?'

'Give it back to Connor? That would be my guess. Let's just see what happens, yeah?'

'Easy for you to say. You're not the one with the noose around your neck.'

'I don't think you're quite at that stage yet, dude. Chill. I'm here, aren't I?'

'Sorry.'

'How are things with Marty?'

'He's a dick, as usual. He came in my room last night, called me a pussy and started flicking my ear lobes.'

'Eh, what's that all about?'

'I don't know. He's a nutter. It really hurt. Luckily Mum came upstairs, so he stopped. Pretended to be all pally, like he does. He claimed to be helping me with homework. As if.'

'You haven't stood up to him yet?'

'With the knife? No way I'm risking that while I'm hiding a dodgy package. Imagine if he grassed me up to Mum or his dad and they searched my bedroom. Or perhaps he'd come back when I was out and start rooting around himself, trying to find the blade. No, it was a stupid idea in the first place. If I'd not bought it, I wouldn't be in this mess with Connor now, would I?'

'I suppose not. You can't let him push you around, though, mate.'

'Who, Marty or Connor?'

Ethan rolls his eyes. 'Both? Although I meant your step-brother.'

A loud mobile phone notification dings.

'Is that...?'

'Yep.'

Liam fumbles in his pocket and pulls out the phone again, only to drop it on the grass. It breaks into two pieces. 'Shit.' He looks down at them without moving.

Ethan steps in, crouching to pick them up, giving himself a muddy knee in the process. 'It's all right. Panic over. It has a removable battery. It's unclicked, that's all. Here.' He fits the pieces back together, finds the power button, presses it and hands the device to his friend.

After waiting for the phone to reboot, Ethan watches Liam's

face, somehow even paler than before, as his eyes scan the message. 'Right,' he says in a tiny voice.

'What does it say?'

'It's an address.'

'Let me see.' Ethan peers at the text on the small screen and then pulls out his smartphone, which feels huge in comparison. 'I'll look it up. Hold on.' He taps in the details. 'Bingo. A sixteen-minute walk from here. Ready?'

'No.'

'Come on. Let's get it done.'

THIRTY-FIVE

Billy

Waiting is hard. He's had to do a lot of it lately. You'd think it would get easier, but this current wait – this nagging uncertainty – feels like the biggest obstacle yet. It's not even been twenty-four hours since he told Beth about the half-brother thing and he already feels like he's climbing the walls.

He's been out for numerous walks today to try to combat this impatience. This need to know what's going to happen next. But it's not something he can leave behind. It's always there, crawling under his skin, like his own private army of ants.

The stakes are so high this time. This is what he's been building towards. He's left the ball firmly in Beth's court. If she doesn't contact him again, what then? Everything is dependent on her doing so. And what if she does contact him but only to say that she doesn't want him in her life?

He's so desperate, he's even been checking on the backdoor he secretly created into her redundant laptop, in case by some miracle she's actually decided to charge up the machine and use it. Fat chance. That's proved as pointless as ever. Definitely not worth coming clean to her about.

Billy wants to scream.

Why did he tell Beth he'd give her space: no rush, no pressure?

Because it was the right thing to say.

And yet still he wishes he hadn't, so that he could be the one to make contact. To go round, knock on her door and ask for her answer. To beg his way back into her life.

Yeah, right. Great idea. Like that would work so much better.

Patience. That's what's needed. Tough but true.

He has to believe in himself. To trust in the backbreaking groundwork he's already put in. And to wait. As long as it takes.

But how long might that be?

He does wonder if he ought to have said something yesterday about the thorny topic of Beth's father's death. *Their* father, rather; he still needs to get used to that. Maybe it would have been good to let her know that he was already aware of the circumstances. That might have given her some peace of mind, perhaps, as she began to weigh everything else up.

Dammit.

Soon he can't bear it any longer. It's suffocating, like the walls are closing in on him, so he grabs his coat and goes outside, not bothering to turn off the television or any of the lights.

He breathes in the late-afternoon air and relishes the cool feel of it sinking into his lungs, even tainted as it is by traffic fumes and wood-burners.

He walks in the direction of Beth's house. He's already passed by several times today, as discreetly as possible. He can't stop himself. Not that he's seen much. Beth told him at dinner yesterday that she and Daisy were planning to have a home pamper session. That will have kept them inside.

As he nears the house again, he slows as he notices two

figures on the pavement at the end of the drive. Shit. Who's that? He really doesn't want to get spotted walking past, particularly by Beth, who already thinks of him as a stalker now. Whoever they are, both wrapped in hooded puffer jackets, they're not looking in his direction, at least. He's still far enough away for them not to have heard the sound of his footsteps.

He ducks down on one knee by the side of a van, pretending to fasten his shoelaces. He can still see the two figures ahead, who he hopes might be a pair of randomers having a stop and chat; he doubts they can see him in this crouched position.

One of them turns their head for a moment, and it's enough for him to see that it's Ethan, who's presumably with a mate. Brilliant. So what now? Should he get back up and continue, say hello to the kid like he just happens to be passing and then keep on going? Or better to turn on his heel and head back the way he came?

Ethan and the other figure appear to be arguing. They exchange several cross words, which Billy can't make out despite their raised voices. Ethan throws his hands in the air, turns and walks back towards the house. The other person remains on the pavement, gesturing after him and saying something else Billy can't hear. Then he turns and starts walking towards Billy, who rises back to his feet in response and continues on his way. They brush past each other, allowing Billy to make out the face inside the hood. It's a lad around Ethan's age: pale complexion dotted with a few angry-looking spots; backpack slung over one shoulder; eyes fixed to the pavement.

Billy slows right down and crosses to the other side of the road.

When he does pass the house, a quick glance tells him Ethan is no longer outdoors. Phew. Close call. He must stop walking by. He needs to do what he promised and give Beth space: no rush, no pressure.

His best bet is to do something else to distract himself. Perhaps he should go to the gym. Or maybe the pub would be better. He might meet someone nice there. Someone to help him forget.

THIRTY-SIX

Beth

I'm in bed and it's just gone ten o'clock. On a Saturday. I'm such a rebel. Ethan, wide awake on his phone in his bedroom, looked at me like I was a weirdo when I said goodnight.

'I'm shattered,' I told him. 'You should be getting ready for bed too.'

'Eh? I never go to bed this early on a Saturday. Dad doesn't—'

'Fine.' I didn't have the energy to argue. 'At least keep it down, please. Your sister is already asleep and I hope to be in the land of nod myself soon. Don't start having noisy showers at midnight.'

'When do I ever do that?'

'Goodnight, love.'

'When do I, though? Seriously.'

'Ethan, just do as I ask, please.'

'Fine.'

It's no wonder I'm so tired after the last twenty-four hours or so. I was way too late to bed and too boozy after Billy's revelation yesterday, followed by my video chat with Mum. Today I had to put my awful hangover to one side for Daisy's sake. We may not have had a magician, but we did have a lovely mother–daughter day of face masks, manicures, pedicures, makeovers and hair styling. I gave it my all, in spite of everything, and I enjoyed spending that quality time with her.

'Good day today?' I asked her while blow-drying her hair after her shower.

'The best.'

I didn't say anything about it being better than the party. There was no need to remind her of that before bedtime. Monday will no doubt be tough, when everyone relives whatever happened at Lori's bash, but we can chat about that on the day. It makes me mad thinking about it again now. I allow myself one frustrated punch of my pillow, then move my thoughts along.

Next to pop into my mind is Billy – shocker – but I'm having none of that. It's been nice being too busy to think about his bombshell. Tomorrow is another day. One when I can also consider what my son might have been doing earlier, out with Liam for hours on end. He seemed annoyed and extra shifty when he got home. Defensive when I asked him the briefest of questions.

'Good day?'

'It was fine.'

'Where did you go?'

'Here and there, just in the area.'

'How's Liam?'

He growled. 'Fine. Why do you have to ask so many questions, Mum?'

'I'm showing an interest, that's all. You're my fourteen-year-old son. I like to have some idea what you get up to.'

'Whatever. I told you, didn't I?'

I'm not thinking about that any more tonight either. I push

it away and attempt to wipe my mind of all thoughts. I picture myself lying on my back in a large empty field of grass. I imagine blue sky above, scattered with a handful of fluffy white clouds; the warmth of the sun on my face. I breathe slowly and deeply. In through my nose, feeling my abdomen expand. Hold. Out slowly through my mouth. And repeat.

It's starting to work until there's a loud knock on my door. 'Mum? Are you asleep yet?'

'What is it, Ethan?' I ask, refusing to open my eyes.

I hear the door open.

'Mum?'

'Yes?'

'Why are your eyes still closed?'

'Because I'm in bed. Like I told you before, I'm shattered. I was almost asleep until you knocked.'

'Oh, right. Sorry.'

'What is it? Make it quick, please.'

'You know how you told me I couldn't have a shower at midnight.'

'Yes.'

'Does that mean I can still have one now?'

I sigh. 'If you must, but you really need to keep the noise down. And now means straight away. Not in twenty minutes or half an hour.'

'Nice one.'

'Please could I get some sleep now?'

'Sure.'

'You're not going to wake your sister up, are you?'

'No. I'll be really quiet.'

'Goodnight, then.'

'Night, Mum.'

Right. Let's try this again. I'm back in that grassy field. Blue sky, fluffy clouds, sun on my face. Deep breaths. Bathroom door and extractor fan.

Oh for goodness' sake.

I pull the quilt over my head and curl into a tight ball.

Please let me get some sleep now.

Is that too much to ask?

I'm so damn tired.

I need to switch off.

THIRTY-SEVEN

THEN

As soon as I found Dean and his mates in the park, my heart sank. They were gathered on and around a bench outside the entrance to the playground, in which I could see my dad and brother using the sandpit at the far side, Sean practising his long jump as planned.

The lads had their backs to me, but it was easy to make out who was there alongside Dean: Sam, Mac and Lenny. Brilliant. They all had cans of lager in their hands, Dean included; Sam and Lenny were both smoking what I hoped were just cigarettes.

Had Dad noticed Dean brazenly boozing in public? I really hoped not. He was looking the other way at that moment, but he was bound to turn round at some point, if he hadn't already, so I decided to act. The easiest thing would have been to call Dean over, but I was afraid Dad might hear that, so instead I crept up behind him.

As I approached on tiptoes, I overheard snippets of a conversation about a fight they were planning, presumably with another bunch of lads.

'You've got what I gave you before, right?' I heard Lenny say in his gravelly voice.

'Yeah,' one of the others answered, although I couldn't make out who.

'It needs to be you, lad,' Lenny continued. 'Can't let them diss you like that. You gotta show 'em who's boss. Stick it to 'em.'

'Totally,' Mac said. 'Us lot don't take shit off no one.'

Right behind Dean now, still unnoticed by any of them, I poked him in the side, making him jump.

'Boo,' I said, flashing him a grin. 'Thought I'd join you after all.'

'Oh, hi. It's you.' His initial frown turned into a somewhat forced smile. A furtive look passed between the other three.

'Well, if it isn't Bubble Butt Beth,' Mac said.

'Well, if it isn't Little Mac,' I replied, waving my pinkie finger at him, garnering an 'ooh' from the other guys.

He grabbed his crotch. 'I might be offended by that, if it was true. I'd be very happy to show you that it's not.'

'No thanks.' I made an exaggerated retching sound.

'Rather have a gang bang, would you? I'm sure we can accommodate you. Right, lads?'

Lenny and Sam laughed, to my irritation. I glanced over at Dad and Sean, glad to see they were busy and apparently oblivious to my presence. Then I scowled at Dean. 'Are you going to let him talk to me like that? Let them all laugh at me. Disrespect me. The disgusting stuff that perv comes out with. I'm only fourteen.'

'Need Deano to fight your battles for you, do you?' Mac said. 'Poor baby.'

'Mac, why are you being a knob?' Dean asked. 'Leave it out, will you? There's no need.'

'You're the one who can't go anywhere without your whiny girlfriend, mate,' Mac said. 'BBM.'

'Yeah, whatever. Knock it off.'

'Can I have a word?' I asked Dean, glancing again at Dad and Sean to check their attention remained elsewhere.

'Sure.' Dean showed no sign of moving.

'In private?' I nodded back in the direction from which I'd arrived.

'Oh, okay.' He put his can of lager down on the floor next to the bench.

'The lad's in big trouble now, boys,' Mac said to the others, all three chuckling as we walked away. 'He'll be grounded if he's not careful.'

Dean said nothing.

'Seriously?' I asked him once we were far enough away not to be heard.

'What? You're the one who walked off.'

'So you thought it would be a good idea to get pissed in public right in front of my dad and brother?'

'Oh, right. That. What was I supposed to do? The lads were already set up there when I arrived.'

'You could have suggested moving somewhere else.'

'Who says I didn't?'

'Hmm. And yet you were happy to keep swigging beer in full view of the playground.'

Dean shrugged. 'I was being discreet.'

'Pull the other one. I saw you before you saw me, remember. Didn't look discreet at all. And what was that about some fight I heard you lot planning?'

'Bloody hell, Beth. Don't go there. Trust me.'

'You're not giving me much reason to do that.'

'What do you want from me? I'm just hanging out with my pals.'

'And don't I know it. What does BBM mean?'

'Sorry?'

'BBM. Mac said it before.'

'Oh, right. It means, um, "bird before mates".'

'Of course it does. Why aren't I surprised? I can't believe how you let him talk to me.'

'Listen, I can't deal with this now, Beth. I feel like piggy in the middle. It's doing my head in. I'm getting out of here. See you later.'

He stormed off; to my surprise, not in the direction of the other lads, but away out of the park, leaving me on my own. 'Where are you going?' I called after him. 'Come back.'

He didn't even turn around.

'Fine. Be like that, Mr Stroppy.' Like I could talk, having done the same to him minutes earlier.

I decided to join Dad and Sean, who'd probably be wrapping things up soon. Unfortunately, that meant passing Dean's three idiot friends, who of course tried to speak to me as I did so.

'Oi,' Lenny said. 'Come here a second. I want to ask you something.'

I ignored him.

'Hey, Bubble Butt,' I heard Mac chip in. 'Lenny's talking to you. I wouldn't disrespect him if I were you.'

'You can piss off, both of you,' I said without looking back.

I walked through the entrance of the playground. Apart from Dad and Sean, still busy in the sandpit at the far side – still facing away from me – there were only a dozen or so others in there. Mainly teenagers enjoying the lazy summer evening, chatting and goofing around. I don't remember much about them other than these two girls about a year younger than me, who stood out because they were practising a dance routine, both wearing big headphones. I remember thinking how weird it looked to see them move in sync without being able to hear the music. I wondered what the song was and if they were connected to the same music player. They must have been. How could they have kept in time otherwise? Strange the things that stick in your mind.

I was looking at those girls as I felt someone grab my wrist from behind and spin me back towards them. I knew instantly it wasn't Dean. The grip was far too tight to be friendly.

As I turned around, I saw it was Mac, flanked by Lenny and Sam.

'What the hell do you think you're doing?' I said. 'Get your hands off me.'

'I was speaking to you,' Lenny snarled. 'I called you over. Wanted to ask you something.'

'So?' I tried and failed to shake myself free from Mac, who was surprisingly strong. 'You're not my boss. I'd happily never speak to any of you again. I've no idea why Dean hangs out with you.'

'I have a question,' Lenny said. He was right in my face now, reeking of cigarettes and beer. I was tempted to call out to my dad for help, but for some reason I didn't.

'When you crept up on us before, what did you hear?'

'What? Nothing. Why do I care what you lot chat about?'

Lenny looked from me to Sam, to Mac and then back to me. 'What do you reckon, boys? Think she's telling the truth?'

'No, I don't,' Mac said. 'I think she's a little liar. She was definitely eavesdropping. What a shame Deano isn't around to protect her now.' He tightened and twisted his grip on my wrist, also clamping a hand on my opposite shoulder. 'I think we should take her somewhere quiet and—'

'Ow!' I said. 'That hurts. Get off me. Leave me alone, you pervy freak.'

'What the hell's going on?' The sound of Dad's voice from behind me cut through everything else. I was mortified – not by his presence, which was a huge relief, but by the fact that he'd found me in this situation.

'Piss off, old man,' Lenny snapped. 'This is nothing to do with you.'

'I beg your pardon, sonny. This is *everything* to do with me.

That's my daughter you lot are harassing. Get your damn hands off her.'

'Or else what?' Mac piped up, holding me firmly in place. 'Think you can take us on, do you? Good luck.'

It's hard to explain exactly what happened next. It was all so fast. Lots of sudden movements and shouting. I couldn't tell you if it was Dad or Lenny who made the first move, but suddenly they were grappling, and punches were being thrown. It was incredibly noisy, violent and scary. I heard my brother scream: 'Get off my dad!' Then he hurled himself at Lenny's legs, thumping, scratching and biting. I screamed too.

I fought to get free from Mac's clutches, but his grip was like iron. 'Stay still, bitch,' he spat in my ear.

Sam wasn't involved initially. I recall he looked out of place, rooted to the spot, while the rest of us were tussling. If only he'd stayed that way. But no. Mac yelled at him to do something. To help Lenny. Because against the odds, my dad – a tall, strong man, yes, but one I didn't think had a violent bone in his body – was taking on that psycho and holding his own.

Sam jerked forward, grabbed hold of my little brother and more or less threw him to one side, provoking yet more screaming and flailing from me, at which point Mac slapped me hard around the face. 'Stay still like I told you, stupid cow. You're not going anywhere. And your prick daddy is dead meat.'

As hot tears ran down my stinging cheek, to my horror I saw the evening sun reflect off a flash of silver in Sam's right hand. He moved back towards where Dad and Lenny were rolling around on the floor, Dad currently on top, and held his knife-wielding arm aloft. 'Sam, no, please!' I screamed. He hesitated, his body shaking. Looked back at me and Mac. Then, as the struggling bodies shifted, he was knocked to one side, the weapon jerking out of his hand and onto the floor.

Before I could even breathe a sigh of relief, I saw Lenny's

hand dart towards the knife. He grabbed it and, with zero hesitation, thrust it upwards with real force into the open sleeve of Dad's T-shirt. I watched it stab twice into the fuzz of hair under his armpit. I heard the devastating sound of Dad wailing in agony when Lenny yanked it out and pushed away his foe's instantly weakened form.

Dad flopped sideways onto his back, blood spurting out from his wounds.

So much blood.

Lenny staggered to his feet, covered in crimson. Everything went blurry, running in slow motion, as if I'd been drugged. 'We need to get out of here,' he barked at the other two, wiping blood from his face and pocketing the weapon. 'Now.'

Mac said: 'What about—'

'Leave her.'

He let go of me and I dropped to my knees, all strength sapped from my body. Sam stood still before me, also splattered in blood, staring down ashen-faced at my father's fast-fading form.

'Shift it,' Lenny said, shaking Sam into action as Mac reached his side and the pair of them dragged him away. The sound of their feet as they started to run echoed in the fresh silence like a galloping horse, fading into the distance behind me.

'Dad!' Sean's wretched voice cut into my dazed consciousness as he ran to our father's side, before looking to me, eyes suffused with terror and panic. 'He's not moving. What do we do?'

My body lurched into gear as the adrenaline kicked in with a surge.

'Someone call an ambulance,' I shouted to whoever else was still in the playground. 'Has anyone got a phone? Our dad's really badly hurt. I think—'

'Yes,' a shaky female voice replied. 'I'm calling now.'

There was blood everywhere, on and around Dad and now both of us; it was still pumping out of him at a terrifying rate. I've never seen so much of the stuff before or since. And I could smell it: a horrible hot metallic tang mixed in with the scent of summer grass. How long since he'd been stabbed? How much precious time had we lost? Hopefully not as long as it felt. I knew it mattered. I knew Lenny must have hit somewhere bad: a main vein or an artery. I knew we had to stop it coming out of him. He was already unconscious, the few unbloodied parts of his skin lily white; his life essence draining away.

'Give me your T-shirt,' I said to my brother. 'We need to try to stem the bleeding.'

'Dad,' I said, keeping my hands pressed on the cloth even as it disappeared under the river of red. 'Can you hear me? We're going to save you. You'll be all right. Help is on the way.'

Did I believe any of that? No, not if I'm honest. Not at that point. It was mainly for Sean's sake, to give him strength to keep going, at least until help did arrive. In my heart of hearts, I knew Dad wasn't going to make it. There was too much blood. And still no ambulance.

When the paramedics did finally arrive, they pronounced him dead at the scene. He was only thirty-four, for God's sake. He still had so much living to do.

Our father was murdered in that playground and the two of us saw it all.

Our lives changed irrevocably that summer evening.

Our childhoods ended.

It's not something you can ever recover from, watching your father be brutally killed, especially when you're the one who caused it. Who led the perpetrator right to him.

I've never set foot in a playground since.

THIRTY-EIGHT

NOW

I wake with a jolt, covered in the usual cold sweat. It's 5.07 a.m. I throw off the soaking bedcovers and, with a jaded sigh, get up, towel myself down and put on my dressing gown. A well-oiled machine. I'll need a shower, but it's too early yet, especially on a Sunday. Too much chance of waking up one of the kids. I hope they're having sweet dreams, unlike me. I hope Daisy's not imagining some nasty scenario involving stupid Lori.

After what Sean and I went through, it's really important to me that my children have a normal childhood. As normal as possible, anyway. The idea of them being scarred by some dreadful trauma, like we were, terrifies me.

Living apart from their father isn't the perfect upbringing I had in mind, but Rory left me with little choice when he abandoned our marriage vows in pursuit of his cheap thrills.

Part of me would love to wrap my children up in cotton wool and keep them close, away from any potential danger. But that would do them more harm than good in the long run. That's not a normal childhood. Rory helped me to understand this fact back in the days when he was a supportive husband rather than a cheating rat.

I do realise that having a mother who's never once entered a playground with you – never spun you on a roundabout or sat you down on a see-saw – isn't a normal childhood either. I wish I could have done that with them, particularly when they were toddlers. At that age, there's little more exciting than a playground. At least they had their dad to take them when I wasn't around. That was hard for me to accept, but Rory insisted. He said I had to allow them some semblance of normality with regard to this, even if I couldn't do it myself. Eventually we settled on the rule that it was okay with Daddy but totally off bounds with Mummy, which they accepted without question when they were small. When they got older and did query it, we told them enough of the truth to explain without scaring them. What child needs to know that their grandfather was brutally killed in front of their mother in a place every youngster should feel safe?

They both now know that my dad died in a playground, but they think it was from a heart attack. I'll tell them the full story eventually, probably before too long in Ethan's case.

I'd been having a nightmare about Dad's murder when I woke up a few minutes ago, which is why all of this is on my mind. It's a subject that's haunted my dreams for years with a frequency that's never abated. In this instance, everything unfolded as it actually did back in the day. Sometimes that's the case; sometimes it's a twist on the theme, often with horror or supernatural elements thrown into the mix.

They're all awful. All terrifying. But the nightmares closest to reality are the hardest to handle. Because it's like I'm there all over again, reliving the worst day of my life: a vulnerable four-teen-year-old with my eight-year-old-brother, witnessing things no one should ever have to see.

I tiptoe down the dark stairs, using the torch on my mobile to see where I'm going. When I enter the kitchen, I put on the light, closing the door behind me.

I open the fridge to take out some milk for a cup of tea. The chilled bottle of white wine inside grins at me; for a second, I consider opening it. Reliving such awful memories has stressed me out. It always does. It makes them fresh again. However, experience tells me that the feeling will fade soon enough, as the remnants of my dream evaporate from my mind's eye and proper perspective returns.

I've had a long time to absorb what happened on that horrendous summer evening. I'll never come to terms with it, but I've learned to live alongside the pain without having to do destructive things like neck a bottle of wine first thing in the morning. Been there, done that. Definitely doesn't help.

I boil the kettle. Soon I'm sitting at the kitchen table, hugging a warm mug and reflecting again on how, at my next birthday in February, I'll be the same age as Dad was when he was killed. What a morbid thought. Next summer will be the twentieth anniversary of his death.

I keep thinking about Daisy and Ethan being roughly the same age as Sean and I were when we witnessed the attack.

I wouldn't wish that on any child. I can't even imagine how Daisy would begin to cope if she saw me or her father stabbed to death. Eight is very young.

No wonder Sean took it so badly. I was floored by it, but he was worse. He was a shadow of himself from that day forward. Barely the same kid. The cheeky joker making smooching noises from the back of the car, snogging his hand when Dad drove me to meet Dean, he was gone.

The new Sean was withdrawn and introspective. As a young teenager, he fell in with a bad crowd and started taking drugs; drinking a lot; getting into trouble with the police for antisocial behaviour and petty crime. He played up with Mum far more than I did – and I was no angel. There was a lot of shouting and screaming on his part for a few years.

Sean left school at sixteen and never really found a vocation. He tried his hand at all manner of jobs: shop assistant, waiter, labourer, kitchen hand, plumber's mate, roofer's mate, mortgage adviser, delivery driver. And that's only scratching the surface. You name it, he probably did it at some point before deciding it wasn't for him and moving on.

He never found a soulmate either. Nor did he get to experience the joy of having children. Would that have changed had he lived longer? I doubt it. He thought the world wasn't a fit place to bring kids of his own into, fortunately without judging any of the rest of us for doing so.

Sean was a gay man who enjoyed the singles scene without ever seeming to want or need to settle down. Sex to him was an act of pleasure to enjoy with like-minded folk. Neither love nor procreation entered the equation. That's what he told me, anyway. As for friends, there were plenty over the years, male and female, but they were transitory. He'd talk about someone constantly for a while, like they were a key part of his life, and then he'd stop mentioning them, as if they'd never existed.

When you asked after such a person, he'd give you a blank look and say: 'Oh, I know who you mean. No, I haven't seen them for ages. No idea what they're up to now.'

Having his father torn away from him so brutally at such a seminal age had made him avoid strong attachments, I think, to reduce the potential pain of further loss.

The only true passions he had in his life were dance music, meaning chiefly the clubbing scene and its associated drug culture, plus motorbikes. He used to tell me with rare enthusiasm how both of these things had the power to elevate his spirit; to lift him out of the dark thoughts he'd struggled with from a young age.

'I can lose myself on a dance floor at a decent club night like nowhere else,' I recall him saying to me on one occasion, not long before he died. 'We should do it together sometime – the full experience. You'd love it, sis. The music becomes transcendent. The only other thing that gets close, in my experience, is—'

'Let me guess,' I said. 'Riding your motorbike too fast on an open road in the countryside.'

'Bang on – and you'd love that too.' He grinned, which probably meant he'd been drinking or had taken some drug or another. By that point, it was rare to see him smile while sober. Apart from when he was with Ethan. His eyes always lit up around his nephew, whom he adored. And Ethan loved him right back. It makes me so sad to think how that connection was lost when Sean died, on top of neither of my kids ever meeting my father. Daisy would have loved Sean too, I'm sure, but she was so young when he left us; they never got a chance to properly bond.

'I'm a mother and a wife,' I told Sean. 'That's what makes *me* happy. Taking drugs and riding motorbikes aren't on my radar.'

Being killed in a motorbike crash was, at least, the way Sean would have probably chosen to go out. Not that this was any consolation to those of us left behind.

Did Mum and I suspect he might have caused the accident deliberately? Killing himself, in other words. Yes. The thought went through our minds initially, even though he'd seemed in good spirits when each of us had last seen him, with no indication that it would be for the final time; no note left behind.

Sean had suffered from depression for years. There had also been an incident about eighteen months earlier when he'd phoned me in the middle of the night saying he was in the bath with a razor blade. I'd managed to talk him down before he actually harmed himself. But he'd confessed it wasn't the first time he'd felt so desperate.

I urged him to get professional help, and he did for a while. But was it enough?

We'll never know for sure what happened to him on his

beloved motorbike. He was alone in a remote part of Cumbria when the accident took place, late at night. No one else was involved and no alcohol or drugs were found in his system, so at least he was sober.

He appeared to have lost control on a sharp bend, although the weather was dry and fine. The coroner recorded a verdict of accidental death, suggesting that perhaps an animal had run into his path, the bike had malfunctioned, or something else unexpected had distracted him.

Mum accepted the verdict as gospel. It was a huge relief to her, which I totally understand. What parent wants to think of their child taking their own life?

As for me, I still have a lingering suspicion that his death may have been deliberate. It could be sisterly intuition. It could equally be the fact that I miss him terribly, and suicide somehow makes more sense to me than it being a random accident. When I stopped him slitting his wrists, I told him he couldn't put me through that again. Not after Dad. Perhaps killing himself alone and with no obvious proof of suicide was his warped, desperate way of sparing me.

So why do I punish myself? Six and a half years on, why can't I accept the coroner's verdict, like Mum has?

I weigh this up while making myself another cuppa, since it's still too early to go for that shower I'm craving.

There's no easy answer.

Maybe it's to avoid letting go of Sean, not only because of who he was, but because he was a physical link to my father. It's not like they looked exactly the same, but you could tell Sean was Dad's son. Sometimes he'd do things without realising – a little mannerism, like raising one eyebrow in a certain way – and it would be like Dad was back in the room. So when Sean died, I didn't only lose my brother; I also lost a final piece of my father.

It dawns on me where this is heading.

We were very different people, Sean and I, but we were in regular contact up to the end. We spoke several times a week by phone and often met up in person. In many ways we were as close as two siblings could be, bonded by the horror we'd witnessed as children. No one else could truly understand what we'd been through and how it would haunt us for the rest of our lives.

I miss my brother so much. I'd do anything to bring him back, although that's never going to happen.

Sean's irreplaceable.

However, that's not to say I couldn't enjoy a different kind of close relationship with another sibling, if I had one.

A half-brother, for instance, who I already know I get along well with, even if I haven't yet thought of him in that context.

Perhaps I could see parts of my father in Billy too. It's possible, even though they never met. Could that be the reason we got on so well so quickly: our shared genetics?

A strange thought. And yet I did mistake him for Dad that first time we met, when I was in the throes of a panic attack.

Oh God, I think I might be coming around to the idea of letting Billy back into my life, and I'm not even drunk.

I sit back down at the kitchen table and stare into space.

THIRTY-NINE

ONE MONTH LATER

Rory

He walks to the front door with Daisy. He carries her overnight bag, even though she said she could manage.

Beth's Fiesta isn't on the drive. Strange.

Daisy stretches up to ring the doorbell and, to Rory's distaste, bloody Billy answers, all smiles and brimming with confidence. Anyone would think it was his name on the mortgage, not Rory's.

'Hi, Daisy Chain. Hi, Rory. How's it going?'

'Hi, Uncle Billy.' Daisy gives him a big hug before striding into the house.

Rory swallows, resisting the urge to punch the oily bastard in the face. He hates hearing his daughter call him Uncle almost as much as he hates the stupid pet name Billy has given her. Daisy Chain? Ugh.

'Hello,' he says, remaining outside. 'Is, um, Beth not home?'

'Sorry, she's popped out to the supermarket. I doubt she'll be long. Come in and wait, if you like.'

Gee, thanks. Invited into my own house on a Sunday by Beth's brother from another mother. 'No, I can't hang around.'

'Fair enough. Anything I can help with?'

Do you live here now? Rory almost asks. Billy seems to be here constantly. It was bad enough at the beginning, before the whole half-brother thing, when he thought the guy might be a potential boyfriend. But at least then he could hope that the relationship might fizzle out. Now that Beth has accepted him as part of the family, however, Billy's going nowhere. His presence has more or less rendered Rory totally unnecessary, other than as Ethan and Daisy's dad. He never thought he'd miss Beth's phone calls about how to do certain jobs around the house: bleeding radiators, topping up the boiler pressure, changing smoke alarm batteries, etc. But such calls have dried up since Billy came on the scene, vastly reducing any chance Rory has of working his way back into Beth's good books.

Rory's family can't get enough of Billy, it seems. Even Ethan has come around to him since discovering he's his uncle. Rory, however, hates the man. It's not like he knows him well, admittedly, and yes, there must be an aspect of jealousy on his part. There's more to it than that, though. It all seems very odd: particularly the way Billy first stalked Beth, then befriended her, before revealing his true identity. Hardly honest, trustworthy behaviour. How Beth got past that so quickly, Rory has no idea. It's not like she talks to him about such things any more.

The first he knew of it was when Daisy started referring to him as Uncle Billy a few weeks back. 'Why are you calling him that?' Rory asked.

'Because he's my uncle, of course.'

'What are you talking about?'

'Haven't you heard?' Ethan chipped in, still sceptical at that point. 'He's Mum's long-lost brother, apparently. He didn't bother telling any of us until the other day.'

'What the hell?' Rory said to Beth on the phone later.

'Don't you think you ought to have told me about this? I shouldn't have had to find out from Daisy.'

Beth apologised. 'You're right. It slipped my mind. There's been a lot to take in.'

'No shit. How is this even possible? Where has he been hiding all this time? What's the story? I didn't want to ask the kids, so I'm totally confused.'

'Dad was a womaniser, it turns out. Mum confirmed it. Not that she knew about Billy. She wasn't exactly surprised, though.'

Beth recounted the whole story.

'How do you know for sure that he's your brother?' Rory asked. 'Are you going to do a DNA test?'

She really didn't like that suggestion. 'What's wrong with you? Why can't you be happy for me?'

'I am happy for you,' he lied. 'But I think it's wise to be cautious. You didn't know him from Adam until recently, and it's creepy the way he stalked you first. Don't let your guard fully down yet. He could be a con man trying to steal your fortune.'

That last bit was meant to lighten the mood, but it didn't have the desired effect.

'The only thing Billy wants is to know his family, you hypocrite. If only you were a time traveller, Rory. You could go back to when you and I first met and warn me not to let my guard down with *you*. Not to settle down and dedicate my life to you, only to be shafted years down the line when you grew bored of me.'

He remained silent.

'Anything else you'd like to add?' she asked. 'Any other sage advice?'

'I've said my piece, Beth. Take it however you like, but it's meant genuinely. And if there are any other big revelations, please don't leave me to find out from our children.'

Back in the present, Billy is staring expectantly at him from inside the doorway.

'Sorry, what was that?' Rory asks, shaking his head to refocus.

'I asked if there's anything I can help with.'

'Right, of course. Sorry. I, er, lost my train of thought. Um, no, I don't think so. I'll speak to Beth another time. Best get going.'

'Fine. See you later.'

Rory nods. 'Bye, Daisy,' he calls.

She's already disappeared upstairs, but he does hear a faint reply: 'Bye, Daddy.'

He makes to leave.

'Hang on,' Billy says. 'What about Ethan? Has he gone to visit one of his pals? Doesn't he usually send his stuff back with you?'

Rory turns back to the open door, frowning. 'What do you mean? Ethan was here last night. He told me he couldn't come to mine because he had some school science project to work on and it was all set up in his bedroom.'

Billy scratches his head. 'I don't know what to tell you. I've been here since first thing this morning and Ethan's definitely not been home. Beth told me they both spent last night at your place.'

'What the hell? Where is he, then?'

'I think you'd better come in,' Billy says. 'We need to get to the bottom of this. It's probably some kind of mix-up.'

Rory steps inside and shuts the door behind him. 'No, there's no mix-up. This is deliberate. He's lied to me and Beth, playing us off against each other. Whatever the reason, whatever he's been up to, that lad is in big trouble.'

FORTY

Beth

I grab a shopping trolley after scrabbling around for a pound coin to release it and head to the fruit and veg aisle. I'm only here to grab a few bits, so hopefully this shop won't take long. Billy kindly offered to wait for the kids to return home, which was a relief. Rory's hard to deal with at the moment. He's been super-weird ever since he found out about Billy being my brother. It seems like he can't come to terms with it.

Of course, Billy's revelation was a massive shock to me. It was an incredibly tough call when I resolved to allow him back into my life – and my children's lives – despite the initial deception. But a month later, I have no regrets. I'm certain I did the right thing, even if Rory thinks otherwise.

Billy and I get on better now than ever before. We see each other pretty much daily. It's a struggle to imagine life without him. He's great with Daisy Chain, as he's taken to calling her, which I find cute; she rarely stops chatting about her amazing Uncle Billy. As for Ethan, despite some initial resistance, he's embraced having a new uncle now too. It warms my heart, hearing their enthusiastic chats about football, video games and such. I hope it gives Ethan back a piece of what he lost when his Uncle Sean died. Billy will never replace Sean for any of us. Obviously. Just like his presence will never bring back my dad. But having him around definitely helps. He offers a wonderful new link back to my father; most importantly, he makes our lives brighter.

I'm reaching for a bottle of milk in the dairy aisle when my phone rings. It's Rory's number on the caller display. My heart sinks. I'm tempted not to answer, but I have to, in case of an issue with one of the kids.

'Hi, Rory. Everything all right?'

'No, it's not. There's a problem with Ethan.'

'What do you mean? What's happened?'

'You thought he was with me last night, right?'

'He was. Both of them were.'

'Daisy was. Ethan told me he needed to stay home with you.'

'What are you talking about?'

'Ethan wasn't with me or with you last night, Beth.'

'Where was he, then? Where is he now?'

'That's the million-dollar question.'

I take a deep breath, fighting the urge to panic. 'Have you tried his mobile?'

Rory clears his throat. 'It rang out, no answer.'

'Where are you now?'

'At home. Um, your home, with Billy and Daisy.'

'Right. Stay there. I'm coming back. Have you asked Daisy if she knows anything?'

'Not yet. She's upstairs. I'll go and check.'

'I'll be back soon.'

I stick my phone into my handbag and abandon my shopping trolley. No time to queue up and pay now. I stride outside to the car park and drive home. All sorts of terrifying thoughts are circulating in my head; I try to focus on the road.

At one point, unable to stop myself, I pull the car over into a lay-by and try to phone Ethan. There's no reply, so I send a text message:

Where are you? Your dad and I are very worried. Please contact one of us ASAP. X

I stare at the screen after sending it, praying for a quick reply, but nothing comes.

Dammit. I continue the drive home. Please let my son be okay.

FORTY-ONE

Billy

Beth and Rory are panicking. Neither has a clue what's happened to Ethan. The lad has properly pulled the wool over his parents' eyes. Secretly, despite the concerned face he's wearing, Billy is amused. Impressed, actually. He didn't think the little ginger nut had it in him.

Daisy has been interrogated by each of her parents in turn. Neither was particularly tough in their line of questioning, quickly accepting she didn't know anything, but she's upset nonetheless.

'Shall I take her for a walk to calm her down?' Billy offers. 'You two can put your heads together in peace and work out a plan of action.'

'Would you like to go for a stroll with Uncle Billy?' Beth asks.

Daisy nods in between sobs. 'Is Ethan going to be okay?'

Billy kneels down in front of her, so their eyes are level. 'I'm sure he'll be fine, Daisy Chain. He might even be home by the time we get back.'

Coats and shoes on, ready to go, he turns back to a pale Beth and gives her a hug. 'You know where I am if you need me. Give me a bell and we'll be back in a flash.'

He almost calls her 'sis'– something he's been working towards – but he holds off. It doesn't feel right in the moment.

'Where are we going, Uncle Billy?' Daisy asks once they're outside, where it's cloudy but so far not raining.

'Somewhere nice. It's a surprise.'

'Oh, goodie. I like surprises.' She takes hold of his hand and squeezes it.

'Would you like to know a secret, Daisy Chain?'

'Yes please.'

'You're my favourite niece.'

'Really?' Her eyes narrow. 'Do you have any other nieces?'

He chuckles as they walk along the pavement. 'There's no tricking you, is there? No, you're my only niece, but if I did have any others, I bet you'd still be my favourite.'

'Is that because you saved me in the playground?'

'Well, it's for all sorts of reasons, but I'm really glad I was there to help you when you were in trouble.'

'Me too. I was so scared.'

'Where do *you* think Ethan might be?'

She shrugs. 'He never tells me anything. Especially secret stuff. He thinks I'm too young. I know where his secret hiding place in his bedroom is, though.'

'Oh? Does he have one, then?'

Daisy nods. 'He doesn't know that I know. I heard him telling his friend Liam about it. He said he doesn't want Mummy to find what he keeps there. I'm not sure what that is, though.'

'Really? You haven't had a peek?'

She shakes her head. 'No way. I'm a good sister. Don't ask me where it is, because I can't tell you.'

'I wouldn't dream of it.' Billy's intrigued what Ethan might be hiding. His first thoughts are a porn magazine or a pack of cigarettes, but do lads of fourteen actually have that stuff these days? Cigs cost a fortune, and there's more than enough sex on the Internet to keep even the horniest teenager happy. So what, then?

'Okay, I will tell you, if you like,' Daisy adds, unprompted, much to Billy's amusement. 'But you have to promise you won't tell anyone.'

'You don't have to tell me if you don't want to, Daisy Chain.'

'I want to, but you have to promise first.'

'Sure. I promise not to tell anyone.'

She stops walking and gestures for Billy to lower his head so she can whisper in his ear. 'Under his bed. But remember: top secret.'

Billy nods. He mimes zipping his lips and throwing away the key.

Soon they arrive at the playground where they first met. There are several other people in there – the usual mix of noisy young children and the adults with them – but it's not overly busy.

'Surprise, we're here.'

Daisy's face falls. 'Oh. I'm not sure this is a good idea.'

'What's up?' Billy asks. 'You're not worried about those boys and their dog coming back, are you? Because you needn't be. I've already had a good look round and the coast is clear. There are no dogs in there at all. Not even tiny ones on leads. And no nasty-looking boys either. Plus, I'm here to protect you.'

'What about Mummy? She really doesn't like...'

Billy waves away her concern. 'Don't worry about that. It's all sorted. You've been here before with your daddy, right?'

'Um, a few times. Not recently.'

'Well, you're with your Uncle Billy now. Trust me. It's fine.'

She looks up at him through squinting eyes, still hesitant. 'Are you sure?'

'Absolutely. Last one to reach the swings is a rotten egg.'

He runs through the playground entrance, leaving Daisy behind on the pavement. After a few metres, he looks back to check she's following him, which she is, and then he races on, before feigning pulling a muscle at the last minute and letting her win.

'Haha, you're a rotten egg,' she tells him, already perched on a black rubber swing seat next to two older girls, who are chatting and listening to pop music from a mobile.

'Oh well. Would you like me to push you, or would you rather push yourself?'

'You push,' she says with a wide grin.

While he's doing that, Billy receives a text. He expects it to be from Beth, hopefully saying they've found Ethan. In fact, it's from Ethan himself.

I'm in trouble with Mum and Dad. Told a fib about where I was last night. Now they're both looking for me. Don't know what to do.

Billy rolls his eyes, but he's chuffed to be the one Ethan has turned to when his back is against the wall. The lad didn't warm to him at all prior to the uncle revelation, and even after that, it took longer than with Daisy and Beth. This is Billy's big chance to cement the relationship.

'I need to make a quick phone call, Daisy Chain.'

She looks back at him with anxious eyes. 'You're not leaving me here, are you? What if—'

'Relax. I'm not leaving. I'm going to walk a few metres over there, where it's a bit quieter. We'll be able to see each other the whole time; if you need me, I'll be back in a flash.'

'Promise?'

'Promise.'

He walks just far enough away to be out of earshot and dials Ethan, who answers immediately.

'Thanks for calling. You're not with Mum, are you?'

'No. What's going on? Are you all right?'

'Yeah.'

'Good. Where are you? Where have you been?'

'It's complicated. I don't know what to do. Can I, um, say I was staying at your house last night?'

'That's not going to work, mate. I was with your mum earlier, round at the house. Why not tell the truth? It can't be that bad, surely.'

'I need to think. Could you do one small thing for me to buy me a bit of time?'

'What's that?'

'Tell her I'm safe and sound. That she doesn't need to worry.'

'When will you be home?'

'Today. This evening at the latest.'

'Are you sure you're all right? If there's something I can do to help...'

'There is. Give Mum that message. Please.'

'She won't be happy. You know that, right? You'll be in trouble when you do get home.'

'I know.'

'But you'll definitely be back today?'

'Yes.'

'Okay, I'll do it. Stay safe. And if you need anything in the meantime, you have my number.'

Billy gives Daisy a wave and a smile. She's still on the swing, alone now, as the two older girls have moved on. 'One minute,' he calls, holding his forefinger aloft.

He rings Beth. 'I've heard from Ethan.'

'What? Where is he? He's not answering any of our calls or messages. Is he okay?'

'He's fine. He didn't say much other than that, though. He asked me to tell you not to worry; that he'd be home this evening at latest.'

'How can he expect me not to worry? What did he sound like? Do you think he's in trouble?'

'It was a short call. He sounded fine. I'm sure he'll explain everything when he returns.'

'He better had do. Rory and I have been tearing our hair out. What on earth is he playing at, Billy? He's only fourteen. And why's he calling you rather than one of us?'

'I'm not sure. I imagine he's worried about getting into trouble.'

'He should be.'

When he returns to the swings, Daisy has been joined by a young lad and his dad, to whom Billy smiles and says hello.

'What next?' he asks. 'Slide, see-saw, climbing frame?'

Daisy flinches at the latter suggestion. They settle on the see-saw, which works well, as it's something they can do together.

On the way home, having taken Daisy on every piece of equipment, including the climbing frame eventually, Billy asks: 'Did you enjoy yourself?'

Daisy nods vigorously. 'Yep. Thank you for taking me, Uncle Billy.'

'You're welcome. It's the first time you've been there since we met, right?'

'Uh-huh.'

'That's why I was keen to take you. I wanted you to know it was safe, so you weren't scared to return.'

'Like Mummy, you mean?' She looks down at her pink trainers. 'Are you sure she won't be cross that we went there?'

'Don't you worry about that.'

FORTY-TWO

Beth

When the doorbell sounds, I pray it's Ethan, even though I know he has a key. It's not him. It's Billy and Daisy back from their walk.

I smile and try not to look disappointed.

'He's not home yet?' Billy asks.

I shake my head and lead them through to the kitchen, where Rory's waiting.

Daisy takes a cup of juice up to her bedroom, leaving us adults to it.

'Beth says you spoke to him,' Rory snaps at Billy.

'Yes. I told her everything he said, which wasn't much.'

'Did you ask him to stop pissing us about and get himself home immediately?'

I scowl at Rory as Billy clears his throat. 'I, er, thought it best not to risk antagonising the lad, since he seemed to be avoiding everyone else's calls. I let him talk. Asked if he was okay. Offered to help.'

'How did he sound?' I ask.

'All right. He knows he's done wrong and there'll be consequences.'

'He's in big trouble,' Rory says.

Billy takes my hand. 'There's something I need to tell you.'

'About Ethan?'

'No, about where I took Daisy just now. We, um, went to the playground. I hope you don't mind.'

'What? Why on earth did you do that? Was it her idea? You know my feelings—'

'No, it was all my idea. Daisy questioned it; I told her I'd square it with you.'

Rory stays silent, but I can tell he's taking a certain pleasure in this, like he's been waiting for Billy to stuff up.

'Can I explain?' Billy asks.

I nod, so he continues: 'I was bothered about the fact that she hadn't been in there since the dog incident. I didn't want her to be afraid to return. And as I helped her last time, I thought it made sense for me to be there again. I didn't mean to go against you or step on any toes. It's not something I planned. The idea came to me when we started walking, and I went with my gut.'

Rory can't help himself. 'Who the hell do you think—'

'Butt out. This is between me and my brother.'

'Daisy is my daughter too.'

'Since when have you had an issue with her going to the playground, Rory? If you've nothing useful to add, you may as well go back to your flat.'

'I thought we agreed to deal with Ethan together.'

'Yes, but who knows when he'll get home? Why don't I call you when he does? We're achieving nothing just waiting here.'

Rory gets to his feet. 'Fine. I know when I'm not wanted. But you'd better call me, Beth. I need a stern word with that boy.'

He lets himself out.

'He doesn't like me much, does he?' Billy says.

'I'm not sure I do at this moment. I really wish you'd run it past me first, taking Daisy to the playground.'

Billy looks down at the tiled kitchen floor. 'Sorry. I did emphasise to her that it was a one-off; that she wasn't to go there at any other time without your permission.'

He looks so crestfallen, I don't have the heart to stay annoyed. 'Look, what's done is done. I know you had good intentions and maybe it was the right thing to do for Daisy. As you know, it's not a subject I can address objectively. Let's drop it now and focus our attention on Ethan. Do you have any idea at all where he spent last night? I already tried contacting Liam's mum, but I only have her landline number and there was no answer.'

FORTY-THREE

Rory

Beth calls his mobile at 6.33 p.m. 'Ethan's just walked through the door. Are you coming back?'

'Give me a few minutes.'

He hangs up without thanking her for calling him. It was the least she could do after the way she humiliated and undermined him earlier; in front of Billy too, making it all the worse. This morning, Rory didn't think it was possible to dislike that weaselly man any more than he already did. Now, having spent far too much time with him today, his opinion of Billy has hardened. He loathes everything about him, from his annoying whiny voice and smarmy smile to his overly fashion-conscious dress sense. Then there's that ridiculously strong, sickly aftershave, like he's covering up a foul stench. He doesn't trust him one bit.

As for Beth, ejecting Rory from his own home like a nuisance, will she ever get past his cheating on her? Will she ever view him again the way she once did?

Billy can barely do any wrong in Beth's eyes. Rory can't

believe she didn't lose it with him for taking Daisy to the play-ground. Unbelievable. It's like that prick has cast a spell on her.

He throws on a coat and grabs his keys.

At 6.53 p.m., according to the clock on the oven, he sits down opposite his son at the kitchen table. Beth also takes a seat. Billy, thankfully, is nowhere to be seen and Daisy is in her bedroom.

'You're all right, then?' Rory asks Ethan. 'In one piece? Your mother and I have been very worried.'

Ethan looks up from the table for a brief moment, revealing the black eye Beth already flagged to Rory. 'I'm fine. Sorry.'

'What's with the shiner?'

He grimaces. 'I got into a bit of a scrap. It was something and nothing.'

'Who with?'

'This lad. No one you know. A couple of punches were thrown. Then it got broken up.'

'Where? Who broke it up?'

'It was, um, a random street. We bumped into each other. Our mates pulled us apart.'

'Why did you fight? Who threw the first punch? I hope it wasn't you.'

Ethan, looking twitchy and sleep-deprived, keeps on staring at the table. 'Dunno. It just happened. We were giving each other grief and it got out of hand. He, er, said something to make me think he might have been one of the lads who set their dog on Daisy in the playground that time. But I was wrong.'

'What did he say?' Beth asks with a furrowed brow.

'Lad stuff I'd rather not repeat. It doesn't matter, anyway. It was a total miscommunication. It definitely wasn't him.'

'How do you know?'

'I just do, Mum.'

Rory frowns. 'Fighting is for losers. We've told you that so many times. Clever people use their heads, not their fists.

Imagine if the fight had turned out differently. If one of you had fallen badly and been killed. Don't you smirk at me, Ethan. It happens. Lives get ruined. What was the other boy's name?'

'No idea. I don't know him.'

Hmm. Rory doesn't buy everything he's being told. He smells a rat. But he also doesn't want to get too distracted from the real reason they're sitting here.

'We need to talk about where you spent last night. What you did, playing your mum and me off against each other, was deceptive, calculated and dangerous. You're going to be punished. I think you know that. But right now, you need to start talking. You have some major explaining to do.'

FORTY-FOUR

Ethan

Mum and Dad are eyeballing him, waiting for him to speak. They want him to explain where he was last night.

Telling each of them he was with the other wasn't the best plan in the world. Getting found out was inevitable. In fact, Ethan's surprised he got away with it for as long as he did, mainly down to luck.

So why did he go with that plan? It was all he could think of at late notice as a way to stay out yesterday. That was the important part. The repercussions were for later. Now.

He could have said he was stopping over at Liam's house. However, Liam had already told his parents that he was staying over at Dad's flat. Ethan was concerned about their mums chatting, knowing they'd been in contact recently. Ironically, playing his parents off against each other seemed the safer bet, based on their current poor levels of communication.

Billy being around can't help. It's obvious Dad doesn't like him, even though he denies it. Plus Billy's handy at DIY, computers and all that, so Mum's less reliant on Dad to do stuff for her. Could that be *why* Dad doesn't like Billy, even though it saves him hassle? Who knows? Adults are weird.

He likes the idea of having an uncle around. Yes, he was a dick to Billy at the beginning, wrongly thinking he fancied Mum. But it turns out he's all right.

Mum and Dad are still eyeballing him. He needs to tell them what happened. Not the truth – they'd go spare – but something they'll hopefully believe. He and Liam put their heads together earlier and came up with a story.

'I'm really sorry,' he says. 'It was a stupid dare.'

'What was?' Mum asks.

'The reason I stayed out all night.'

He goes on to tell them a load of bullshit about how there was a rumour at school that one of the parks nearby was haunted; someone dared him and Liam to spend the whole night there to prove they weren't scared. So they did, making up false stories to their parents because they knew they'd never agree to it.

'You stayed out all night in the park at your age, at this time of year?' Mum says. 'You must be joking. How did you stay warm?'

'It wasn't that cold. We wrapped up.'

'And what did you do there all night?' Dad asks.

Ethan chews the corner of his lip. 'Um, chatting, playing games on our phones. That kind of stuff.'

'You didn't sleep?' Mum says.

'A little bit. We took it in turns while the other one kept a lookout.'

Dad frowns. 'A lookout for what?'

'I don't know. Police, weirdos, pissheads, wild animals. In case we needed to get out of there fast. We weren't bothered about ghosts, if that's what you mean. They don't exist.'

Dad looks over at Mum before adding: 'And that's honestly

what happened? You were there all night? Why did you come back so late today?'

'I was scared. Worried about how to tell you and what you'd say, especially after you both started calling and messaging me.'

'So where have you been all day?'

'Out and about. Seeing other mates. In a few shops. A couple of cafés. Back in the park for a bit.'

'Silly boy,' Mum says, slowly shaking her head. 'You're lucky you didn't catch your death of cold, or worse. Anything could have happened. You could have been targeted by paedophiles.'

'What? How would they have known we were there?'

'Don't answer your mother back,' Dad says. 'You're not in any position to be a wise guy. I think we've heard enough. Do you agree, Beth?'

She nods.

'Upstairs to your bedroom, please. Your mother and I will discuss your punishment in private.'

Ethan's glad to get out of there. He almost skips up the stairs. That couldn't have gone much better. It looks like they believed him.

'How come you're smiling?' Daisy asks, appearing at the door of her bedroom as he reaches the landing. 'I thought you were in big trouble.'

'Mind your own business.'

'Everyone was really worried about you.'

'Well, I'm back now.'

'Where have you been?'

'Why are you so nosy? It doesn't matter where I've been. I've got stuff to do. I'll see you later.'

He continues to his own room, closing the door firmly behind him and breathing a sigh of relief. He leans down and pulls the envelope of money out from one of his socks, his knife out of the other. Quickly, before anyone can come in to interrupt him, he stashes them away under his bed.

Then he lies down and drops Liam a text:

Done. Think they bought it.

Once he sees that Liam's read it, he deletes the message.

FORTY-FIVE

Billy

He knocks on Ethan's bedroom door.

'Who is it?'

'Billy.'

'Come in.'

He turns the handle and swings open the door. Walks inside Ethan's stuffy room, which could do with a window opening to dissipate the smell of body odour and farts. 'How are you on this marvellous Monday evening?' he asks.

'Hmm. I feel like I'm at the start of a long prison stretch. How come you've got your coat on?'

'I'm off home. I've been chatting to your mum; I asked if I could bother you for a minute before leaving to see how you're doing.'

Billy looks for a spot to sit, but other than the bed, on which Ethan is already sprawled, everywhere is covered in junk. He remains standing, hands in his coat pockets.

'They grounded me for a month.'

'I heard. Could be worse.'

'How? A month is forever.'

'You still get to go out to school.'

Ethan leans forward. Holds his head in his hands. 'Yeah. Brilliant.'

'Is it right that you and Liam spent all night in the park for a dare?'

He clears his throat. 'Um, yeah.'

'Hope it was worth it. Is Liam grounded too?'

'Yes, also for a month. Our mums coordinated our punishments. Can you believe it?'

'As much as I can believe you wanted to spend a cold night outside in the park.'

Ethan looks at the floor.

'You're only young once, I guess,' Billy adds. 'Listen, sorry I couldn't help more when you called me yesterday. I would have if I could. I'm glad you know you can turn to me when you feel like your back is against the wall. That's what uncles are for, right?'

Ethan manages a weak smile. 'Don't worry about it.'

'I've got you an incarceration gift.'

'What does that mean?'

'A present to mark the beginning of your punishment. To take the edge off, if you like. Don't get caught with it. If you do, it's nothing to do with me.'

Ethan looks perplexed until Billy pulls the large can of lager out of his inside pocket and hands it to him, eliciting a wide grin. 'It's still coldish. Best I could manage in the circumstances.'

'You're a legend. Thanks, Billy.'

He nods. 'I thought it might help. Our little secret, yeah?'

'Totally.'

Billy glances under Ethan's bed, remembering Daisy's claim that he hides things under there; wondering what those things might be.

'Are you into that vaping all the kids seem to be doing nowadays?' he asks in a low voice.

'Um. I, er...'

'I'm not going to tell your mum, mate. Look at what I've just handed you. I'm interested, that's all. I was wondering what the fuss is all about.'

'I've tried it a few times.'

'What's it like? Similar to cigarettes?'

'Dunno. Probably a bit. Do you smoke, then?'

'No, mate. I dabbled when I was younger but knocked it on the head years ago. That shit's bad for you. So do you get a buzz when you vape, from the nicotine?'

Ethan shrugs. 'I guess.'

'Right. Anyhow, just wanted to see how my favourite nephew was getting on. I've gotta shoot off now. Chin up, yeah? And don't get caught with that beer.'

'I won't. Thanks, Billy.'

'No sweat.'

Billy pops to the gym after leaving. While he's there, mind free to wander as his body works away, he weighs up Ethan's story about spending the night in the park with Liam. Beth and Rory believe it, apparently, but Billy's not so sure. The tale doesn't ring true to him. It doesn't fit in with how het-up Ethan sounded when he phoned yesterday, hoping to lie about staying with him. It sounds like a story he and Liam concocted to cover up whatever they were actually doing. Oh well, the truth will out eventually. At least he's still got the ginger nut on side. He knew the beer would go down well, having previously slipped Ethan a couple of bottles while they watched sport together at his place. Fourteen-year-old lads are easy to please. Fingers crossed he's smart enough not to get busted.

As for vaping, he's pretty sure Ethan does it more frequently than he let on. He probably has a vape tucked away under his bed. And the rest, whatever that might be.

After working out, he shoots the breeze with Ed, the burly bald bloke who runs the gym, and then walks home. His phone vibrates as he lets himself into the house. Once inside, he pulls it out of his pocket: withheld number.

'Hello?' He remains cagey until he knows for sure who's calling.

'It's me. Can you talk?'

'Yep.'

'And? I've given you the space you said you needed. Now I'm getting itchy. What's happening?'

Billy takes a deep breath before replying.

FORTY-SIX

Beth

Hi! Are you free for a chat?

I send the message and wait. A reply soon comes in the form of a video call.

'Hello, Mum,' I say as her image appears on my phone screen, as clear as if she was next door. She looks toasty in a bright red woolly jumper.

'Beth. How are you?'

'Not bad.'

'Have you been eating properly? You look skinny. And tired.'

'Yes, Mum. Thanks for that. Are you and Roger both well?'

'I'm fine. He's feeling sorry for himself with a cold. How are the children? How's work?'

I still haven't told Mum about being off with stress. It's ridiculous, but I'm not going down that rabbit hole today. My employers leave me alone for the most part, other than the odd checking-in email. Last time I spoke to my GP surgery was the other week, by telephone appointment. The locum doctor took little persuasion to extend my sick leave. I told her I still felt faint, like I was about to vomit, every time I thought about my job; that I couldn't bear the thought of returning. All true.

'Work's fine. Same old, same old.'

I tell Mum about Ethan's night in the park.

'Oh dear,' she says. 'Boys have a tendency to do silly things at that age. Sean gave me a weekly heart attack when he was a teenager. Anyhow, you see what Ethan was doing, right? He was exploiting a weak spot caused by your split from Rory.'

I blow out a puff of air. 'Wow. That's one way of looking at things, Mum.'

'How is Rory? I haven't seen or heard from him in ages.'

'Why would you? We're separated. You're *my* mother.'

'Yes, dear, but he's still part of the family. He's Ethan and Daisy's father. He's also still your husband, unless you've secretly got a quickie divorce.'

'We might be married on paper, Mum, but we're very much separated. He doesn't seem to like Billy, which is awkward.'

I've been trying to get Mum to meet Billy over one of these video calls for weeks. She always makes some excuse why she can't, which I assume means she doesn't want to. I do get it. They're not related, plus he's living proof that Dad used to cheat on her. It ought to happen at some point soon, but I won't force the issue.

'He's probably jealous.'

'But Billy's my brother, not a love interest.'

'And? He gets to spend lots of time with you and the children, at the house Rory lived in for years.' Mum wrinkles her nose. 'Things are going well with Billy, then? No regrets.'

'He's great. The kids love him too.'

'Does he remind you of your father?'

'I think so, sometimes. He definitely has a look of him, with his brown eyes and thick beard. You've seen a photo of him. Don't you agree?'

'Yes, maybe. A photo only tells you so much, though.'

I resist the temptation to suggest a video call meeting yet again. 'It's been so long since Dad died. I don't always remember the fine details. Does that sound awful? I do also find it hard thinking about him now that I know the truth about him.'

Mum looks misty-eyed. 'Sorry I had to tell you about his, um, not-so-charming side. Try to focus on the happy memories and your father's many good qualities.'

I run a hand through my hair. 'I've spent so long thinking of Dad as a hero. This amazing, flawless guy who selflessly put his life on the line for me, only to have it taken from him in one brutal moment by a mindless thug. That's been the one great truth of my life. And now I find myself questioning it. What if Dad hadn't been so hot-headed? What if rather than getting into a fight with Lenny, he'd tried talking his way out of the situation?'

'Your father was who he was, for better or worse. He was an impulsive, emotionally driven man. That's what made him such fun to be around. It's also what made him behave irrationally at times. What-ifs won't bring him back.'

I nod. 'I keep recalling times during my childhood when I heard you two arguing. You often seemed to be cross with him; I used to think you should give him a break. Now I realise your anger was probably justified.'

Mum scratches her chin. 'That's water under the bridge, Beth. I made the decision to stay with him when by rights I ought to have kicked him out. More fool me.'

'So why should I give Rory another chance? Why would you want me to repeat your mistake?'

Mum moves her face closer to the camera. 'Rory is nothing like your father, Beth. Trust me. Yes, he made a huge mistake, but I honestly believe he's learned from it and would never do such a thing ever again.'

'You saw that in your crystal ball, did you?'

'Oh, come on. I know Rory well enough after all these years. He's a good man at heart. He worships you, Beth. He always has. If he really was a womaniser, he'd have cheated far sooner into your marriage. And he'd never have come clean by choice, like he did. It was a drunken, foolish cry for help. Attention-seeking. A decent marriage counsellor could fix this.'

'No thanks. How could I ever trust him again? And without trust, what's the point?'

Mum lets out a wistful sigh. 'It's your life, Beth.'

FORTY-SEVEN

Billy

'Things are going well,' Billy says into the phone. He takes off his coat and hangs it up.

'What does that mean?'

'She's accepted me as her brother.'

'Does she trust you?'

'Yes. Enough to add me as a driver on her car insurance.' He sits on the sofa to stop himself from pacing up and down. To make sure his voice stays calm and steady, even though he feels the opposite. Rather than sitting back in the chair, he leans forward on his toes, calves tight, mind focused.

'And the rest of the family?'

'The two kids are sorted.'

'Calling you Uncle?'

'Daisy does, yes. Pretty much all the time. Ethan doesn't use that word, but I wouldn't expect him to: he's fourteen. I'm in his confidence, one hundred per cent. He trusts me.'

'And the husband?'

'Rory's not so easy to convince. He seems jealous of how

close I am to his family. I'm round at the house far more than he is. Beth doesn't have much time for him.'

'He doesn't trust you?'

'No, I don't think so.'

'Is he going to be a problem?'

'Absolutely not,' Billy says. 'Everything is in hand. It's unfortunate that getting to this stage has taken longer than expected, but I'm happy where we're at.'

'You're not getting too attached?'

'No. Why would you think that?'

'Because of the delay.'

'Don't worry. We both want the same outcome.'

'Good. When?'

'Soon,' Billy replies. 'It depends on how things pan out.'

'We're talking days rather than weeks, yes? You've been there a long time. I'm all out of patience.'

Billy takes a deep breath. 'Yes.'

'Don't keep me waiting.'

'You can count on me,' Billy says, only to realise the call has already ended.

FORTY-EIGHT

Ethan

He meets up with Liam on Tuesday morning on the way to school.

'How's it going?'

Liam hangs his head. 'Still grounded. You?'

'Same, obvs. I never thought I'd be glad to go to school, but here I am, enjoying the fresh air. I feel like a lifer on day release.'

'I know what you mean.'

'How's Marty? Still leaving you alone?'

Liam nods. 'So far. He's barely said a word to me since Saturday. He's stayed out of my way.'

'While keeping his mouth shut with your parents?'

'As far as I know.'

'It was hopefully worth me getting this black eye, then,' Ethan says.

Liam looks at it and pulls a face. 'Again, I'm really sorry about that, mate. Does it hurt?'

'Not much, unless I touch it.'

'It's more yellow than black now.'

'I know. Hopefully it'll fade soon. In the meantime, at least I've got my model good looks to fall back on.'

Liam laughs. 'Yeah, right. You're definitely a model dickhead.'

'Cheers, dude.' Ethan stares at him, deadpan. 'What happened to being sorry?'

'I am sorry. Sorry for you, having to look at yourself in the mirror every day. It must be awful.'

'It's your mum I feel sorry for,' Ethan replies. 'She has to look at you over breakfast every morning and see what a loser she brought into this world. That must be tough.'

'Very good.'

'Hey, guess what.'

'Go on.'

'My uncle sneaked me a beer in my bedroom last night.'

'Billy did? Seriously?'

'Yeah.'

'Wow. I wish I had relatives like that. Instead, I get manky Marty.'

'He might not bother you any more, thanks to me.'

The story the lads told their parents about how Ethan had got his black eye was as fake as their supposed overnight stay in the park.

What had actually happened was an unforeseen run-in with Liam's idiot stepbrother right at the worst possible moment.

They'd popped back to Liam's house in the afternoon, while his mum, stepdad and half-sister were out, to pick up the parcel they needed to deliver. As they were about to head out with it, Marty got in the way.

'What are you pricks up to?' he asked, blocking the doorway of Liam's bedroom.

'Nothing,' Liam replied. 'We're going out.'

'Says who? You'll need to get past me first. Been sucking each other off again, have you?'

'Don't be a wanker all your life,' Liam said. 'We don't have time for this.'

'Ooh. Got somewhere important to be? I'll let you past if you show me what's in that bag you're holding.'

'Get lost, Marty.'

'What's in there, ladies? A pair of gimp suits? Come on, you can show me. I won't tell.'

Ethan looked at his watch. 'We need to go,' he whispered to Liam.

'Sorry, what was that?' Marty smirked. 'Neither of you is going anywhere until I say so.'

'Come on.' Liam tossed Ethan the bag and strode forward.

Next thing, he and Marty were wrestling in the doorway. Liam held his own for a minute or two, but then Marty got him into a headlock and Ethan realised he'd have to get involved. He dashed forward, left hand gripping the all-important bag, right ready to strike. For his trouble, he got an accidental elbow in his eye from a struggling Liam.

'Ow! Bloody hell,' he cried out, much to Marty's amusement.

The smug look on that loser's face as he continued to restrain Liam while laughing at Ethan's pain was too much. Ethan took a step back, dropped the backpack on the floor and in one smooth, practised move, pulled out and brandished his knife.

Confusion and doubt flashed across Marty's face but were quickly replaced by bravado. 'Ooh, big man with a likkle knife,' he said, shifting his position slightly but not letting Liam go. 'Is that even real?'

Ethan glared at him, using the throbbing pain from his injured eye to focus his fury. 'It's very real, trust me. And very sharp. Now let go of him, shithead, or I'll give you a taste of it.'

'Yeah, right.'

Spurred on by a waver in Marty's voice, Ethan lunged at him, knife first, belting out a surprisingly ferocious war cry.

It was enough. A fearful Marty released Liam and backed away onto the landing.

'You're a psycho,' he said from a safe distance.

'What if I am? Stay away from Liam in future or you'll find out for sure. If you say a word about this to anyone, I'll come for you in the night and slit your throat. Got it?'

Marty didn't reply; the sound of his bedroom door closing behind him was answer enough.

Liam, back on his feet, looked at Ethan in awe. 'Where did that come from?'

Ethan shrugged, signalling they should leave straight away. He was wired: pulse racing, every inch of his body pumped with adrenaline. It wasn't until they'd walked a fair distance from the house that he finally started to unwind. Liam, who'd already apologised numerous times for elbowing his eye, asked if they should find some ice for it.

'No need,' Ethan said, 'although it is sore. How does it look?'

'A bit red and swollen. Hang on. I've got an idea.'

Liam darted into a nearby takeaway, returning with an ice-cold can of lemonade. 'Hold this on it. Might help with the swelling.'

Ethan took it, appreciating the cold feel of the smooth metal against his burning skin. 'How long until the train leaves?'

Liam looked at his watch. 'About fifty minutes. Still up for it?'

Ethan nodded. Like they had any choice.

'Do you reckon this will really be the end of it with Connor?'

'It has to be, mate.'

Having been sucked into this mess alongside Liam just over a month ago, Ethan knew it needed to end. Sure, they'd made some cash from the dodgy drop-offs and pickups they'd carried out for Connor, no questions asked. But it was putting a strain on their friendship. They were living in constant fear of landing in trouble: either with the police, or at the hands of some of the shady types they'd already encountered.

Liam hadn't dared to say anything to Connor, afraid of how it might go down. So it had fallen to Ethan to tell him, having arranged a post-school meet-up in the park.

'We want out,' he'd said, getting straight to the point.

'Why? Don't you like the bills you've been earning?'

'Not enough to carry on. We're not built for this. Sorry.'

'Hang on. Are you trying to rinse me for a rise? Is that it? Cheeky bastards.'

'No, that's not it. Not at all. We genuinely want out. Right, Liam?'

A pale Liam, looking ready to throw up, had managed a nod in reply.

Connor had sighed. 'I'm disappointed, lads, I'm not gonna lie. I had high hopes for youse. But at least you had the balls to come to me rather than trying to slink off. And you've been good workers. So how about this: one more job, then quits?'

They'd agreed without hesitation, surprised he was being so reasonable; expecting a similar task to previous ones.

Then he'd mentioned the bit about it being an overnighter, involving taking a train down to London. Brilliant.

FORTY-NINE

Billy

He's agreed to walk Daisy to school this morning. Beth has an early appointment at the dentist.

'Are you sure you don't mind?' she asked him the other day. 'I'm overdue for a check-up and it's the only appointment I could get at late notice. I meant to book one the last time I was there with Daisy – the morning you rescued her, as it happens – but I forgot. Yesterday I got a final reminder message.'

'It's my pleasure,' he told her, delighted to be asked ahead of Rory. 'I'll be working from home that day anyway.'

Daisy gives him a huge smile and a big hug when he rings on the doorbell to pick her up. 'Hi, Uncle Billy. I'll put my shoes on, then I'm ready. Mummy's going to the dentist.'

'I know, Daisy Chain. Take your time. No rush.'

'I had to get a special filling when I was at the dentist,' Daisy says. 'But it didn't hurt and it still feels good when I run my tongue across it. Do you think Mummy will need a filling too?'

'Hopefully not. I bet she brushes her teeth really well. Am I right?'

Daisy nods. 'She watches me now to check I do it well too.'

Later, as they're walking hand-in-hand along the pavement, the roads full of commuters, Billy asks her how things are going at school.

'Okay,' she says in a glum tone. 'I don't like it as much as I used to.'

'Why not?'

'Lori.'

'Seriously? Is she still being nasty? I thought that was all over with now?'

Beth told Billy a few weeks back that she'd dealt with this. Soon after Lori's birthday party – the one singled-out Daisy hadn't been invited to – she'd decided enough was enough and spoken to the teacher. Mrs Williams had raised the matter with Lori and her parents and she'd assured Beth it would no longer be a problem.

'She's not as mean as she used to be,' Daisy says. 'But she still does things sometimes.'

'When? What does she do?'

'Um, when Mrs Williams isn't there, at playtime and stuff. Last week she kept whispering "loser" when she walked past me. And yesterday she pushed me over in the toilets and laughed. She pretended it was an accident, but it wasn't.'

'Have you told your mummy or daddy?'

'Not yet.'

'Why not?'

She shrugs, a sad look on her face. 'Dunno.'

As they approach the school gates, Billy hears someone say his name from behind him. He turns around to see Ed, the guy who runs the gym he uses. Billy helped him out recently with a minor IT issue that was causing him a headache; they've been quite pally ever since.

'Hi, Billy. How's it going? I didn't know you had a kid at this school.'

'Ed, fancy seeing you here. This is actually my niece, Daisy.'

'Hello, love.' Ed flashes her a warm smile. He nods towards a girl walking alongside him, almost twice the size of Daisy. 'This is my not-so-little one, Flick.'

Billy says hello to Flick.

'You coming along later?' Ed asks.

'Yeah, probably.'

'Nice one. I'll catch up with you then. Gotta dash.' He rolls his eyes. 'Teacher wants to see me about something.'

'You know Flick Webster's daddy?' Daisy asks Billy once the other two are out of earshot.

'He runs the gym I go to.'

'She's a karate champion,' Daisy whispers. 'She's the toughest girl in Year 6. Everyone's scared of her.'

'Hello again,' he says to Ed, entering the gym's reception area that evening.

'Billy. How's tricks?'

'Not so bad. You?'

'Can't complain.'

'Computer still holding up?'

'It's not given me any grief at all since you worked your magic. I wish you'd let me pay you.'

Billy deliberately hadn't charged him a penny, despite spending a couple of hours fixing the issue. He thought perhaps Ed might be a useful man to have owing him a favour, which it's turned out he is, although not how Billy imagined.

'Glad to hear it. Listen, mate, I was wondering if you might be able to help *me* out with something.'

Ed grins. 'Of course. Name it.'

FIFTY

Beth

When I pick Daisy up from school on Thursday, she runs out with a huge grin on her face, which makes a nice change.

'Hi, Mummy.'

'Hi, love. Good day?'

'The best.'

'Excellent. What made it so good?'

Daisy looks around, then whispers: 'Let's start walking. I'll tell you in a minute.'

I'm intrigued; even more so when she eventually bursts out with it, saying: 'Uncle Billy is the best.'

'Right,' I say, confused. 'That's nice to hear. What is it he's, er, done to make you so happy? You are talking about the reason school was so good today, right?'

'Of course, Mummy. You'll never believe what happened at morning break.'

'Tell me, love. I'm dying to know.'

'It was so cool. You know Flick Webster?'

'Um.' The name doesn't ring any bells. 'I'm not sure. Should I?'

'I've told you about her.'

'You have? Sorry, you'll have to remind me.'

'She's a karate champion from Year 6. She did a demo for us once in assembly when she broke some wood with her bare hands. She's really tough. Everyone's scared of her. Even some of the teachers, I think.'

This I do remember from a while ago. I recall warning Daisy not to try it herself at home. 'Ah, yes. So what was so cool, involving Flick Webster and your uncle?'

'You won't believe it, Mummy.'

'Try me.'

'Well, Lori was being mean to me again at break time—'

'What?' I can't stop myself. 'You're kidding. I thought that was all over and done with. What's that horrible girl done now? I'll be speaking to your teacher again—'

'Mummy, listen. There's no need. Flick sorted it. Everything's fine.'

I bite my tongue and let her continue.

'Lori tried to trip me over in the playground when no teachers were watching. It's okay, I didn't actually fall over, but I nearly did. She called me Dumbo again and I was about to start crying. Then Flick turned up. First she checked I was all right. Then she gave Lori this scary look, like she was about to chop her head off. She asked her why she was being mean to me. She said I was a good friend of hers and if she ever saw or heard from anyone else about Lori picking on me ever again, she'd make her regret it. Lori looked so scared. I've never seen her like that before. I thought *she* was about to start crying. Then Flick spent the rest of break with me. She was so nice. She promised I wouldn't have any more problems from Lori.'

'Wow,' I say. 'That's incredible. This Flick sounds amazing.

But you'll have to forgive me, love, I don't understand. What's Uncle Billy got to do with any of it?'

'It was him who asked Flick to help me, Mummy. He knows her dad from the gym. Can we go and see him? I want to say thank you.'

'Um, sure, if he's around. He might be at work.'

It bothers me that this is the first I'm hearing about Lori being back to her old tricks. Why didn't Daisy tell me sooner? I say nothing, for now at least, not wanting to spoil her good mood. But it's strange that Billy knew about this recurrence while I didn't. What about Rory? Did he know too?

At home, Daisy badgers me to find out if Billy is around, so I call him to ask.

'No, I'm afraid not,' he says. 'I'm in the city centre today seeing clients. I'm on a break right now. Is there anything I can help with over the phone?'

'Bear with me,' I say. 'There's someone here who wants to talk to you. I'll put you on speakerphone.'

'Hello, Uncle Billy,' Daisy says after a nudge from me. 'Guess what.'

'What is it, Daisy Chain? Everything all right?'

'Uh-huh.'

Why do kids clam up as soon as you try to get them to speak on the telephone?

'She wants to say thank you because of something that happened today at school,' I say, encouraging her with my eyes to continue.

'Uncle Billy,' she says. 'Flick Webster helped me today. She was amazing.'

'Ah, I was hoping it might be that. She came through for you, did she? Put whatshername in her place, I hope.'

'Daisy's nodding and smiling,' I explain.

'Uncle Billy can't see you when you do that, love,' I tell Daisy. 'It's not a video call. You can only hear each other.'

'So today was a good day at school, Daisy Chain?' Billy asks.

'The best. Thank you for asking Flick to help me, Uncle Billy.'

'You're welcome. I couldn't have you getting pushed around, could I?'

'Can I go now, Mummy?' Daisy whispers in my ear. 'I need a wee.'

I nod, and off she pops.

'Daisy's gone,' I tell Billy, switching the call off speakerphone. 'She needed the loo. She was so excited to speak to you. You should have seen her when she came out of school, like a different girl from how she's been recently. The size of the grin on her face. It made my day.'

'That's cute,' he says. 'I hoped it would work out.'

After Billy's explained how it came to pass – how he only learned about the recurrence of the Lori problem while walking Daisy to school on Tuesday – I feel better. He doesn't think she told anyone else before then, because it was only just starting up again.

'Hopefully it'll be done once and for all now,' he says. 'Teachers and parents only have so much sway with bullies. You can't beat a threat from the toughest kid in school. Luckily, her dad owed me a favour.'

'How did we ever manage without you, Billy? You're a star.'

He laughs down the line. 'I do my best. Anyhow, gotta go. Work calls.'

After I've hung up, I look at the clock. Ethan should be home any minute. I'll give him ten; if he's not back by then, I'll chase him up on his mobile. Grounded means grounded.

FIFTY-ONE

Billy

He walks back into the pub. 'Sorry, work call,' he says to the woman sipping on a gin and tonic at the bar. 'Something I couldn't ignore.'

She frowns. 'Are you going to be taking many more calls?'

'Nope. In fact I'm turning my phone off now. Better?'

'We'll see.'

Billy wasn't lying to Beth and Daisy about being in the city centre – he is – but he's definitely not working. Well, unless you count grafting the woman he's currently on a first date with as work. It does feel a little that way. She has such a mardy look on her face right now. Hopefully, things will improve without any more interruptions. She's almost as smoking hot in person as she looks in the app, which is rarely the case. All being well, after a few more drinks she'll be up for inviting him back to her place for some no-strings, one-off fun.

'So, you work in TV?' she asks him, smiling again, thank goodness.

'That's right, for my sins.'

He put this down on his profile after once meeting a guy at a party who actually did work in television and said the ladies loved it. 'They imagine it's really glam,' he told Billy, laughing. 'They assume we're best pals with celebrities and always at swanky parties or premieres. Yeah, right.'

'What programme are you working on at the moment?' Billy's date asks.

He's forgotten her name. He could remind himself by looking on his phone, but he's made a thing of turning that off. Dammit.

'This and that,' he replies. 'It's all contract work these days. I seem to be forever in meetings. I'm hoping to start a shoot on the Yorkshire coast soon, but I can't really talk about that. It's all very hush-hush, because of the stars involved. That was what the phone call was about.'

'Sounds exciting,' she says, wide-eyed.

'It pays the bills. I'd tell you more if I could, but my hands are tied. Between you and me, though, it could be big, this one: a potential BAFTA winner, if everything slots into place.'

She falls for it, hook, line and sinker, much to Billy's amusement.

'Enough about me, anyway.' He changes tack before he gets out of his depth. 'Tell me about you.'

Not that he cares. He smiles and nods in the right places, but he's not listening. He's imagining what she'll look like naked and wondering how long it will take until he finds out.

Meanwhile, in the back of his mind, he returns to planning his endgame with Beth and family. Nearly there now. He has them all, except one, eating out of his hand. He's picked his moment to strike, and barring any last-minute hitches that could force a delay, it's almost upon him. That's why he's out with this woman today. It's a chance to unwind ahead of the stress to come when he finally pulls off his mask and reveals his true self; the real reason he came to the area in the first place.

It all has to happen in a short stretch of time. He must move each piece into the right place at the right moment. And it needs to start with Rory. He's the wildcard that Billy can't control. So, step one is to remove him from the equation.

FIFTY-TWO

LAST SATURDAY

Ethan

They're on a train heading to London. It's busy but they have allocated seats next to each other. Their return tickets were handed to them by Connor.

'I was hoping we'd be on a table,' Liam says as the train glides away from the station.

'Why?'

'It's better, innit? Everyone knows that. Like the back seat of a bus. If it's free, you always take it.'

'Why's a table better when there's only two of you? It means you probably have to share it with other people, which is rubbish. We've got our own foldaway tray tables now, like on an aeroplane.'

'A proper table is better,' Liam continues, looking towards the nearest one, across the aisle. 'Check them out over there. Loads of room. When was the last time you were on a train?'

'Years ago, with my parents.'

'Same. Do you reckon it's safe to put the backpack in the baggage rack?'

Ethan, who has the window seat, looks where Liam currently has it, between his feet. 'I'd keep it where it is.'

'It's a bit of a squash.'

He lowers his voice. 'Better than losing it. I don't think Connor, or whoever we're taking it to, would be too happy about that.'

Liam chuckles. 'I'm not scared, knowing I have you on my side.'

'What are you on about?'

He speaks in a Batman growl, quoting Ethan's earlier words to Marty: 'I'll come for you in the night and slit your throat.'

'Shut up.'

'Even I was terrified when you said that. And I remember you dressed as a penguin in that school play at primary school.'

'Whatever. I was too busy saving your arse to think about the exact words that came out of my mouth. It was automatic. I was trying to put the wind up him, that's all.'

'You succeeded.'

'Do you think he'll tell anyone?'

Liam scratches his nose. 'Doubt it. He'll be too embarrassed. Hopefully he'll leave me alone from now on. That would be nice. Do you reckon there's a buffet car on this train, and what about first class? Shall we have a look for it; see if we can get away with sitting there?'

'Yeah, let's do all we can to draw attention to ourselves.' Ethan rolls his eyes. 'Or how about we sit tight, stay out of trouble and concentrate on minding this bloody package?'

'You don't even want to find the buffet car?'

'No.'

'Right. I might go to the loo, then.' Liam mimes puffing on a vape.

'Don't. There'll be a sensor in there, dickhead. Stop being a liability. You're winding me up.' Ethan pulls out his earbuds.

'I'm going to chill and listen to some tunes. Why don't you do the same?'

'Okay. How's your eye?'

'Not too bad. How does it look?'

'Sore. Doesn't it hurt?'

'I'm trying not to think about it.'

A couple of hours later, Liam nudges him awake. 'I think we're nearly there. Do you remember when we were in London on that school trip in Year 6? It took ages on the bus. The train's way faster.'

Ethan nods while having a yawn and a stretch. It's already dark outside. 'How long was I asleep?'

'Most of the journey.'

'Guess I was tired.'

'Apparently. Have you been to London since that trip?'

'Nope. Not before or after. You?'

'Same. The big wheel by the river was good, but I wasn't into that musical with the green witch.'

'*Wicked*? I enjoyed it. The views were decent from the London Eye, but it moved so slowly. I remember it taking forever because I was bursting for a piss.'

'Anyway,' Liam says, 'remind me what's happening when we arrive. I still don't get why we have to stay overnight.'

Ethan sighs. How has he become the one in charge, when all of this started out as Liam's problem? 'We look for the guy in the red puffer jacket outside the toilets; we do what he tells us. I've no idea why we have to stay overnight or where we'll be staying. You were there when Connor told us everything. If you had questions, you should have piped up then.'

After the train arrives, they're quick to find the meet-up location, even though the station is heaving. Way busier than back home. Another level of fast-moving crowd. It might be early evening on a Saturday, but everyone looks like they're running late for something.

'There's no one in a red coat,' Liam says.

'I have eyes. We're early. Relax. He'll be here.'

Ethan struggles to follow his own advice when he sees two police officers walking in their direction. Thankfully, there's no sign of a sniffer dog, which could have been disastrous, considering the package in Liam's bag.

They still don't know what it is they've been delivering for Connor. It's probably better that way. However, the signs definitely point to drugs; particularly the decent money they've been getting in return.

Ethan usually tries not to think about it. This time feels much higher-risk, though, considering the long journey and the fact they're in the capital city. The package is larger than normal, plus they're both carrying a knife. They debated beforehand whether this was a good idea, in light of how tough police are on knife crime, especially in London. But bearing in mind they'd be screwed anyway if they got stopped with the package, they figured it was safer to have some form of protection in case things turned nasty.

Now they're here, cops already breathing down their necks, Ethan's not so sure they made the right decision.

How the hell did he get himself into this situation? Mum would blow her top if she had even the smallest clue what he was up to. Only the other day she said something to him about kids carrying knives. She asked if any of his mates had one, making him fear that she knew something. Thankfully, he played it cool, telling her no and calmly asking why she wanted to know. Apparently, she'd seen some special report on the TV news.

'It's a real issue,' she said. 'They're terrible things, knives. They can kill someone so quickly if they catch an artery or a major organ. The idiots who carry them to feel tough would do well to remember that. A knife fight is a whole different ballgame to a punch-up. Steer well clear.'

The mere thought of that conversation makes him feel awful, but he pushes the guilt away. No time for that now.

The sooner this red-coat guy turns up and they get out of here, the better.

'Shit,' Liam says under his breath once he too clocks the police.

'It's fine. Chill.'

'You're not the one holding the bag.'

Ethan glares at his pal to get him to hush.

The police continue to approach, seriously making Ethan sweat. But at the last minute, one of them takes a call on her radio, leading them to rush off in the opposite direction.

'See,' he tells Liam, feigning calmness. 'Told you it would be fine.'

'It'll be a lot better when this bloody bloke shows his face. We're like sitting ducks.'

'Don't be dramatic.' Ethan sees someone in a red puffer jacket approaching: a tall, chunky man with a shaven head and a goatee beard. 'Is this the guy?'

'I hope so. About damn time.'

The man stops outside the toilets, looks at his watch and then stands still with his hands in his coat pockets. Liam's quiet all of a sudden – surprise, surprise – so Ethan takes the lead and walks over.

'I'm looking for a grandfather clock,' he says, exactly as Connor instructed. He resists the urge to add that this isn't a wind-up.

'I can help with that,' the man, who looks in his late twenties, replies in a gruff voice. 'There are two of you, right?'

'Yeah.' Ethan nods in Liam's direction.

'Follow me.'

The man walks off at a pace. Ethan and Liam follow, sharing looks with each other but saying nothing.

Ethan's heart is racing. Where the hell is this stranger going to take them? Connor didn't elaborate beyond the meet-up, although he did warn them the exchange wouldn't happen at the train station, as it would be too risky there.

'They'll take you somewhere else,' he said. 'Do as they tell you and it'll be fine.'

They follow the man in the red coat out of the train station into the fume-filled evening air, where it's busy as hell. After looking back to check they're still with him, he leads them across the road and down several side streets, to the point where Ethan would struggle to find his way back without using his phone or asking for directions.

They keep going for a good ten minutes, bright lights and noise on all sides, in fine rain that doesn't feel much but soon has them soaking. Eventually, the man, who hasn't said a word since they started walking, turns into the dimly lit entrance of a small multistorey car park and leads them up a grotty staircase that reeks of urine. On the third floor, he approaches a battered green Citroën with another man in the front passenger seat, and gestures for them to get into the back.

Ethan and Liam share yet another concerned look, but they do as requested.

'Hi,' Ethan says. The other bloke, a skinny older man in grimy grey joggers and a matching hoodie, doesn't look back at them. He's busy on his phone.

'Where are we heading?' Ethan asks after they've been driving for a few minutes.

'Not too far,' Red Coat replies.

This is starting to feel like a bad situation. All kinds of fears are running through Ethan's mind, but he tries to block them out and focus on this being their final delivery: their way out. This time tomorrow, whatever happens, it will all be over. Hopefully.

'Are we nearly there?' he asks after another ten minutes.

'Uh-huh.' Red Coat reaches across to the glovebox and pulls

out two small bottles of lemon and lime-flavoured water, which he passes back to them. 'Here. For you. On the house.'

The silence in the car is oppressive. Even the guys in the front don't speak to each other. No radio or music. Nothing other than traffic noise. It feels off. But what the hell are Ethan and Liam supposed to do about it, other than be patient while sipping on their complimentary water?

Where even are they? Ethan's tried looking at street signs, but none of them make any sense.

Finally, after driving for the best part of an hour, the car pulls up in a litter-strewn street of terraced houses, none of which look well cared for.

The one they're parked nearest to has a boarded-up front window; there's an old pink bath, basin and toilet looking sorry for themselves in the front yard.

Liam looks pale and scared, his hands shaking, like he's about to fall apart. Ethan is far from comfortable, but someone needs to stay in control. He focuses on getting from one minute to the next.

'What's going on? What now?' he asks in the deepest, most confident voice he can muster as a fourteen-year-old in a strange city with a pair of scary criminals.

'We go in,' Red Coat replies. To Ethan's dismay, he gestures towards the peeling green door of the manky house they're parked outside.

Ethan takes a deep breath, gives Liam a 'we'll be fine' look and moves to open his car door. The handle doesn't work.

'Wait,' Red Coat says. 'We need to let you out. Child lock.'

Ethan tries not to read anything into this.

When they enter the damp-smelling house, it's as dilapidated inside as out: tatty bare floorboards, torn wallpaper, patches of black mould, and a threadbare floral carpet on the stairs. He can't imagine anyone actually lives here.

They're led through to a back room where two burly mid-thirties men, both in need of a wash and a shave, are playing cards and drinking whisky under a bare light bulb. They're sitting at a circular dining table that's seen better days, cardboard wedged under one leg.

The men don't acknowledge them immediately, but after playing his hand, one of them, who has several gold teeth and two fistfuls of matching rings, looks in their direction.

'What?' he says to Red Coat in an unexpectedly high-pitched voice. 'Who are these kids?'

'They're the lads you asked me to pick up from Euston, Frank.'

'That's today? I thought it was tomorrow.' Frank lets out a weary sigh. 'Have a seat, boys.'

As directed, Ethan and Liam take the two empty chairs at the table, so they're sitting opposite each other, between the two men.

'How was your journey?' Frank asks.

'Fine, thanks,' Ethan replies.

'You have something for me, yes?'

'We do.' Ethan looks at Liam. 'Give him the bag, mate.'

'What's up, lad?' Frank asks Liam, his high voice sounding increasingly creepy. 'Cat got your tongue? Or is he your spokesman?'

Liam shakes his head, still looking nervous as hell. He hands over the backpack.

Frank unzips it and pulls out the package. He inspects it for a moment, turning it around in his hands without unwrapping it, and then places it on the table. 'Know what this is?' he asks Liam.

'No.'

'You?' he asks Ethan next.

'None of our business. We just deliver it.'

'You're not curious? Not in the slightest? I'm not sure I believe that.'

'Honestly, I'd rather not know,' Ethan says. 'I think it's better that way.'

Frank nods. 'I hear you want out. That you don't want to make any more deliveries. Why? It's easy money, no?'

Ethan suddenly feels woozy. 'We're school kids.'

'Exactly. I bet you're from nice families. Middle class? Comfortable? That's what makes you perfect for this. You're invisible. Can't we change your minds? Would a little pay rise help?'

Ethan and Liam's eyes meet before Ethan replies: 'No, sorry. Thank you, though.'

'That's unfortunate,' Frank says. 'The problem now is that we need to know you won't ever say anything about any of this to anyone. Understand?'

Ethan gulps. 'We won't, I promise. Not a word. Ever. Right, Liam?'

'Yes.'

'It's good to hear you say so, boys.' Frank nods slowly. 'I'd like to believe you, but sadly, in my experience, people often say one thing and do another.'

'We won't.'

'Shh, quiet now.' He holds a forefinger up to his lips. 'I've developed a system for dealing with this. A way to ensure former employees definitely do keep quiet. Does that make sense? No words, please. Nod if you agree.'

The lads both nod.

'Good. Then let me apologise in advance for what's about to happen. It's a necessary inconvenience, I'm afraid.'

Before he's finished speaking, both boys are grabbed from behind by the two men who brought them here in the car. They whip their arms behind their backs and, with practised ease, fix cable ties around their wrists. They blindfold Liam and stick thick tape over his mouth. Then they do the same to Ethan, before pulling another cable tie around his ankles. All attempts to struggle and cry for help are futile.

'Calm down, boys,' Frank's eerie voice says. 'It'll all be over soon.'

Ethan feels himself being strong-armed out of the chair and dragged to another room as Frank asks: 'Did they both drink the water?'

'Yes, boss,' Red Coat replies.

'Good. They should be out of it soon, then.'

FIFTY-THREE

NOW

Rory

He drives away from the office, relieved that the working week is finally over. It's been a busy, demanding one; he's looking forward to a drink. No kids this weekend, so tonight, and maybe tomorrow too, he intends to get trolleyed all by himself at the apartment. He still struggles to think of it as home, but it's the best he's got.

Is it sad to drink alone in front of the telly? Probably, but he doesn't care. He's not got the energy or desire to go out and socialise. He's knackered. Perhaps he should go to the GP and get signed off with stress for a bit. It's a fleeting but tempting thought that he'd never say out loud, least of all to Beth, who'd think he was making light of her own very real struggle.

He does genuinely feel stressed, although it's not just work – it's everything. Ethan going missing last weekend was particularly challenging, not helped by the fact that it led to Rory having to spend time with Billy. Bloody Billy the wedge, gradually pushing him further and further away from his family.

He stops en route at the supermarket. Buys a crate of beer, a decent bottle of red and a discounted single malt. Plus a pepperoni pizza, crisps and chocolate. All bases covered.

Half an hour later, feet up in the lounge, he's supping on his first beer.

Nothing on TV grabs his attention, so he puts on a playlist called, appropriately, Cosy Evening Chill, a soothing mix of electronic soundscapes and lo-fi beats. Just what the doctor ordered.

He nods off while drinking his third beer, like a lightweight, only to be woken up half an hour later by someone pressing his buzzer at the front door of the apartment block.

No one ever comes to see him here apart from the kids, so his initial reaction is to ignore the sound. It's almost certainly a mistake or someone messing about.

But when the buzzer sounds for a fourth time, he gives in and walks to the intercom.

'Yes?'

'Is that Rory?'

'Who's asking?'

'It's Billy.'

Shit. What's he doing here?

'Oh, um, hi. What's going on? How can I help you?'

'Sorry to turn up unannounced. I was hoping for a chat. Any chance I could come in?'

Rory stares at the wall for a long moment. He's sorely tempted to say that now's not convenient, but he can't really do that, can he? Billy's a part of Beth and the kids' lives now, whether he likes it or not.

He presses the buzzer to open the outside door.

A moment later, Billy's standing there, larger than life, in Rory's hallway. He has a backpack over one shoulder.

'Can I take your jacket or your bag?'

'No thanks. I'm fine.'

Feeling awkward, Rory puts his hands in his trouser pockets, where he comes across his car and door keys. He pulls them out and hangs them in their usual place on the wall hook.

It feels strange letting this man he doesn't like or trust into his flat, but he shows Billy into the lounge nonetheless. 'Have a seat. Can I get you a drink?'

'Thanks. Whatever you're having.'

'Beer?'

'Great.'

Rory nips to the kitchen to retrieve a fresh one from the fridge.

'Thanks,' Billy says, taking it. 'Sorry again for turning up unannounced.'

'I'm surprised you know where I live.'

'Beth gave me the address. I told her I wanted to try to smooth things out between us.'

'Right.' Rory scratches an itch on the side of his nose. 'So that's why you're here?'

'Something along those lines.'

Billy seems nervous. His voice is wavering and he's fidgety. Is it really so important to him that the two of them iron out their differences?

'You've never liked me,' he says. 'Have you?'

'Why do you say that?'

'It's obvious. The rest of the family have welcomed me with open arms, but not you. You've always been cold, no matter what I say or do.'

Rory shrugs. 'Let's say you're right. Why do you care? You've got what you want, haven't you? Beth and the kids can't get enough of you. They think the sun shines out of your backside. That you can do no wrong.'

Billy grins in a way that Rory hasn't seen before, like he's drawing back the veil and revealing a hidden part of himself. It's almost... menacing. 'They do, don't they? You must hate that.'

Rory's unsure how to respond. Is Billy here to goad him? Did he imagine that manic flash in his eyes just now?

'Look, what's going on?' he asks, taking a sip from his beer and then placing it back down on the coffee table. 'What's with the weird looks? Why are you actually here?'

'Weird looks?' Billy appears confused. 'I'm not sure I understand what you mean, Rory? How much have you had to drink?'

'What?'

'Well, I don't mean to pry, but I saw all that booze you have in the kitchen as I walked by. Beer, whisky, wine. Looks to me like you're having a party, but there's no one here apart from us and you didn't know I was coming. Party for one? Oh dear. Do you think perhaps you have a bit of a problem, Rory?'

'How dare you—'

'How dare I what? Steal your family from under your nose? That's why you don't like me, isn't it? Let's be honest. With me around, there's no point to you, is there? Not since you blew it with Beth by cheating on her. I'll tell you what, before I told her I was her brother, she'd have blown me in a second. She was mad for it.'

What the hell? Rory can't believe his ears. As much as he's always disliked Billy, he never expected this kind of behaviour from him. If only he'd thought to record their conversation, so Beth could hear it for herself. He doesn't even have his phone on him; it's charging in the bedroom.

'Well, you're certainly showing your true colours at last,' he says.

'You have no idea.' Billy bares his teeth.

'I think it's time for you to leave.' Rory gets to his feet. 'You're not welcome here any longer.'

Billy remains seated. 'I'll be the judge of that. Sit back down.'

'I beg your pardon. Who the hell do you think you are,

ordering me about in my own home? Boy, was I right about you. Wait until I tell Beth—'

'Tell her what? Like she'd believe you over me. I said sit back down.'

'Out. Now. Before I turf you out.'

'You and whose army?' Billy reaches into the inside pocket of his jacket and, to Rory's horror, pulls out a handgun, which he points straight at him. 'Even if I didn't have this, you wouldn't have a chance, mate. But I do have this, so sit.'

'What's that: a fancy cigarette lighter? A replica? Like you'd have a real gun.'

'Oh, it's real, don't you worry. They're not that hard to lay your hands on if you have enough money and know the right people, which I do. I mean, I'll prove it to you, if you like: shoot you in the leg as a taster. Or you could sit down and shut up, like a good little boy.'

Rory's heart is pounding. He does the only sensible thing in the circumstances and sits back down in his chair.

'Good choice.' Billy keeps the gun trained on him. 'Now, here's what's going to happen...'

FIFTY-FOUR

LAST SUNDAY

Ethan

When he comes to, his cheek is pressed against the side window of a moving car. Still groggy, his vision sliding in and out of focus, he looks over and sees Liam to his left, fast asleep with his head hanging forward. They're in the back seat of what looks like the crappy green Citroën they travelled in before. The one that took them to that horrible house where... Oh shit.

The last thing he recalls is being bound and gagged, dumped on what felt like a mattress in a nearby room, terrified for his life, then passing out. They must have drugged them both with that flavoured water they gave them on the way. He did think at the time that it had an odd taste, but it never even occurred to him that this might be the reason why.

He moves his arms and legs to check they're no longer restrained, which they're not. Nor is his mouth taped shut. Liam looks all clear too, as far as he can tell.

It would be tempting to believe he imagined the entire ordeal, but his sore, bruised body tells him otherwise.

He hasn't a clue how much time has passed, but it must be

quite a while, since it's already light outside. Sunday morning? Surely no later than that.

What the hell happened between then and now? Why did Frank and his henchmen do that to them in the first place? And where are they being taken next?

He peers into the front of the car, blinking to try to get his see-sawing vision back under control.

Red Coat's driving again, but there's someone different in the front passenger seat; not the skinny, silent man from last time. Oh crap. It's Frank.

'The chatty one's awake, boss,' Red Coat says after glancing in the rear-view mirror.

Frank turns around and flashes his gold teeth at Ethan. 'Morning, sleepyhead. You probably have a few questions.'

Ethan nods.

'Wake your pal. I don't like repeating myself.'

Ethan reaches over, his arm smarting from the movement, and gently shakes Liam by the shoulder. 'Mate, wake up.' His mouth is dry as a bone, his swollen tongue like sandpaper, so his voice comes out raspy.

Liam gasps as his eyes snap open and he jolts upright. He looks first at Ethan and then at Frank, the sight of whom makes him jerk backwards in the seat. 'No!' His voice is crackly and hoarse. 'Where are we? What the bloody hell is going on?'

'It's okay,' Ethan says, like he has all the answers. 'Calm down. Take a breath.'

Liam checks to see if he's still restrained, before shaking his head and rubbing his eyes.

'Back in the room?' Frank asks in his creepy high-pitched voice.

Liam replies with a timid nod.

'Excellent. We're returning you to Euston. Then you can get your train home. Good news?'

Both of them nod this time.

'You see, I'm not an unreasonable person. However, as I mentioned yesterday, precautions are necessary to ensure former employees never become a problem. This is why Connor sent you here. Call me a control freak, but I like to oversee these things myself. Anyhow, I doubt you remember much, if anything, from the past several hours. You were drugged, more than once, but it was done cleanly; you might feel tired for a bit, but there will be no other lasting effects. Nothing to be concerned about.'

Easy for you to say, Ethan thinks.

'So what happened in that time?' Frank continues. 'What precautions did I take? That's what you're wondering, right? That's what you're racking your teenage brains to try to recall. Well, relax. We've not harmed you in any way, other than perhaps the odd cut and bruise, which I apologise for and assure you wasn't deliberate. We needed you fully compliant, that's all, because what we did do was take copies of your fingerprints and several DNA samples. We also took some blood from you both. Not enough for you to notice, and I can assure you it was done in a clean, hygienic manner – fresh needles and so on – nothing for you to worry about health-wise. We're not animals. All of those samples are now stored safely and securely, which is where they'll remain as long as you do nothing to upset me or anyone who works for me. Clear?'

Ethan looks over at a confused, anxious-looking Liam before replying: 'I think so.'

'Why don't you explain it to your friend so I know you both understand? What could I do with those samples, should I choose to?'

'Set us up. Like at a crime scene or something.'

'Bingo. I could frame you in an instant for anything I wanted to.' He eyeballs Liam. 'Are you keeping up?'

'Yes,' Liam replies like a mouse.

'Samples or no samples, to be clear, I could arrange for you to be killed like that.' Frank snaps his fingers in front of Liam's face, causing him to recoil. 'I have eyes and ears everywhere. I could have killed you both last night. Made you disappear without a trace. But why would I do that unless I had to? No, I only gave you a taste of my power and took my precautions, because that's the generous kind of person I am, unless people cross me. When that happens, whole different ballgame. You wouldn't like me when I'm disappointed by people. Anyway, how are we doing so far? Questions?'

Ethan and Liam shake their heads in unison.

Frank grins, nodding. 'I'll jump straight to the conclusion, then. You never worked for Connor and you never worked for me. You wouldn't recognise me in the street, nor any of my colleagues. This trip to London, it didn't happen. Got it? None of it did.' He holds his forefinger up to his lips. 'You stay quiet, everyone's happy. You talk, even a little bit, and there's trouble. Before you know it, you'll be some big ugly bloke's prison bitch, staring down the barrel of a life sentence. Or dead. Are we clear, Ethan?'

'Yes, absolutely.'

'Are we clear, Liam?'

'Um, yes.'

'Um, good,' he says, mimicking Liam's scared reply. 'Glad to hear it, boys. Talk over. Not far to go now. Sit back and enjoy the ride. I'd offer you a drink, but I don't have one, and even if I did, I'm not sure you'd want to take it from me, would you?'

Less than half an hour later, the car pulls up at the side of the road. 'Right. We're here,' Frank says. 'Near as dammit, anyway.' He points to the right. 'Head that way and you'll be back at the train station in a few minutes. Goodbye, lads. All being well, we'll never meet again. You should steer clear of Connor too. He'll blank you in future, for all our sakes.'

He reaches into the glovebox and, after slipping on a pair of thin leather gloves, pulls out a small plastic bag containing their phones, earbuds, wallets, vapes and knives. He hands them over, knives last. 'Careful carrying these. If the police catch you with them, you'll be in deep shit. And never start a knife fight unless you know you can win.' Lastly, he gives them each an envelope. 'Parting gift. Now off you pop before we get a parking ticket.'

Red Coat jumps out from behind the wheel and opens the door on Ethan's side. He gets out, closely followed by Liam. Red Coat shuts the door, gets back in the car without saying a word, then drives off.

Ethan stares at his friend. 'Are you all right? You look terrible.'

'No. I think I'm going to—' Liam bends forward and vomits on the pavement, narrowly missing his trainers.

Ethan grabs him around the waist to support him. 'Are you okay?'

'Give me a minute,' Liam puffs, pushing him away, before retching again.

Afterwards, he stands upright, hands on his hips. 'Sorry. I think I'm all right now. Shit.'

'What?'

'My backpack. They didn't return it.'

Ethan can't believe his ears. 'That's what you're worried about? I'm missing twelve-plus hours. You?'

Liam scowls. 'Yeah, me too. I was already feeling weird when they jumped us at the table. I think I blacked out as they were tying us up.'

'I thought we were both going to die,' Ethan says. 'Game over. Seriously, the last thing that went through my head, before whatever drug they gave us took effect, was how Mum would cope. She's already lost her dad and her brother. I don't think she could handle losing me too.'

'I was proper shitting it.'

'We ought to have realised something was up beforehand,'

Ethan adds. 'Coming all the way down here overnight, it should have triggered alarm bells. I was too focused on getting free.'

'Well, we are now, aren't we?'

'I guess. At a cost. Hopefully there are no more surprises. Hopefully everything really was as hygienic as he said, unlike that filthy house. What time is it, actually? How long until our train?'

Liam looks at his phone. 'We've got about forty-five minutes. Do you have any missed calls or messages from home?'

'Not so far. You?'

'No. Phew. My battery's nearly dead, though.'

'Same. Where's your charger?'

'It was in my backpack.'

'Great. We'll have to see if we can borrow one on the train. Unless...' Ethan opens the envelope Frank handed him and counts the notes inside. 'Shit. There are five hundred bills in here. I might buy a new charger at the station. And breakfast.'

Liam's already tearing open his own envelope, which he's chuffed to find holds the same.

Walking to the station, Liam says he's surprised Frank gave them their knives back. 'How did he know we wouldn't use them on him?'

'Really?' Ethan replies. 'After everything he just put us through? Like that was ever going to happen.'

'I suppose. I can't lie, I wish we'd never got the knives now. They're what landed us in this bullshit mess. I might get rid of mine soon.'

'I know what you mean. At least we did get to scare Marty, even if it was me rather than you.'

'Bloody Marty.' Liam lets out a long sigh. 'All this is basically his fault. If only he wasn't such a knobhead.'

'I know.'

'Do you reckon they cloned our phones while they had them?'

'What? Why?'

Liam blinks. 'It happens in films.'

Ethan squints at him, deadpan. 'I think it's more likely they shoved a butt plug up your arse.'

'Don't even joke about that. They could have done anything to us while we were out of it. I tell you what: I'm never saying a damn word to anyone. I do not want to get on the wrong side of that guy. I thought Connor was scary until I met psycho Frank with his freaky voice. He was another level.'

Vaping, Ethan points towards the station entrance as it comes into view. 'Yeah, totally. This whole thing – all of it, start to finish – needs to stay on the down-low for good. Like it never happened.'

'It doesn't feel real,' Liam says. 'Last night, I mean. Like it was a bad dream or something. They drugged us. We were tied up, blindfolded and gagged. What the hell? We're fourteen. How did that happen to us? If we weren't both there, I'd doubt my memories.'

Ethan rotates his stiff wrists. 'I have the aches and pains to prove it.'

'Me too. It was a bit extreme; don't you reckon? Even if they did want to take samples or whatever.'

'They delivered a message we wouldn't forget.'

'True. I'm surprised I didn't shit myself, literally.' Liam follows Ethan through the doors into bustling Euston station. 'Are you seriously hungry for breakfast? I think I'd puke again if I ate anything. I can't even face vaping yet.'

'I'm famished. I fancy a bacon butty. You should eat too.'

'No thanks.'

FIFTY-FIVE

NOW

Rory

'You're going to listen while I talk, okay?'

Rory nods slowly in response to Billy, not taking his eyes off the handgun pointing at him. He's still not convinced it's real, as opposed to a replica or whatever, but he's far from an expert in such matters. What's he supposed to do, other than what Billy tells him, unless he potentially wants to get shot?

'You've been a thorn in my side ever since I first got to know Beth,' Billy says. 'To be clear, every time I smiled at you, like I was keen for you to like me, it was an act. I actually wanted to punch you in the face.'

'So, I was right all along. I always knew there was something off about you.'

'Shut up. I'm the one talking now.'

'Are you even related to Beth? I bet you're not. What's your ga—'

'Wouldn't you like to know?' Billy leans forward in his chair, stretching his gun-toting arm closer to Rory, a maniacal grin carved into his face. 'I could tell you, but then I'd have to kill you. Oh, wait...' He breaks off to laugh.

'I'm glad you find this so funny,' Rory says.

'Am I going to have to shoot you in the mouth to make you be quiet?'

'I think if you were going to shoot me, Billy, you would have done it by now.'

No sooner has Rory said this than he regrets it. Billy's face forms into a furious frown and there's a sudden flurry of movement followed by an explosion of pain in his temple and cheek as Billy smashes the gun against his head. An eruption of terrifying power.

Rory cries out as he collapses back into the chair and into the rear of his mind while the agony surges. He's not yet unconscious, but he's seriously dazed by this unexpected and brutal blow. If there was any doubt before whether Billy meant business, that's gone.

'Did that sting?' Billy growls, back in his seat again. 'Poor you. You're a bit of a loser, all in all, aren't you, Rory? I imagined your flat would be pathetic, but this is even worse than I thought. No surprise it winds you up being stuck here while I'm round at your old house, having fun with your wife and kids. There was me, wondering the whole time what I'd got wrong; why I couldn't get you on side. But you'd have hated me whatever I did, wouldn't you? It surprises me you had the balls to cheat on Beth, or that you could find someone willing to take part. I bet she was ugly. Was she desperate, like you are now?'

Rory wants to reply – to tell Billy to go to hell – but he's still overcome by the pain. The whole side of his face is thumping. Keeping conscious, listening to what Billy's saying, is sapping enough of his remaining energy already.

'Nothing to say for yourself?' Billy asks, shaking his head. 'Why would I waste a bullet on someone so easy to put down? Is that it? Are you done? No fight left? What about if I told you that Beth's in for a lovely surprise tonight? She's going to have to make a choice – and it won't be easy. Spoiler alert: there are going to be tears, and much worse.'

'Why?' Rory manages to say in a low croak.

'Sorry, what was that? Why? Good question. I bet you'd love to know, wouldn't you? The thing is, I'd rather you didn't. I'd prefer to leave you wondering. It's more torturous that way and – news flash – I kind of get off on seeing you suffer. You've been irritating me for ages now with your yapping and whining, trying to warn Beth off me, interfering with my plans. I've been biting my tongue for so long, I'm surprised it's still in one piece. You were never a real threat. More of an annoyance. But still, I don't like being annoyed. And this would all have been much easier without having to account for you.'

Billy pauses for a moment to clear his throat. 'That's better. I'm not used to all this chatting. Anyhow, I've not got much more to say. In a moment, I'm going to hurt you – more than I have already – and then I'm going to leave you to rot while I go and hurt the rest of your family.'

He leaps to his feet and steps towards Rory, who in a last-ditch attempt to stave off the attack hurls himself forward, fuelled by pure desperation, and rugby-tackles him to the floor.

The gun flies out of Billy's hand as his legs give way.

Rory gives it his all, thumping and scratching and grabbing and squeezing any part of Billy he can get hold of. It feels for a moment like he has the upper hand. Like he's going to over-power him.

Then Billy strikes back with a perfectly delivered right hook to Rory's chin, which sends him sprawling. Next thing, Billy's on top of him, pinning him down with a strength he can't match; snarling like a wild animal and pummelling him with blow after blow to his body, his arms, his face, pretty much everywhere.

Rory tries to defend himself, but it's useless. He hasn't been in a fight since school, and he was hardly a scrapper then. As intensely as he wants to stand up to this charlatan, whoever he really is – to defend his family from him – he doesn't stand a chance.

As the punches continue to rain down, he feels himself going numb, slipping away, like he's no longer fully present in his body. Finally, after what feels like forever, the blows stop.

Is that it? Is the attack finally over?

His eyes are closed, but he feels Billy's weight on top of him shift to one side, like he's reaching for something.

Oh shit.

The gun.

One final crushing blow of cold, hard metal against his skull and it's all over.

Rory slides into nothingness.

FIFTY-SIX

Beth

I'm expecting Billy at any moment. He has a surprise for me. I've no idea what, but I guess I'll find out soon. It's so lovely having him around. After losing one brother, I never imagined I'd experience that special sibling bond again, but here we are.

Billy's frequent presence has made me think of Dad a lot. It's a mixed blessing, because whenever I recall the good times, thoughts creep in about his cheating on Mum. Did he have daydreams of other women while he was with me and Sean? Did he use dropping us off at friends' houses and so on as an excuse for a quick fumble with whoever he had on the go at the time?

How was I so blind to that side of him? Because he was a good father, I guess, even if he wasn't a good husband. He was always there for me, no matter what. I knew he'd run to my side if I was in trouble. As he proved on the day he was so cruelly, brutally taken from us.

I can't unsee the image of Dad lying in the playground, covered in blood, his life draining away from him. It's etched into my mind. The days, weeks and months that followed that, before Mum moved us out of the area to try to escape and rebuild our lives, are one huge blur. I remember Dean calling around at the house and me screaming at him to leave; telling him I hated him and never wanted to see him again; meaning every word and sticking to it.

I also remember Dad's funeral, of course, which Dean thankfully didn't attend. It crushed me, the idea of my beloved father's broken body in the coffin, which looked far too small to contain a man so much larger than life. That and the awful guilt I felt, still years away from coming to terms with any of it. There was a massive attendance, including members of the press outside, for whom Dad's death was a major story. You hear about families hating the intrusion of journalists. Not me. I welcomed their presence. I wanted the world to know what that evil monster Lenny had done.

I didn't cry at the funeral, despite feeling the most devastating sense of loss. It was like I put on a mask for the day, because I wanted to keep that part of my grief private. I did cry tears of relief when, nearly twelve months later, Lenny was found guilty of murder and given a life sentence with a minimum seventeen-year jail term. Sam and Mac were also locked up for lesser offences. I cried with frustration a year later when Lenny's sentence was reduced to fifteen years on appeal, only a few years before the government introduced tougher new penalties for knife killers, raising the minimum term to twenty-five years.

That welcome legal change may have come too late in the case of Dad's killer. However, it helped fuel the successful campaign I ran as an adult, in conjunction with several newspapers, to block Lenny's release on licence after those fifteen years had passed. He died in prison a few months later, stabbed by a fellow inmate with some kind of improvised blade. I wish I could say I took no pleasure from this, but that would be a lie. I never found it in my heart to forgive him for what he did – what he took from me and my family – and I secretly smiled to myself when I heard of his demise. It felt like justice at last. Not that I said this to the press when they inevitably came calling. Some things are best kept to yourself.

I haven't yet properly discussed with Billy what happened to Dad. I'm not sure why. I know he knows Dad was murdered, but is he fully versed on the ins and outs of what happened? There's plenty of information online, which he's probably read, but I couldn't say for sure. He's never specifically brought it up, as in: *let's talk about it in depth, please, because I have questions.* He must have questions, though. He was robbed of a father too and I was an eyewitness to the crime. He could be waiting for me to bring it up. Perhaps I should, but it's never felt like the right time so far.

The doorbell sounds. That'll be Billy now. I probably ought to get a house key cut for him. He's already a named driver on my car insurance, since he doesn't have transport of his own and I barely use the car. Maybe I could convince Rory to give him his key. Like he'd surrender that without a fight, least of all to my brother.

I swing open the front door expecting the usual big smile, but instead Billy looks flustered – and on closer inspection, injured.

'Are you okay?' I ask as he enters stiffly, some fresh cuts on his face, the right side of which looks swollen. 'My goodness. What happened to you?'

'Don't worry,' he says. 'It looks worse than it is. I got jumped by a couple of scrotes who wanted my phone and wallet. I sent them packing, but not before they managed to have a dig.'

'You're joking? When? Not on the way here from yours, surely?'

'I've been in town. It was on my way back: a quiet spot near the tram stop.'

'It might be on CCTV. Have you reported it to the police yet?'

'What would be the point? They didn't get anything and they had hoodies on. I couldn't even tell you what they looked like. Also, I walloped them before they ran off. I could end up being the one in most trouble.'

'Are your hands injured too? Let's have a look.'

He shows me.

'Oh dear,' I say. 'They look sore. At least let me clean you up a bit.' I head for the first-aid kit. 'I have some antiseptic wipes and cream I can use.'

Once that's done, he tells me to stop fussing. 'I'm fine now, Beth. Where are the kids?'

'In their rooms.'

'Could I nip up and have a word? It's about the surprise I mentioned.'

'Of course.' I scratch my head. 'You still want to go ahead with this surprise thing after what just happened? Please don't feel like you have to for my sake.'

'Oh, but I do.' He disappears upstairs with a wink, carrying the backpack he arrived with in one hand. I almost ask him what's in it, but I guess that might spoil the surprise.

He's up there for a good ten to fifteen minutes. When he returns, it's with a grin on his face.

'Not quite there yet,' he says. 'Another twenty minutes or so, I reckon. Then I need you to trust me. I'll be nipping out first with both the kids while you sit tight here and await my instructions.'

'What? But it's Friday night and time's getting on. Daisy needs a shower or bath soon. Where are you taking them?'

'If I told you that, it wouldn't be a surprise. Listen, Beth, you need to trust me, please. If you don't, you're going to ruin all my hard work. You wouldn't believe how long I've been planning this. Seriously, it's going to blow your mind. I can't wait to see the look on your face.'

He's so enthusiastic. I can't believe he's put in this much effort. No one's done anything like this for me in ages. Rory and Sean once teamed up to throw me a surprise birthday party, years back. It wasn't even a traditionally big birthday. Was it my twenty-third or twenty-fourth? Something like that. It was lovely, anyway. Made me feel really special. And now, all these years later, here I am feeling special again, thanks to another brother. The one I didn't know I had until recently.

'When you put it like that, how can I say no?'

'Excellent.'

Despite the enthusiasm, something about Billy this evening seems odd. It's probably down to his run-in with those thugs earlier. Or maybe he's just distracted by planning the surprise.

'Are you sure you're all right?' I ask him. 'You're definitely up to this?'

'Absolutely,' he replies, with such conviction I think I must be imagining things.

FIFTY-SEVEN

Ethan

Once Billy has gone back downstairs, Ethan opens the beer he gave him. It's some kind of fancy home-brew, Billy said, explaining the unbranded glass bottle and swing-top lid. He was apparently given several bottles as a thank-you gift from one of his work clients.

'Get it down you before we head out,' Billy told him. 'It'll give you a nice buzz. But as usual, don't tell your mum or I'll be in big trouble.'

'What are we doing again?'

'You and Daisy are coming with me in the car first so we can get everything in place to surprise your mum.'

'Yeah, but how exactly are we going to surprise her?'

Billy winked and tapped the side of his nose. 'All in good time, my boy. It'll be great, trust me. Ready in twenty minutes?'

'Sure.'

'Good. Your sister will be ready by then too.'

Alone in his room, Ethan sniffs the beer. It smells weird. Billy said something about it being stronger than regular shop-bought beer. He has a small mouthful and that tastes weird too. It reminds him of something. He can't put his finger on what, but it has definite negative connotations. Enough to make him hesitate.

Something about tonight feels off. It's not only the fact that it's all so hush-hush, whatever Billy is planning, either. He seems different to normal: kind of distracted. Mind you, he *was* jumped on the way over. He's shrugging off the attack, saying he gave as good as he got, but it must be playing on his mind. The injuries to his face and hands look sore. That'll be it. That'll be all Ethan's sensing. The rest will be paranoia. He's felt that way a lot since London.

He walks through to Daisy's bedroom, where she's colouring on the floor, surrounded by an array of crayons and pieces of paper. 'All right?'

She smiles. 'Hi, Ethan. Are you excited? I am.'

'For what?'

'Mum's surprise. Uncle Billy says it's going to be amazing.'

Ethan notices an empty plastic bottle next to her on the floor. 'What's that you've been drinking?'

'Oh, chocolate milk, from Uncle Billy,' she says. 'It was the yummiest ever. I couldn't stop drinking it. Look: it's given me a brown tongue.' She sticks it out as proof.

'Right,' Ethan says. 'Do you know where he's taking us; what we're doing?'

'Of course not, silly. It's a surprise.'

'Yeah, for Mum, not us.'

Daisy shrugs. 'Dunno. I bet it will be fantastic. Uncle Billy is the best.'

Ethan nips to the toilet before returning to his own room, where he has another sniff and small taste of the beer, which is no better than before. What *does* it remind him of? It's not good, whatever it is. He puts the cap back on and tucks the bottle under his pillow. Maybe he'll be more in the mood for it when he gets back.

'Ethan? Daisy Chain? Are you nearly ready to go?'

Billy's calling them from downstairs.

Daisy quickly replies that she's coming.

'Two minutes,' Ethan calls back. He's confused that he's allowed out on a Friday night, considering he's grounded. This appears to have been forgotten in the excitement of Billy's mysterious surprise. Ethan's not complaining; he certainly won't be the one to bring it up with his mother.

Once the three of them are in the car – Mum left behind, bemused – Billy asks: 'Did you both enjoy your drinks?'

'Mine was yummy,' Daisy says from the back seat.

Ethan, who's up front with his uncle, lies. 'Yeah, mine was very nice too, thanks.'

'Did you have chocolate milk too?' Daisy asks.

Billy throws him a discreet wink.

'Strawberry milk, actually,' Ethan says.

'Yuck.' She yawns. 'I'm tired.'

'Have a snooze,' Billy says. 'I'll wake you up when the time's right.'

'Are you going to tell me where we're going now?' Ethan asks as Billy reverses Mum's Fiesta off the drive.

'Patience. All in good time. Feel free to have a snooze yourself.'

Ethan raises an eyebrow. 'I'm not tired.'

'Really? You look shattered.'

'Well, I'm not.'

'Okay.'

'Hey,' Ethan says. 'Wasn't that Dad's car we passed? Why's it parked at the end of our road?'

Billy coughs before replying: 'No, it was just a similar model, I think.'

'I guess.' Ethan texts his dad a minute or two later, regardless. It was definitely his father's number plate.

Why's your car on our street, Dad? We're not home, in case you're planning to call by. Billy's arranged some surprise for Mum.

'What are you up to?' Billy asks, looking across at him.

'Messaging Liam. He owes me a fiver.'

Ethan turns around to see how his sister's doing. She's already fast asleep with her mouth wide open.

'She'll be snoring next,' Billy says.

Ethan laughs, but it's not genuine. He has a bad feeling in the pit of his stomach: a growing sense that something's definitely not right. He looks at his phone screen again, careful to keep it out of his uncle's view without looking suspicious. No, Dad hasn't read his message yet.

There's a thought gnawing away at the back of his mind that Ethan can't quite bring into focus. He racks his brains trying to get to the bottom of it as Billy starts talking again. 'So, tell me. What did you think of that beer I sneaked in for you? Good, yeah? Has it made you a bit tipsy? I'm not sure how strong it is, but it's definitely got some kick to it, right?'

'Yeah, it was great. Quite different to the beers I've had before. Not that I've had many.'

Suddenly it dawns on him.

The penny drops.

He can't believe he didn't realise sooner what was right in front of him.

The 'home-brew' beer from Billy.

What he didn't like about it.

There was something funny about the smell and taste. Something familiar – and not in a good way.

Now he knows exactly what that was.

It reminded him of the bottles of flavoured water Red Coat gave him and Liam in London last Saturday; the ones that knocked them both out. Fast asleep, like his sister is in the back of this car, having also been given a drink by Billy.

What the hell?

If he's right, what does that even mean?

Why would their own uncle drug them before taking them out on a Friday night to some unknown, mysterious location?

He must have it wrong. Surely. It makes no sense.

He can absolutely trust Billy.

Can't he?

'Everything all right, mate?' Billy pulls the car up at a set of traffic lights. 'You're quiet.'

Ethan fakes a yawn. 'You know what? I am pretty tired all of a sudden. Maybe I will rest my eyes for a few minutes.'

Billy nods. 'Of course. No shame in that, buddy. I'm sure you've had a busy week. Don't fight it. I'll wake you when we get there.'

Ethan squeezes his eyes shut, leans back into his seat and does his best impression of someone nodding off.

Meanwhile, his mind is in overdrive.

FIFTY-EIGHT

Beth

The house is eerily quiet after Billy and the children have left in my car. I have no idea where he's taken them; what comes next.

I feel excited and a little nervous.

What does Billy have in store for me? I really don't have a clue.

It's too late for a surprise party, surely. So what, then? It can't even be a fancy meal, since we've all eaten.

'Sit tight,' he told me as they left. 'It won't be long. Someone's coming for you soon.'

'Am I wearing the right clothes?' I asked. 'Do I need to dress up? Down? I'm totally confused. And who is it that's coming for me?'

'You're fine as you are. I can't tell you who's coming without ruining the surprise, but relax: it's someone you know.'

'What? Like who?'

'Patience. Now I have to go. See you soon.'

Waiting in the hallway, sitting on the bottom of the stairs, already in my coat and shoes, I decide it must be Rory that's coming for me. It doesn't make much sense, considering he and Billy don't get on. But who else is there?

I peek out of the window every couple of minutes. Eventually, to my surprise, a large black Mercedes pulls up in front of the drive, which blows my Rory theory out of the water. Unless it's a hire car.

In fact, it looks to be chauffeur-driven, as a youngish chap in a smart black suit, matching hat and gloves steps out of the driver's door and walks towards the house.

'Good evening, madam,' he says as I answer the front door, cursing Billy for not advising me to smarten myself up. And so much for this being a person I know. What was that: deliberate misdirection?

'Hello,' I say. 'Are you sure you have the right address?'

He pulls a small card out of his inside pocket and reads out my name and address. 'Is that correct?'

'Yes. Could you tell me where you're supposed to be taking me?'

'I'm afraid my instructions are not to divulge that information, madam. Is that, er, going to be a problem?'

I sigh, rolling my eyes. 'No, no. All part of the fun, right?'

I exit the house and lock the door before following the chauffeur to his vehicle, which has tinted privacy glass on the rear windows. That combined with the way he opens the door for me, revealing the plush beige leather interior, makes me feel like a celebrity. I'm impressed so far. If the rest of what Billy has planned is of a similar standard, I should be in for a proper pampering.

Once I've buckled up, the car glides down the street, faint classical music playing in the background.

We drive for a few minutes, then the chauffeur says: 'We'll be stopping in a moment for a quick pickup.'

'Right,' I say, too busy pondering Billy's plans to give it any real thought.

The next minute, the car pulls in to the side of the road; the opposite rear door opens and a man I don't recognise gets in, giving me a minor heart attack. Who the hell's this? Is this some sort of budget chauffeur-driven car service where you share the ride with other passengers? Way to ruin a luxury experience.

The man looks around my age, maybe a little older, wearing a navy wool overcoat with a black scarf and leather gloves; he's bald, with pockmarked skin, chewing gum. To my dismay, he smells strongly of cigarettes.

'Evening,' he says.

'Sir,' the driver replies.

'Sorry for barging in on your ride,' he tells me, throwing a brief smile in my direction.

I nod, too perplexed to reply, before shifting my gaze away from him and out of the window.

The car pulls away again and heads in the direction of the motorway. Is that where we're going? I was expecting somewhere local.

'Excuse me,' I say, leaning forward towards the chauffeur. 'How long's the journey likely to take?'

'Oh, don't worry, not too long,' my fellow passenger replies, still reeking of smoke.

'Sorry,' I say, avoiding eye contact. 'It was the, er, driver I was asking.'

'I know,' the man next to me answers. 'But he works for me.'

'Sorry? I'm, er...'

'No need to keep apologising. Not for this, anyway. You must be confused.'

I look at him at last. 'Yes, I am. Is there something I'm missing? Are we sharing a lift here, or—'

'Oh, I'm coming with you, Beth. All the way. I had hoped you'd recognise me – I can't lie. It has been a long time, though. You look a lot older now. I'm not sure my nickname for you is apt any longer.'

I freeze.

Daren't breathe.

Stare straight forward, terrified.

Who the hell is sitting next to me?

He knows me, so why don't I recognise him?

Or do I?

Then he says two words that chill me to my core: 'Bubble Butt.'

Only one person has ever called me that, and the last time I heard him do so was nearly twenty years ago, minutes before I watched my father get stabbed to death.

'Mac,' I whisper. Saying that name makes my lips feel dirty.

'Oh, don't you know it, baby girl,' he says. 'Have you missed me? Because let me tell you, I've been dying for this reunion.'

Desperate to get away from him, I try my door handle, even though the car is moving, but it doesn't work. The same goes for the electric window, much to my frustration.

'Yeah, we already thought of that, I'm afraid,' Mac says.

I don't want to look at him, but at the same time, I can't stop myself. Armed with the knowledge of his identity, I can now just about recognise the teenage boy I once had the misfortune to know. He turns my stomach even more today than he did back then.

I want to start shouting and screaming – to try to alert someone to my plight – but as the car turns onto the motorway, I talk myself out of it. If I kick off here, I'm likely to cause an accident, which I can't afford to do. I have to think of my children. The last thing I want is for them to have to grow up without a mother.

It's only at this point that I have time to put two and two together. Mac's appearance must be somehow linked to Billy and his surprise for me. I'd love to believe that he has nothing to do with this and Mac has merely hijacked whatever transport

Billy arranged. But equally, I'm not an idiot. Mac has to be the 'someone' Billy was talking about. Shit.

I try telling myself that Mac must have tricked him into believing we were old friends; that Billy would never have set me up like this. I desperately want to give him the benefit of the doubt. But it's a tough theory to swallow, especially in light of the weird way Billy suddenly appeared in my life.

I can't think about that now. Billy has my children. It's too much to process without losing my mind. If I'm to stand any chance of getting myself and my family through this – whatever the hell *this* is – I need to focus on the situation at hand.

'What's going on?' I ask Mac in the calmest voice I can muster. 'What is it you want? You, your brother and your cousin took my father from me all those years ago. Wasn't that enough?'

'We all served our time for what happened that day. Unfortunately, we didn't all make it home.'

'This is about *him*?' I avoid saying the name of my father's killer out loud. 'I heard he died in prison.'

'Thanks to you.'

'Sorry?'

'If it wasn't for you and your bloody campaign to block his release, Lenny would have been out of there before he was attacked. My brother would be living his life now.'

I want to say I'm glad he isn't – that he deserved to die – but I stop myself.

'Why did you have to get involved?' Mac continues. 'Why couldn't you leave it alone?'

'Because he killed my father, for no good reason, right in front of me and my brother. He didn't deserve to be released after what he did; the lifelong pain he inflicted on my family.'

'It was a fight. Your dad gave as good as he got. If he'd been the one to get his hands on the knife first—'

'He'd have never used it. Not in a million years. Don't start up with the whole self-defence thing again. It didn't work in court and it won't work on me, ever. Your brother was found guilty of murder, because that's what it was. He took my dad's life, and as far as I'm concerned, it was only right that he spent the rest of his own life behind bars.'

'I'm afraid I strongly disagree with that,' Mac says. 'And I'm not the only one.'

'Where are you taking me? Where are my children?'

'Ah yes,' he says with a creepy smile. 'Ethan and the lovely Daisy. They're on their way to the same place we're heading: your surprise. You think I'm going to ruin that now? You don't have to be patient for much longer. We'll be there in no time, and then it'll be all fun and games.'

I must raise the alarm somehow. My phone. I need to use it without him knowing, so I can call for help.

Maybe I can discreetly send a text message to Rory, telling him to call the police.

Or perhaps I should dial 999 whenever I can and scream. Even if the call gets cut off, that might be enough for them to trace me.

As if he can read my mind, Mac asks the driver: 'Have you got her phone yet?'

'Yes, sir,' he replies, to my shock. 'I swiped it when I picked her up; turned it off straight away.'

My hand automatically travels to the pocket I put it in, and sure enough, it's gone. Dammit.

Mac chuckles, the creepy sound reminding me of what he was like as a pervy teenager.

I want to scream.

FIFTY-NINE

Billy

He pulls Beth's car into the small dark, deserted car park and turns off the lights and engine.

Here at last, after all this time. All this planning.

He's wanted revenge for so long. Finally, it's within touching distance.

There would have been far quicker, easier ways to punish Beth, of course, but they wouldn't have been anywhere near as satisfying or effective. That's what this whole exercise has been about: from the early observation stages, via gaining everyone's trust, through to now. He wanted to give Beth hope, in the form of an all-singing, all-dancing new brother, so that he could then tear that away from her and leave her shattered into tiny little pieces.

Why? Because that's exactly what happened to him, thanks to Beth's unwanted interference and lies.

Hope, like trust, isn't something you can create out of nowhere. It needs time to grow. And that's what he's been doing these past several weeks: weaving himself into Beth and her family's lives. Gradually getting them all to trust and rely on him. Well, all bar one, but that's been dealt with now.

Time to bring it all tumbling down like the house of cards he always knew it was. Tricking them into thinking otherwise – believing the crap he's fed them – has been his greatest achievement so far. An acting performance like no other.

He looks across at Ethan, and then into the back at Daisy. Both zonked out. Perfect.

Ethan had him worried earlier. Despite saying he'd drunk the beer, he didn't appear tired when they first set off. Billy feared he'd messed up the dose, but then, to his considerable relief, it finally kicked in, knocking the boy out as intended.

As his eyes adapt to the dark, he can make out more and more of the secluded spot to which he's brought Ethan and Daisy, his supposed nephew and niece. Swings, slide, climbing frame, roundabout. Where else, other than a playground? What better place to torment Beth than one she fears and avoids at all costs?

The tricky thing was finding a playground where they wouldn't be disturbed.

Ideally, he'd have taken her back to the one where her father died, near where she used to live. But that would have been too risky, bearing in mind the public nature of the spot, a popular evening haunt for teenagers. The same applies to their current local playground, where Billy made his first move by seizing the opportunity to rescue Daisy. What a stroke of luck that was, to be in the right place at the right time. It couldn't have worked out better if he'd planted the mutt and the young morons there himself.

Finding this location, where there is little to no chance of them getting interrupted tonight, was another stroke of luck. He came across it while watching some urban explorer videos online. Less than a twenty-minute drive along the motorway, it's part of an abandoned television set in a field in the middle of nowhere.

He mentioned it to Mac, with whom he had stayed in occasional phone contact while 'undercover', and Mac came to check it out. After making enquiries with the right people, via an old contact, a sum of cash got them access for the night, no questions asked and no security cameras operational.

As far as he can tell from inside the car, the playground looks to be in a decent state, despite sitting unused for however long. It backs onto a small row of terraced houses, which he assumes to be hollow shells, once used for the purposes of outside filming. There's even a mock corner shop. Driving in, they also passed the fake frontages of a small supermarket, a factory and a petrol station. Not that either of the kids will have noticed, being too busy sleeping.

It's all a bit creepy. Ideal.

He's exhilarated ahead of Beth's arrival. What will she make of the real Billy when she finally meets him? Playing the nice guy has been exhausting. She'll already be in the car by now. Her face when Mac appeared must have been a picture. What's she thinking at this moment? Does she have any idea yet what's coming?

Mac did promise not to give much away before they got here. Billy wants to be the one to explain the hows and whys. Fingers crossed Mac stays true to his word, although he does get carried away when he's excited.

And what could be more exciting than a chance to exact revenge at last?

It's finally time for the bitch to pay.

SIXTY

Beth

I have no idea where we are. It's hard to keep track of directions from the rear of a car when you're being driven at night, especially when your head is all over the place and you're terrified what the future might hold.

A few minutes ago, we turned off the motorway into an area with barely any street lights: somewhere rural at a guess.

Eventually the car pulls into what I first think is a village. It can't be, though, as it's totally dark and deserted, like an eerie ghost town. Plus, the layout makes no sense. Rather than the usual cohesive mix of residential properties and businesses, it's an illogical hotchpotch.

'Where are we?' I ask Mac.

He throws his head back and laughs. 'I thought this place would confuse you. Great, isn't it? Like something from a zombie movie. I could just picture a herd of walkers shuffling around that corner by the petrol station.'

'Where is it? What are we doing here?'

'I could tell you,' he replies, in between chewing gum. 'But it's more fun not to. I'm enjoying that look of raw confusion on your face.'

They drive a little further and then stop in a small car park. Beth sees her Fiesta already there – stationary and, as far as she can tell, empty. The sight fills her with momentary relief, knowing Ethan and Daisy must be close, but it quickly turns to dread.

Mac leans forward to speak to the driver. 'No need for you to hang around. We'll be some time. Go for a drive. Keep your phone on. I'll call when I need you back.'

'Of course, sir. Would you like me to keep her phone, or...'

'No, give that to me.'

The driver opens the glovebox and hands my phone to Mac, who slips it into the inside pocket of his coat before winking at me. Bastard.

Then he reaches into another coat pocket and pulls out a handgun, which he points at my head. 'You're going to do exactly as I tell you. Got it?'

I'm too shocked to answer. What is he nowadays: some kind of gangster? I have no idea what happened to him – what he's been up to – in the years since serving his custodial sentence. I don't even know whether he still lives in the area where we grew up. I've had no inclination to find out, hoping never to see him again. He may not have been the one to kill my father, but he was complicit in the act. He restrained me while they were fighting. He ran off with Lenny and Sam afterwards. He did nothing to save Dad.

'Did you hear me?' he asks, waving the gun even closer to my face. 'Do you understand? This is loaded. I'd have no hesitation in using it.'

A nod is all I can manage.

'Good. Now get out.'

I'm about to say I can't – that the door is locked – but the driver is already outside, opening it.

I do what Mac says and he shuffles across the seat after me, gun still in hand.

What's he afraid of: that I'll hit him, or run off somewhere?

Right now, all I want to know is where my kids are and if they're okay.

Outside in the dark, I scan all around for them, but I can barely see or hear anything.

'Let me guess,' Mac says as the Mercedes drives away. 'You're wondering where those children of yours might be.' He nods to our left. 'Walk over that way.'

It only takes a few strides through the car park for me to see where he's leading me, and as soon as I do, I gasp and freeze.

It's a small playground. Billy's standing in the middle of it, my two children lying lifeless at his feet.

'What have you done?' I cry.

Billy laughs in a way I've never heard him laugh before. It's a nasty sound that grates on my ears.

'Why don't you come over here and have a look, *sis*?' The way he says that last word, it's like a taunt.

My feet are glued to the spot. I'm literally petrified. It's happening again. I'm going to lose another person I love in a playground. It's like all my nightmares have merged into one and burst into real life with a vengeance.

Why are Ethan and Daisy on the ground? Are they unconscious? What has he done to them?

'I see you picked up the gun okay,' Billy says to Mac.

'I did. Your instructions to find it weren't bad. It's firmly trained on this one's head. I'm not taking any chances. You could have cleaned it, though. I guess that was her husband's blood I had to wipe off. Rory, right? Looks like you had some fun with him.'

What's he talking about? Surely that can't be true. Can it? I need to stay strong. But the tears come anyway, trickling down my cheeks.

'What have you done, Billy?' I ask. 'What is all this? Why would you—'

'What? Pretend to be your brother? Kidnap your children? Lure you to this remote playground, like something out of one of the bad dreams you love to whine about having? Attack Rory? Where do you want me to start, Beth?'

'Are my children still alive?'

'I think they're still breathing,' he replies. 'Come and see for yourself. What are you most afraid of: me or the playground?'

It dawns on me that the minor wounds I treated earlier on his face and hands weren't really from being jumped by yobs. I want to throw up. 'Is Rory still alive?'

Billy gives a dramatic shrug. 'Honestly, who cares about him? I'd been dying to give him a good thumping ever since I met him. I'd focus on your kids, if I were you.'

'Move, bitch,' Mac says from behind me. I feel him press the gun, which I now know may have been used to kill my husband, into the middle of my back. I have no choice but to continue forward. As we draw close to the playground, my heart is thumping in my chest. I slow down until I'm barely moving.

'Why are you stopping?' Mac asks. 'Do you want me to shoot you? It would be my pleasure, honestly.'

I draw to a halt at the edge of the walled playground, in front of the open gate. 'I... I can't do it. I can't go inside. I haven't been able to since—'

'Yeah, yeah,' Mac says. 'Spare me the sob story. Billy's already told me. I wasn't interested then and I'm even less bothered now.' I feel him remove the gun from my back, and from the corner of my eye, I see that he's pointing it at Daisy instead. 'How's this for motivation? Walk inside, bitch, or I'll shoot the little one.'

'No! Leave her alone. Leave both of them alone. Do what you like to me, but spare my children. Please, Mac. Billy, tell him.'

Billy laughs. 'Tell him what, Beth? I'm not on your side. Haven't you realised that yet? Are you a bit slow? Should I spell things out for you? Okay, spoiler alert: I'm not really your brother either. Surprise! I can't believe how easily I got you to swallow that garbage. Is it because I've got a beard a bit like your poor dead daddy's? Nice suggestion of yours for me to grow it, Mac. But I can't wait to shave it off. Too damn itchy.'

Mac, still pointing the gun at Daisy, says: 'Last warning. Walk through that gate right now or I'll put a bullet in your daughter's head.'

My brain is at war with itself. I know I have to do what that monster Mac says, for Daisy's sake, but at the same time my circuits have been hard-wired to stop me ever entering a playground again. The mere suggestion of it floods me with fear. The feeling pulsing through my body as I try to force it forward is like that of two strong magnets being pushed together. I desperately try to step inside the playground.

But

I

just

can't

do it.

'Oh, bloody hell,' Mac says. 'Screw this.'

A hefty shove from behind sends me sprawling forward against my will. Through the gate. Onto my hands and knees on the soft, springy surface of the playground.

I'm gasping for breath.

The world's spinning all around me.

I'm gasping for breath.

I can't move.

I can't think as they laugh and jeer at me, ready to do their worst.

I'm overpowered. Helpless. Terrified of what comes next.

'Please, no,' I whimper, still floored and lacking the strength or courage to get back up. 'Please don't do this.'

But as these desperate words leave my trembling lips, to further jeers, I accept they'll make no difference. There is no sympathy here. Only hate.

I can't let this happen. I can't.

I must find a way to stop them before it's too late.

My eyes focus on Ethan's inert form, mere metres away from me by Billy's feet, and for the briefest of moments, I swear his eyes flicker open and he looks straight at me; stares into my soul.

Pull yourself together, Mum, he seems to say. *Save us.*

And even though I'm not wholly sure this really happened, something clicks. It's enough to jolt me out of my brain spasm, allowing me to take control again.

It's just a playground. A voice from the past bravely echoes through the halls of my head. *It's only a place. You mustn't fear it any longer. Focus on the real threats: Billy and Mac. Your children need you. You may be the only parent they have left. Do what you must. Save them.*

Although I don't give my enemies any sign whatsoever that something inside me has changed, hardened, *I* know it has. And that's enough for now. Inspired by the power of my love for my kids, I've unlocked a fearless part of myself I barely even recognise any longer, it's been gone so long. That's the single weapon I have at my disposal to help me stop these deranged thugs.

So I need to use it.

SIXTY-ONE

'Why, Billy?' I ask, still on my hands and knees, just inside the entrance of the playground. 'Why would you do this? Why would you pretend to be my friend, then my brother? Why would you act like an uncle to my children; let us welcome you into our family, only to turn on us so brutally, working in cahoots with a man like Mac? You know he was there when my dad was killed, right? He held me back while his brother stabbed him. Then he helped him escape. How do you even know a scumbag like that?'

I feel a sudden sharp pain as Mac kicks me in my side. It makes me yelp, but after that, I grit my teeth and try to swallow it down. I don't want to give him the satisfaction of knowing how much it hurts.

'That's for calling me a scumbag,' he says.

'What else would you call a man who kicks a defenceless woman when she's already on the ground?' I throw Billy a pleading look, but the man who stares back at me with an ice-cold glare is like a different person from the one I thought I knew.

'Mac is the closest thing I have to a father, thanks to you,' Billy says. 'He's my uncle. Lenny was my dad.'

'What?' I'm struggling to comprehend his words. They can't be true, can they? I've never heard anything about Lenny having a son. He was only twenty-two when he killed my father, nineteen years ago last summer, and he spent the rest of his life behind bars. Mind you, I was quite a bit younger than that when I had Ethan, so his age back then is irrelevant. Or is it? Billy is thirty, right? So how does that work? Yet another lie?

Billy sighs. 'You're doing the calculations in your head, but they don't add up, right? Let me save you the bother. I'm not really thirty. I made that up at the beginning, before I told you the crap about being your half-brother, so you wouldn't think I was too young to be a potential boyfriend. What can I say? The stupid beard adds a few years. Plus Dad was young when he got Mum pregnant. Just a kid really. Way before you knew him.'

'And the bit about your mother dying of cancer? Was that also—'

'That was true.' Billy's face softens, only to harden again a second later. 'If it wasn't for you, I'd still have one parent at least. Now I have none.'

'I genuinely don't understand,' I say. 'Why do you blame me for your father's death? I didn't kill him. I had nothing to do with it. How can you think otherwise? He was the killer, not me.'

'Shut it,' Mac says, still hovering over me. 'And get yourself up off the ground.'

'I, er, don't know if—'

He presses the barrel of the gun against my temple. 'Now, bitch.'

As he hauls me to my feet, an intense feeling of revulsion surges through my body. If I wasn't trying to hide the level of my defiance, I'd bark at him to keep his filthy hands off me.

However, I must sustain the illusion that I'm broken, having been forced against my will into this playground.

In truth, now that I'm here – now that I've broken the mental barrier that's kept me out of playgrounds all these years – I can see they're just places like any other. I can't believe it's taken me nearly two decades and a gun pointed at my daughter to reach this point. But I know now that what happened to my father was never about a place. It was about people. One evil psycho in particular, whose legacy continues to threaten me and my family to this day. This moment.

Mac walks me forward so I'm standing opposite Billy in the empty centre of the playground: swings immediately to my left, slide to my right. Ethan and Daisy lie on the ground between us. They're within touching distance, both apparently unconscious. I want to kneel down and tend to them, but I daren't. Did I actually imagine Ethan opening his eyes and looking at me before? It's hard to know what's real and what isn't in this freakish, terrifying situation.

Mac steps to one side while keeping the gun trained on me.

'What's wrong with them?' I ask, a lump in my throat and tears pricking my eyes. 'Why are they—'

'I drugged them, that's all,' Billy says.

'That's all? What the hell with? When will they—'

'Quiet,' he snaps. 'I am *so* done with listening to you. Thank God I don't have to pretend I care any more. You asked why I blame you for my dad's death. Are you serious? How can you not see the role you played? He'd come such a long way over the years. He was a reformed character by the time he was finally up for release. He was nothing like the angry, impulsive person who fought with your dad.'

'Who stabbed my dad to death, you mean.'

'He didn't mean to kill him. It was self-defence. If he didn't grab the knife, your dad would have.'

'Really? That's what he told you, I guess. Well, it wasn't the verdict in court, was it? And rightly so. I was there when it happened, don't forget. A fourteen-year-old girl. I saw how Lenny stabbed him: twice, without hesitation, using his own knife, which he'd earlier handed to Sam because of a fight they were planning. Angry and impulsive doesn't cover what he was back then. Yes, they were brawling. My dad was protecting me. But Lenny's life was never in danger. He had Mac and Sam by his side.'

Billy sneers.

How can I compete with years of brainwashing by his father and uncle?

'Whatever you think happened,' he says, 'my dad changed a great deal during his time behind bars. He found religion, saw the error of his ways. He wanted to meet with you to beg for your forgiveness, but you refused. Said you never wanted anything to do with him. Wouldn't even receive a letter. Then, after serving his time, when he was finally eligible for release, you and your bloody campaign with the press put a stop to it. You took away his hope – mine too, of finally having a normal life with a father out of prison – and that's what drove him to drugs. It was all downhill from there. Only a matter of time until he got himself into trouble with one of the gangs. Then, like that, he was gone – taken out by some other desperate junkie. I think it was what he wanted, one way or another. He couldn't hack it inside any longer. He escaped the only way he could. And yes, I blame you for that. You may as well have killed him with your own hands, you heartless whore.'

'I don't know what to say,' I tell him.

'That makes a change.'

'I'm sorry that you—'

'Honestly, I don't want to hear it. I want to make you pay.'

'Hear, hear,' Mac says, clapping. The gall of the man.

'If your father truly reformed, Billy, as you claim, would he have wanted any of this? What would he say if he saw you now?'

'Yeah, whatever. Where did any of that crap get him? It made him weak.' Billy rubs his bearded chin. 'Anyway, listen. I have a question for *you*, Beth. What kind of person do you think carries a knife?'

'An idiot. A mindless thug looking for trouble.'

He reaches into his trouser pocket and, to my alarm, pulls out a wooden-handled pocket knife, which he unfolds to reveal a substantial blade.

'You'll never guess where I got this from.' He leaves a dramatic pause, making a tutting sound before going on: 'I found it stashed under your precious son's bed. Ethan keeps it in the same place he stores his vape. Surprise. It wasn't hard to find. Lucky that Daisy never got her hands on it. She could have really hurt herself. Oh, I helped myself to an envelope of cash hidden there too, which was an unexpected find. Looks like you don't know your son as well as you think you do, Beth. It seems he's been keeping rather a lot from you.'

I glance down at my son to see if there's any further hint of him being secretly conscious, but his eyes remain firmly closed and his body still. I'm so confused.

What's all this about him having a knife, a vape and secret cash? Is Billy messing with me or telling the truth? At this point, I have zero clue.

Hiding a vape isn't great, but that's what an awful lot of teenagers are doing these days, right? I'd rather that than smoking or drugs. I have no idea where an envelope of cash would have come from or what that might mean. As for him owning this knife, if it's true, I'll be devastated.

The mere idea of him carrying that thing in his pocket terrifies me almost as much as being here now, at gunpoint. I should have told him the truth about what happened to his grandfather. I should have further emphasised how strongly I feel about

knives and how incredibly dangerous and stupid it is to carry
one. Foolishly, perhaps, I thought he was still too young for that
to be an issue. If he knew about Dad, what I had to witness at
his age, surely he wouldn't go anywhere near a knife.

Slow down, I tell myself. You don't even know that it's true.
Pretty much everything else Billy has said so far has been a lie,
so why should I believe this?

I don't want to, and yet a nagging feeling in my gut tells me
that it probably *is* true. Ethan having a secret place to hide a
knife and a vape would make sense in light of how furtive he's
been lately. Why didn't I go looking in his room, under his bed?
I considered doing so on several occasions, but ultimately I held
back, choosing to give him the benefit of the doubt.

'Nothing to say?' Billy asks, holding the knife aloft, a
menacing look on his face.

'What do you want from me and my family, Billy?' I ask.
'And what the hell have you done to poor Rory?'

'Poor Rory?' Billy rolls his eyes at Mac. 'She can barely look
at the guy since he cheated on her. She told me countless times
how she'd moved on, but he wouldn't get the hint and leave her
alone. Now that I've shown him who's boss, he's "poor Rory".
What a crock of shit.'

'I told you what she's like,' Mac says. 'She's always been a
self-serving, prick-tease slut.'

I shake my head in despair.

'To be clear,' Billy continues, 'I want you to suffer, Beth. As
much as possible. I want you to pay for what you did to my
father. What you took away from him. And what you took away
from me. I also want you to admit that you lied as part of your
campaign with the press to keep him from his freedom.'

'Lied?'

'Oh, don't play dumb. You know what I'm talking about:
your claims that he harassed you from jail.'

'All I told the reporters was the truth: that he tried to

contact me, in writing and by requesting a meeting, when I had no desire to ever see or hear from him again. The rest was their interpretation.'

'Which you didn't dispute,' Billy yells. 'Bloody hell! He was trying to apologise to you.'

'So you say. I didn't have a clue what he wanted. I wasn't interested in hearing anything from the man I'd watched kill my dad. Dammit, Billy. What's this all about? Please let Ethan and Daisy go. This has nothing to do with them. They're children. How could anyone want to harm them? Especially you. You know them. They adore you – or at least the man you pretended to be.'

'Shut your mouth,' Billy says. 'I feel nothing but hatred for any of you. I want you to suffer like my father did. Like I'm suffering without him. I want you to pay.'

'You don't think I've suffered enough? Thanks to your father, I grew up without mine. I'm haunted to this day by the memory of seeing him killed. My kids have never known their grandfather.'

'Oh, here we go again,' Billy snaps. 'Heard it all before. Yawn. Enough. You really want to know why we're here? Fine, I'll tell you. One of your children is going to die tonight. I'm going to slit their throat with this knife. Your job is easy: you need to choose which one to save and then watch me kill the other.'

SIXTY-TWO

Ethan

He's not sure how long he can keep up the pretence of being unconscious. He's surprised he's got away with it for this long.

The hardest bit was when Billy carried him out of the car into this weird deserted playground, of which he's only had a brief glimpse. He tried to stay loose-limbed in the process, even while Billy reached into his pocket to take his phone. Luckily, that approach seemed to work. Since then, other than the odd sneaky glimpse through his lashes, he's fought to keep his eyes firmly closed. Only once did he take the risk of fully opening them, for the briefest of moments, and that was for his mum's benefit: to try to give her some hope as they forced her against her will into the playground, knowing how painful that must have been.

When the man with the gun – Mac – kicked her, it was all Ethan could do not to spring to her defence. Somehow, he stopped himself, knowing that his being conscious was too important a secret to throw away in anger. He needs to bide his time in order to maximise this advantage, which might be the only chance they have to wrong-foot Billy and, hopefully, escape his and Mac's clutches.

The mind-blowing things Ethan has heard while lying here on the ground next to his genuinely unconscious sister. His grandad was stabbed to death while his teenage mum watched. What the hell? How did he not know about this? Meanwhile, that scumbag Billy has been lying this whole time; rather than being his long-lost uncle, he's a psycho who now wants to kill him or Daisy. And what about Dad? What on earth has Billy done to *him*? No wonder Dad didn't reply to the earlier message about his car, which Ethan now suspects Billy of stealing after visiting the flat. Please let him be all right.

The fact that Billy found his hiding place, revealing the contents to Mum and stealing his shady wad of cash, would usually be a major concern. Now it pales into insignificance.

This is life or death.

For real.

No games.

Soon he'll have to make his move.

And there's no room for error.

SIXTY-THREE

Beth

I can't believe what I heard. From Billy's mouth too. The man I initially fell for, then learned to accept as a brother. The man I was starting to love as a welcome addition to the family, who I pictured as a key part of our lives moving forward.

Now he's talking about slitting the throat of one of my children.

Asking me to make the impossible choice of which one he should kill.

How have we ended up here?

How is this actually happening?

My best hope is that he's bluffing. That this is one big, horrible act designed to terrify and break me, rather than what he really intends to do.

However, this is Lenny's son we're talking about, mentored by Mac, his unhinged uncle. He's already drugged Ethan and Daisy. He's brought us to this sinister, isolated spot under cover of night, having previously stalked us and fed us a pack of lies. Hardly the actions of someone well balanced.

'So?' he snarls. 'What are you waiting for? I said choose. Which one is it you want to save?'

'Come on, Billy. Enough is enough. I get that you want to frighten me, but you can't mean this. How could you want to kill an innocent child in cold blood? I know you. I've spent lots of time with you. You're not capable of this.'

'You don't know anything about me, Beth. You saw what I wanted you to see. Mac, could you remind her how serious we are, please?'

Mac walks up to my side and holds the gun right next to my head, so I can feel the cold, hard metal pressing through my hair into my scalp. 'Do what you're told and choose.'

'Or what? You'll kill me instead? Fine, do it. I'd give my life in an instant to save theirs.'

'And let them grow up without parents?' Billy asks. 'Is that what you want for them?'

'What do you think? Dammit, Billy. You've made your point. Stop this now, before it goes too far and someone really gets hurt.'

'It's a bit late for that.' Billy bares his teeth at me in a horrible twisted grin. 'I'd say ask your husband, but... oops. My bad.'

He makes a nodding gesture in Mac's direction. I feel the gun being moved away from my head; there's a whoosh of air in my ear as it comes swinging back, followed by an explosion of pain.

Then nothing.

When I come round, my whole head is thumping with pain and my vision is blurred, swaying all over the place. I've no idea how much time has passed, but I don't think it's too long. I'm in a heap on the floor, my head next to Daisy's trainer-covered feet.

'Welcome back, bitch.' Mac's ugly mug swims into view before me, his ashtray breath in tow.

There's a damp patch on the side of my face; when I wipe at it, my hand comes away red.

'Do you understand how serious we are now?' Billy asks as I try to look at him and struggle to bring the picture into focus. 'That was a taste of what Rory got earlier.'

Shit, my head hurts like hell. Poor Rory. Please let him be all right.

'I asked you a question,' Billy continues.

'Yes,' I croak.

'Yes, what?'

'I understand.'

'Good. Now I'll ask you again. Choose. Which one lives, which one dies? To clarify, if you don't choose, we'll kill them both as you watch.'

'No, please. Anything but this. Billy, I'm begging you.'

'You want me to listen to you, like my father wanted you to listen to him as he apologised? Nope, I don't think so. Choose: Ethan or Daisy. Who do you love the most? Who do you want to save?'

'I... don't. I can't. It's an impossible choice.'

Billy sniggers. 'No shit. That's kind of the point. But you still need to make it, doesn't she, Mac?'

The older man is standing over the two children now, pointing the gun from one to the other. 'Eeny, meeny, miny—'

'Enough,' a new voice calls out from the shadows, startling everyone. 'Stop this madness now.'

A dark figure appears at the edge of the playground and slowly steps towards us, holding a stick-like weapon in one hand.

'What the hell are you doing here?' Mac spits. 'I thought you didn't want anything to do with this.'

'I don't,' the stranger replies, continuing forward until I can finally make out his face. The years have taken their toll, but I recognise him nonetheless. It's Sam, Mac and Lenny's cousin; Dean's school friend. The boy who dropped Lenny's knife within his reach, enabling him to kill my father. Now a thirty-something man. 'That's why I'm here. To put a stop to it. Beth? Are you all right?'

'I think so.' It feels wrong to speak to him when he once almost stabbed my dad in the back. But what am I supposed to do: ignore the only sane man in the vicinity?

'And the kids?'

'I'm not sure. Billy says he drugged them.'

Billy waves the knife in Sam's direction. 'Leave. This isn't your business.'

'Yeah, piss off,' Mac adds, pointing the gun at his cousin.

'I don't know why you're waving that thing around like you're a gangster,' Sam says. 'We both know it's not real.'

'This knife is very real,' Billy says.

'So is this baseball bat.'

The gun's not real? Well, that's a relief, for our sake as well as Rory's. It sure packs a punch, though, when used for clonking someone about the head. I'm still reeling from that blow.

'What do you want, Sam?' Mac asks.

'I want you to leave her and the children alone and get out of here.'

'That's never going to happen,' Billy replies. 'She's going to pay for what she did.'

'What are you on about? Mac, what have you been whispering in his ear? My God, if only I'd found out what the pair of you were up to sooner. I'm so ashamed to be related to you. Beth is a victim in all of this. We should be asking for her forgiveness, not abducting her and her kids; not threatening more senseless killing. A day doesn't go by when I don't regret my part in what happened to her dad. If I hadn't been there – if

I hadn't lost my grip on that knife and dropped it – both men would probably still be alive today.'

Sam's words are still sinking in when, suddenly, everything erupts. It starts with Ethan, who must have been secretly conscious after all. He reaches up and thumps Billy hard in the face, knocking him over and sending his knife skating across the ground in my direction. Meanwhile, Mac rushes Sam, tackling him so they both end up rolling around on a patch of artificial grass near the roundabout.

'Mum,' Ethan shouts. 'Grab the knife.'

I do as he says, fighting to ignore the sense of revulsion I feel as I grip the wooden handle. Then I see Billy pick himself up and dive on my son. They both start throwing punches, thankfully well away from Daisy. But as fast and scrappy as Ethan is, Billy soon gains the upper hand.

'Get off him!' I shout from the depths of my lungs. Next thing I know, I'm standing over the pair of them as they continue to struggle, Ethan, as determined and ferocious as he appears, weakening by the second in the face of Billy's superior weight and strength.

I have a clear view of Billy's back, and without thinking, I raise my knife-holding arm above my head, ready to bring it down with all my might.

Before I can do so, though, there's a loud roar as Mac, momentarily free from Sam's clutches, barrels towards me, head first. He knocks me to one side, and the knife flies out of my hand and disappears into a large, thick bush.

Mac's on top of me, pinning me to the ground, breathing his foul breath in my face. 'You're going to pay, you slag,' he pants, blood and sweat dripping from his sallow, pitted face.

From the corner of my eye, I see a reinvigorated Sam approaching with his baseball bat. 'Please, my son!' I scream. 'Don't let Billy hurt him.'

Sam turns back towards the other two, heeding my plea but

leaving me to the mercy of Mac, who clamps his hands around my throat, spits in my face and starts to choke me. 'You're not leaving here alive,' he growls. 'You don't know how long I've waited to do this.'

And you don't know how long I've waited to do this, I think, spotting a glorious window of opportunity to knee the sadistic prick in the balls and going for it with every ounce of strength I still possess. As he cries out in agony, I feel the power drain from his arms. I smash my forehead upwards, hard, into his nose, which cracks audibly and starts gushing blood. I push him off me and stagger to my feet.

My first thought is for Ethan. But once I'm free of Mac, who I leave curled up in a foetal position, whimpering, I see that my son is safe, thanks to Sam, who's sitting on Billy with the baseball bat pressed against his throat.

'Are you okay, love?' I ask, rushing over to Ethan. He's kneeling, catching his breath.

'Yes,' he puffs. 'What about you? You have blood all over your face.'

'It's not all mine.'

'When he hit you with that gun, I didn't... I thought...'

'I'm fine. What about Daisy?'

We both dash to her side. She's still out for the count but otherwise unharmed and breathing normally.

'Watch over her,' I say.

I walk back to where Sam is still holding Billy down.

'Thank you,' I tell him. 'You—'

'You don't need to thank me for anything, ever,' Sam says. 'I wish I'd got here sooner or been able to warn you beforehand. I've call—'

Billy suddenly twists and flips his body in a way that throws Sam off him, mid-sentence. The pair wrestle for the baseball bat; to my dismay, Billy wins. He slams it at short range into the back of Sam's head, knocking him out cold. Then he shifts his gaze to me and slowly rises to his feet while I back away.

As I put one foot behind the other, I stand on something unexpected, almost twisting my ankle. I look down at the ground and see the heavy metal gun that, fake or not, proved a useful weapon when Mac slammed it into my head earlier.

I reach down, grab it and hurl it towards Billy's head.

The spinning gun seems to fly through the air in slow motion as I hold my breath, hoping and praying it will land on target; knowing that if it doesn't, we're almost certainly screwed. And then – *bam* – it hits him full force right between the eyes, stopping him dead in his tracks. He stands there, stupefied, for a long moment before keeling backwards onto the floor.

Before I can stop him, Ethan races over to check on him, slapping his face before announcing: 'He's out for the count. Nice shot, Mum. Looks like we're the last two standing.'

'What about him?' I nod in the direction of Mac. 'Did I see him move?'

'I'll check.'

'Be careful.'

Ethan takes the baseball bat out of Billy's limp hand and strides purposefully over to Mac. 'This is for my mum and my grandad,' he says, standing over him and raising the bat like he's about to bring it down on his head.

I gasp. 'Ethan, no. You can't.'

But instead of using the bat, he gives Mac another kick between the legs, causing him to howl like a dying wolf.

'I don't think he'll give us any more trouble,' Ethan says, matter-of-fact, as he returns to his sister's side. 'Daisy? Are you all right? Can you hear me? Mum, I think she's waking up.'

As I move to join them, I hear sirens in the distance. Flashing blue lights soon flood the darkness.

'Thank goodness. Did you call the police, Ethan?'

'No, Billy took my phone.'

'Who, then?'

'I did,' Sam wheezes, conscious again. 'Before I got here. I didn't want to take any chances with those two, family or not. They totally lost the plot. Sorry I let Billy get free. I'm an idiot. Are you...'

'We'll live, thanks to you.'

'I didn't even—'

'You gave us the chance we needed. If you hadn't turned up when you did...' I stare into the distance, slowly shaking my head. 'Listen, Sam, I can't forgive or forget the role you played in Dad's death. Not yet. Maybe never. But I suspect we owe you our lives today, and for that you have my immense gratitude and my respect. Thank you.'

'Thank *you*,' he whispers.

SIXTY-FOUR

SEVERAL WEEKS LATER

Ethan

It'll be Christmas in six days' time, but he doesn't feel festive at all. This will be the first one he's ever spent without his father.

There are a few decorations up around the house, but nothing like normal. Not even the usual big tree: the one he and Dad went to the garden centre to choose in previous years. Mum said she couldn't face it; she bought a small potted one from the supermarket instead. He didn't have the heart to argue. He never wants to argue with any of his family again. They mean too much to him. Life's too precious to waste time bickering about small stuff.

At least school has finished now. They broke up at lunchtime today for a fortnight. It's a shame he won't be around to see Liam and his other mates for most of that time, but it'll be easy enough to keep in touch on his mobile, hopefully. There's Cynthia too, a girl from his class who he's been messaging a lot recently. Although he hasn't admitted it to anyone – not even Liam – he totally fancies her and hopes it might develop into something more than friendship.

They got to know each other after Cynthia asked how he was coping in light of everything that had happened. It was common knowledge at that point, following all the news reports. Unlike others, she seemed genuinely concerned, rather than a rubbernecker. Now he finds himself opening up to her about personal things – how he's feeling and stuff – more than he has before with anyone else. She's really supportive.

Secretly, so no one took the piss, they exchanged Christmas gifts at school this morning. He got her a silver necklace with her name on it, which he really hopes she likes; she hasn't opened it yet, as she wants to wait. Since he'll be away, Ethan opened her present just now, here in the privacy of his bedroom. It's a nice bottle of aftershave. A brand he's seen advertised. He really likes the smell, but he hopes it's not a subtle hint that he has BO.

'Ten minutes, you two,' Mum shouts from downstairs. 'Please be ready in time.'

'I will, Mummy,' Daisy replies from her bedroom.

'Me too,' Ethan adds, before tapping a thank-you message into his phone.

Just opened my gift. Absolutely love it. Really nice smell. Thanks so much. X

Cynthia replies immediately.

You're welcome. Not a hint you stink, btw. Lol. Can't wait to open mine. Miss you already. Have a great trip. X

Ethan smiles while replying that he misses her too.

He's shared so much of himself with Cynthia over the past few weeks, it's scary. The one thing he hasn't told her, nor anyone else, is what happened with Connor, culminating in the nightmare trip to London. He daren't mention that to anyone,

ever. He and Liam haven't even discussed it in ages, which
seems the most sensible course of action. They have both seen
Connor a few times since. That was inevitable. But he blanked
them and they did the same.

An adult would no doubt have advised them to go to the
police. But adults don't always know what's best.

Mum has, of course, asked questions about his knife, his
vape and the cash Billy took from him. She was surprisingly
chilled about him vaping, although she advised him not to and
has since drawn his attention to various studies about potential
health dangers. As for the cash, he told her it wasn't that much.
Thankfully, she bought his story that it was the proceeds from
selling an old pair of designer trainers and his previous mobile
to younger kids at school.

The knife, on the other hand, she was mad about, understandably. She wanted to know where he'd got it from and why;
what on earth he was thinking, etc. He told her as much of the
truth as he dared, without risking anyone else getting into trouble. Swore he'd never have one again. Nonetheless, she
continues to send him frequent links to news articles and
websites about knife crime, detailing youngsters who've been
killed and emphasising the severity of punishment for even just
carrying a blade.

They've also talked in detail about the murder of his grandfather. If Ethan had known about that in advance, he would
never have touched a knife. He certainly won't now, to the point
where he's made Liam hand his blade in to the police via an
anonymous amnesty scheme. They already had Ethan's, which
was recovered from the playground after Billy and Mac were
arrested.

The pair are yet to face trial. However, Mum said officers
had privately assured her that neither stood a cat in hell's
chance of getting off, particularly in light of Sam's testimony on

top of hers and Ethan's. Billy and Mac should both be safely behind bars for a long time to come.

'Are you ready?' Mum calls again from downstairs.

'Coming.' Ethan grabs his backpack, turns the light off and heads to Daisy's bedroom. She's trying to stuff one of her soft toys, a large pink rabbit, into her own brightly coloured bag.

'Here, do you need a hand with that?' he offers.

'Yes please.'

A minute later, he follows her down the stairs.

Thank goodness Daisy was unconscious when everything went down, Ethan thinks, not for the first time. She doesn't remember any of it, which is definitely for the best. The one thing she struggles with is Uncle Billy not being around any more, having missed the part where he revealed his terrifying true colours. They've tried to shelter her from the horror of what he did, as far as possible, until she's older. They've told her he's had to go away for a long time; that he was a 'naughty fibber' and never a genuine member of the family.

Daisy bought Billy's act more than anyone, not least because of how he helped her deal with her school bully, which still doesn't make much sense. Why did he bother when he'd already won her trust? Did a part of him really care for her? Was he bullied at school too? Ethan suspects they'll probably never know for sure.

'Right, the taxi's here,' Mum says, taking a deep breath. 'Got everything?'

'Yes,' Daisy says.

'I think so,' Ethan adds. 'You have our passports and stuff, yeah?'

'Of course.' Mum winks at him. 'But thanks for checking, love. You're a great co-pilot. Right, let's go. Canada here we come.'

SIXTY-FIVE

Beth

We're sitting down to a lovely brunch at Mum and Roger's huge house, having arrived here last night.

'How's everyone feeling this morning?' Roger asks. 'Any jet lag?'

'I'm a bit tired,' Ethan says, 'but I slept pretty well. I read that jet lag is worse on the way home.'

'I'm wide awake,' Daisy says. 'Can I play outside soon? I want to make snow angels.'

'Of course.' Mum beams a radiant smile. She and Roger are holding hands at the table. So sweet. 'I've borrowed a special snow suit for you from one of my neighbours. She has a grand-daughter a little older than you, who's about your size. Hopefully it will fit like a glove.'

'Yay,' Daisy replies. 'Do you have a sledge?'

'Hey, come on,' Roger replies, winking at me. 'What do you think? This is Canada. We most definitely do. In fact, we have several. You can choose your favourite. You too, Ethan. You're not too old for sledging, right?'

'Sure.' Ethan looks the most relaxed I've seen him in ages.

When Mum first suggested we should come to stay for Christmas, my instinct was to say no, even though she and Roger wanted to gift us the flights. I thought it might be too much. But now we're here, it feels perfect. It's lovely to be away. I forgot how liberating that can be.

Mum hasn't let me lift a finger so far. She's been really worried about us. It was all I could do to stop her flying back to the UK once she heard what had happened; she's been calling me daily ever since. Honestly, the tight hugs she gave us all at the arrivals gate yesterday. I thought she was going to break some ribs.

I'm pouring maple syrup onto a delicious pancake when my mobile rings. I drag the slider to accept, breaking my own rule of no phones at the table.

'Is that Daddy?' Daisy asks.

'It sure is.' His face appears on my screen. 'Hey, Rory. How are you?'

'I'm good, thank you. How was the flight? How's Canada?'

'Excellent, thanks.'

'It's really snowy, Daddy,' Daisy calls from across the table. 'I'm going outside to make snow angels soon and they have loads of sledges.'

'Wow. That's brilliant.'

'Can I speak to him for a minute?' Ethan asks, so I hand over my phone.

Rory looks tired. You can see that even on a small screen. He is doing well, but he still has a way to go to get back to full health. The scars on his face remain visible, although the doctors say they'll fade with time. That bastard Billy really laid into him, before stealing his car to drive to my place. The police got paramedics out to him quickly after I raised the alarm. He might not have made it otherwise. I well up every time I recall how Billy left him lying alone in his flat, battered and bleeding, barely conscious and unable to move. It makes me sick to my stomach to think how I then tended to the minor wounds Billy had picked up during his attack.

That guy was warped. Pure evil. And I fell for his charms like a sucker as he preyed on my loneliness. I believed every single lie. Welcomed him into my home and my family. Trusted him to take care of my children. It's terrifying what he got away with. Never again will I allow myself to be manipulated like that.

We're all lucky to have escaped with our lives. And Sam's role was key: something I'll never forget. He told me later that he was still in contact with my old boyfriend, Dean, who'd recently moved to Berlin with his German wife and family. He said Dean had never forgiven himself for leaving me in the park on the day Dad was killed; he had permanently cut all ties with Mac and Lenny. He hadn't given up on Sam, though. Dean's friendship and regular visits while Sam was locked up had played a key role in his rehabilitation, apparently, which was nice to hear.

Sam was the silver lining. The glimmer of hope that emerged from this whole nightmare. The proof that sometimes, despite the weight of evidence to the contrary, people *do* deserve a second chance, no matter what they've done in the past. Some people *can* change.

I often consider this when I think of Rory. Should I give *him* a second chance? Not only because of what we've been through, but because he deserves it. Maybe. For a long time he's been trying to tell me and, more importantly, show me how he's changed. I just haven't wanted to listen or to see it. Previously, I was still too angry and hurt. I didn't want to admit that any part of me still loved him. But that's shifted now. I'm not there yet. But I am at least starting to feel open to the possibility. Perhaps I'll talk it through with Mum at some point while I'm here.

Rory was also invited on the trip. I wouldn't have minded

him coming in the least. Travelling internationally, alone with two kids, is no picnic. Plus, I can't remember the last time I spent Christmas without him. However, he declined. He said he wasn't physically up to it yet and had already arranged to have Christmas with his hippy sister, Karla, who'd appeared out of the woodwork when he was recovering in hospital. After years abroad, having quit the rat race to live and work at various yoga retreats in Bali and then India, she'd shocked us all by jumping on a plane and returning to look after him. Karma, as she's now calling herself, believe it or not, has even moved into his flat with him for the time being. So at least I haven't had to worry about him managing alone. The kids were wary of her initially – understandably, after Billy – but they're coming around. She's quite a character and hard not to like.

Would I have still come here if that had meant leaving Rory home alone? Not a chance. I wasn't even sure at first about leaving him with his sister, knowing how much he and the kids would miss each other, but he was insistent we should go.

'It'll be good for you all,' he said. 'Just what you need.'

'What about what *you* need, Rory?' I asked.

'What I need is for my family to be happy. And I think this trip will really help with that.'

After brunch has been cleared away, Roger takes the kids out into what he calls the yard, although that doesn't do justice to the large garden that surrounds the property.

It's the first time Mum and I have got to talk in private since we arrived.

'How are you, love?' she asks as we sit together on her predictably spacious, comfy couch, both with a brew from the large box of tea bags I brought over. 'Oh, this is a great cuppa,' she adds. 'I haven't had one like this in ages.'

'I'm doing okay, considering,' I tell her. 'We all are. The important thing is that we got through it in one piece, more or less. Plus Billy and his nasty uncle are now safely behind bars – hopefully for a very long time.'

'That's good to hear, love, but how are you *really* doing? You've been through so much. I worry about you all the time. I feel guilty for being so far away, like I've abandoned you. I still think I should have flown back after that night.'

'No, you shouldn't, Mum. That's why I told you not to. There was no need. Besides, you flew us here instead.'

'It means the world to me to have you with us for Christmas.'

'Me too. I'm glad we've come.'

'But how are you in yourself, love? Tell me.'

'I'm getting there. What doesn't kill you makes you stronger, right? I'm trying to focus on the positives. I came close to losing everything: Ethan, Daisy, Rory. Any or all of them could have died that night. So could I. But we didn't. We survived. I want to channel that to appreciate every single day we have together, now and in the future.'

Mum nods. 'It's wonderful to hear you being so positive.'

'I'm not saying I always feel that way, Mum. There are highs and lows, but I do feel like I've turned a corner somehow. Like going through this horrendous ordeal has finally given me perspective on everything, right back to Dad.'

'Really?'

'Yeah, in recent times I've questioned Dad's actions leading up to his murder. At certain confused moments, I've even felt angry with him for getting into that fight with Lenny, because it led to him being taken from us. But now, having witnessed my own children being threatened before my eyes, I know exactly what must have gone through Dad's mind that evening. He was trying to protect his daughter. Nothing else mattered. I was ready to sacrifice my life in a second to save Ethan and Daisy. That's what it means to be a parent. That's what Dad did for me. If he hadn't, who knows what might have happened to me in psycho Lenny's hands? So I've made a decision. From now on, I'm going to try to honour Dad's memory – Sean's too – by aiming to live my life to the max, in the now, rather than being defined by the ghosts of my past. Their lives are over, but mine isn't. Far from it. I need to make it count.'

There are tears in Mum's eyes as she pulls me into a warm, comforting hug. 'You don't know how happy I am to hear you say those words, Beth.'

We go on to discuss Ethan, Daisy and Rory. I say I'm keeping my eye on them to ensure they're genuinely coping as well as they seem to be. I update Mum on the latest in terms of the criminal proceedings against Billy and Mac.

Inevitably, the conversation eventually turns to my work. I tell Mum at last how I've been off with stress for ages.

'What?' She squeezes my hand. 'You poor thing. Why didn't you tell me sooner?'

'I didn't want you to worry. To think I couldn't cope.'

'What now, then? Do you plan to try going back?'

'No. I plan to try going forward. I want to open my own playground.'

Mum's jaw hits the floor. 'I'm sorry, what?'

I grin. 'That was a joke. I have overcome my fear of playgrounds, though. I pushed Daisy on the swings last weekend. I've taken her several times now. Better late than never.'

'That's amazing. I'm so pleased for you, darling. I never thought I'd see the day.'

'Me neither. Seriously, though, I do have a new job in mind.'

'Go on.'

'I want to pack in my old, meaningless role and retrain as a counsellor. I'd like to specialise in grief and trauma.'

'Right. Wow. That's... unexpected. Big. Is it something you've thought about for a while? Have you discussed it with anyone? Rory, for instance.'

'Yes, and yes. He's all for it.'

'But I thought you weren't a big believer in all that. I'm sure I've heard you call it "therapy nonsense" before now. You certainly weren't interested when I mentioned you and Rory seeing a marriage counsellor. And I don't recall you ever being keen to talk to anyone about your own issues. Wouldn't it be stressful?'

I shrug. 'It's what I want to do. It came to me one day and I knew in my gut it was right. Like a calling, I suppose. I want to channel what I've been through into helping others. What better way to stop me dwelling on the past, which has got me nowhere over the years, than to focus on other people's problems? Anyway, I've signed up for an introductory course at a nearby college, which they recommend as a way to decide if counselling is right for you. It starts next month. I'll take it from there and see what happens.'

Mum says nothing for a long moment, staring into the distance. Then she turns to me and nods. 'Fair enough. Do you know what? Scratch everything I just said. Suddenly I have a great feeling about this. I can't remember the last time I saw you so upbeat. It's an amazing response to the hell you've been through. If you think it's the right move, you go for it, love. I'll back you all the way.'

'Thank you. That means the world to me.'

'Happiness is a choice, Beth. It comes from within. Bad things can happen to anyone at any time. How we respond is down to us. I reckon a positive mindset is the first step towards a happy ending. I've found mine here with Roger. By the sound of things, you're on the way to finding yours.'

I smile, enjoying a deep, relaxing breath. 'Let's hope so. I'm done with moping on the sidelines. It's time to make the future my playground.'

A LETTER FROM S.D. ROBERTSON

Dear Reader,

Thank you very much for choosing to read *The Playground*. If you enjoyed it and want to keep up to date with all my latest releases, just sign up at the following link. Your email address will never be shared and you can unsubscribe at any time.

www.bookouture.com/s-d-robertson

This book marks an exciting shift in focus for me as an author towards psychological suspense. I was keen to expand on the darker side of my writing, which has always been lurking in the shadows. However, at the same time, I wanted to stay rooted in the domestic sphere of my previous novels and to continue exploring the themes that intrigue me, like the unexpected nature of life, the power of the past and the unique bond between parents and their children. It's felt like a natural development and I've really enjoyed weaving more gritty crime elements into my plot this time.

So where did the story begin? With playgrounds, of course: key locations in most youngsters' formative years. Children adore them. Parents and carers tend to love them too, because of how they occupy and amuse their little ones. They're great spots to meet and make friends; to relax and unwind.

Anyway, I thought to myself: how about turning that traditional experience on its head? What if something horrific happened to a family in a playground? Something that left my protagonist with a lifelong phobia, to the extent that she's never since dared to enter any playground; never pushed her own children on a swing or helped them down a slide.

Beth was born out of this concept, followed in quick succession by her children, Ethan and Daisy. The rest of the cast and plot grew from there. Eventually, on the back of the blood, sweat and tears that are built into the fabric of every creative endeavour, this book was formed.

I hope you loved *The Playground*; if you did, I would be very grateful if you could write a review. I'd really like to hear what you think, and it makes such a difference helping new readers to discover one of my novels for the first time.

It's always great to hear from my readers – you can get in touch on my Facebook page, through Twitter, Instagram, Threads or my website.

Thanks again,

Stuart

www.sdrobertsonauthor.com

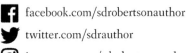

facebook.com/sdrobertsonauthor

twitter.com/sdrauthor

instagram.com/sdrobertsonauthor

ACKNOWLEDGEMENTS

Hats off to everyone who's helped produce this, my seventh published novel. It's a particularly significant book for me because it's my first release with my brilliant new publisher, Bookouture, as well as my first psychological thriller.

Special thanks to Lydia Vassar-Smith for her savvy editing skills and for providing such a smooth transition into my new publishing home and genre. Lydia has been a real guiding light throughout this process. I'm very grateful to have her in my corner, along with Kim Nash, Jess Readett and Noelle Holten from the publicity team, plus editorial manager Hannah Snetsinger and all the other dynamic Bookouture staff.

Next I must mention my amazing agent, Pat Lomax. She's been at my side, through thick and thin, since day one of my publishing journey: a constant champion, confidante and adviser for the past decade now. Thank you so much for everything.

Thank you also to all my family and friends – especially my wonderful wife, daughter, parents and sister – whose unwavering support, patience and positivity keep me going like nothing else. Claudia and Mum have been particularly dedicated in terms of proofreading, answering strange book-related questions, and helping me to overcome various character and plot predicaments. That assistance is, as always, massively appreciated.

Finally, thank you to my readers, new and old, for investing your time in my work and for helping to spread the word via recommendations and enthusiastic reviews. Your support means the world to me.

Printed in Great Britain
by Amazon

28700959R00179